PHANTOM PANTHERS®

DAVID SHULTZ

This is a work of fiction. The events and characters described herein are imaginary and are not intended to refer to specific places or living persons. The opinions expressed in this manuscript are solely the opinions of the author and do not represent the opinions or thoughts of the publisher. The author has represented and warranted full ownership and/or legal right to publish all the materials in this book.

Phantom Panthers®
All Rights Reserved.
Copyright © 2014 David Shultz
v4.0

Cover Photo © 2014 David Shultz. Thanks to Eileen Brown at BuddyWebGrapics.com for contributions to the cover. All rights reserved - used with permission.

This book may not be reproduced, transmitted, or stored in whole or in part by any means, including graphic, electronic, or mechanical without the express written consent of the publisher except in the case of brief quotations embodied in critical articles and reviews.
Outskirts Press, Inc.

http://www.outskirtspress.com

ISBN: 978-1-4787-2739-2

Outskirts Press and the "OP" logo are trademarks belonging to Outskirts Press, Inc.

PRINTED IN THE UNITED STATES OF AMERICA

CHAPTER 1
Western Russia, Summer 1944

Lt. Grisamov congratulated himself on another day of cheating death. He raced over the Russian countryside, the belly camera in his Yak-9R tactical reconnaissance aircraft snapping photos of the Germans three thousand meters below, now the German flak batteries opened up. Grisamov took evasive action and proceeded on with his mission.

Having memorized his route from the sector map, he recognized a bend in the river ahead that marked the end of his last leg. He clicked off the power switch for the camera and felt the mechanism quit whirring behind his seat. He keyed his throat mic and radioed a coded message, "Alpha Four. Status White." Meaning that he was returning to base, mission completed.

The reply from Aerial Reconnaissance dispatch scratched through his earphones. "Alpha Four, acknowledged."

Within a half hour Grisamov would be back in the squadron mess, cheering himself with hot tea, a slug of vodka, and a slice of fried American Spam.

Then a glint in the mirror atop his canopy told him that Fate may have changed his plans.

Grisamov glanced into the reflection, suddenly worried.

The too familiar shape of an ME-109 fighter grew in the mirror. A second Messerschmitt trailed as wingman.

At this altitude, his Yak-9 had the advantage in speed. The Germans knew this and had dove after him to gain superior velocity and overtake his plane.

Grisamov's mouth seemed to fill with dust, and his throat tightened in dread. He pushed the throttle and banked east, straight toward friendly lines.

Another glint to his left warned that the enemy pilots had outfoxed him. The enemy fighters were like fingers closing into a fist with him in the middle.

Grisamov jammed the Yak's Kimov engine throttle to emergency power. The twelve-cylinders screamed in protest, the tachometer and manifold pressure gauges redlining. Better to sacrifice the engine than get shot down and lose the mission.

The cowling machine guns and bursts of 20 mm cannon of the ME-109 on his tail winked fire. His nemesis now made his final approach for the kill, Grisamov felt the Luftwaffe pilot was close enough to wring his neck.

White tracer bullets streaked by.

Grisamov rolled right. In the next second he glimpsed the shark-like snout of another Messerschmitt lunging for him. His guns barked of lead laden flames and this volley of tracers zoomed toward him, appearing big as flaming torches.

The enemy bullets and explosive shells struck home. The Yak shuttered. Its controls slammed against his hands and feet. Black fumes belched from the engine's exhaust ports and sheets of smoke spiraled alongside the fuselage.

His airplane crippled and within seconds of losing power, he gripped the control stick with both hands and executed the one maneuver that would either save or kill him.

He dove straight down and dared his attackers to follow. The needles on the altitude indicator spun in a wicked, dizzying circle. The dying engine spit oil on the windshield and seized. The propellers snapped to a halt.

All Grisamov could see through the grimy windshield was wooded landscape. He hauled back on the control stick and fought to bring the Yak's nose to the horizon. Blood rushed from his head and his vision narrowed as if staring through a shrinking keyhole. Suddenly dizzy, he grunted to keep from passing out.

The airplane shuttered beneath him, pitching upward. He centered the controls and the Yak aligned with the horizon, wings level. Blood surged back into Grisamov's head. The tiny keyhole opened until his vision widened completely. The smoke trailing from the engine had thinned to tattered plumes. He saw familiar landmarks and knew he was over friendly territory.

He keyed his throat mic. "Alpha Four. am going in and ditching in Sector One-Three-Seven." He didn't know if he had transmitted anything but he had to try.

Up ahead, it was all trees. Grisamov had no choice but to crash through them. He pulled the slack from his safety harness, locked it tight, then aimed for a space between the trees and let the battered Yak glide toward the earth.

Grisamov hadn't flown a glider since early pilot training and the silent no-engine descent became eerily strange. His pulse quickened the closer he got to the trees.

The Yak lanced through the gap in a blur of color and noise. The wings snagged the trees and tore loose. The airplane plowed through the grove and speared a dirt embankment. Grisamov was thrown forward. The anchor points of his safety harness ripped loose and he smacked the instrument panel with his face, killing him instantly.

Corporal Belakov and his comrades stood motionless as they witnessed one of their comrades crash land, Corporal Belakov and his platoon sprinted to the crashed Yak. The airplane had settled with its belly against the ground like a dismembered bird, its nose covered in dirt, the propellers twisted like fractured bones, the open wing roots gaping like wounds. Smoke feathered from the exhaust stacks and from under the mangled engine cowling. Up close, the wreckage stank of burnt oil, leaking gasoline, and spilled radiator coolant.

Belakov slung his carbine over one shoulder. He used ragged holes in the fuselage as hand holds and hauled himself to the cockpit. The canopy was cracked and smeared with oil. Inside, the pilot was slumped against the instrument panel.

Corporal Belakov hammered his fist against the canopy and yelled to get the pilot's attention. The man didn't move.

Belakov fumbled with a latch along the bottom of the canopy's frame. He yanked on the latch and the canopy popped up a few centimeters. He shoved his hand beneath the frame and heaved the canopy backwards until it tumbled to the ground.

Belakov pulled the pilot's jacket collar, lifting the head. The man's bloody face resembled ground beef and he was certainly dead. Belakov sighed and eased the pilot's face back against the gore on the instruments. He had seen the dogfight and cheered when his comrade airman had escaped the Hun once more time. What irony to have survived that chase, only to die in the crash.

Corporal Belakov now motioned for his radioman, grabbing the radio he keyed the hand phone and waited impatiently for base to come on line. Base, this is patrol company "C" in sector one three seven, we are at a shot down aircraft, I believe it is a photo reconnaissance, we need a security officer to proceed, the reply come over the line, we are awaiting for further orders.

Corporal Belakov now orders the members of his patrol to execute a routine action and station soldiers on a perimeter to detect any enemy activity.

Corporal Belakov dropped from the cockpit. "The poor bastard is dead."

They stared at the wreckage, awaiting the arrival of G2 and not certain what to do next.

A small truck rumbled through the trees and approached. Someone in the vehicle shouted at them.

Corporal Belakov and the others readied their weapons just in case the intruders were Germans.

The truck appeared on a trail between the trees. It was a Red Army personnel carrier, a soldier driving with two officers as passengers, one in the front, the second in the back.

The vehicle halted close to the wrecked Yak. The two officers dismounted, one a Soviet Sector Commissar of the counter-intelligence branch and an infantry officer with the red star sewn above each sleeve cuff. He carried a submachine gun.

Corporal Belakov and his comrades remained on their stations on the perimeter this close to the frontline, to stand at attention or salute would invite the attention of a Nazi sniper and these officers wouldn't appreciate getting shot through the head.

The Major hurried to the Yak. "The pilot?"

Belakov replies, Comrade Major, "He died in the crash", the Major crouched beside the belly of the airplane just behind the cockpit. He tapped his finger against slotted bolts arranged around an oblong panel. He ordered Corporal Belakov. "Open these." Fuel puddled around the corporal's boots. "Quickly comrade, before the plane catches fire."

"Shouldn't we remove the pilot, sir?"

"You said he was dead. If we don't recover this equipment, then he will have died for nothing." The Major gestured to another soldier. "You, fetch the pilot's identity tag and retrieve his maps and code books. If he has personal effects—and he shouldn't—retrieve those as well."

Corporal Belakov unsheathed his bayonet and used the tip to turn the slotted bolts. When he loosened the final bolt, the panel fell to the ground. A gray box rested snug inside a compartment. Stenciled markings on the face of the box read: USSR Aviation Reconnaissance Command. Motorized Aerial Camera Type CC2 and Film Magazine. Handle With Care.

Corporal Belakov grasped a metal handle on the box and jerked it loose. The box was the size of a milk crate and heavy. He slid it halfway out when the Major had him stop. The Soviet Commissar studied the box and ran his hands along its sides as if it contained treasure. He tapped the bottom.

"The lens is damaged," he points out to the others, "but the mechanism is in a serviceable condition." The Major orders, Belakov, "Now pull the camera out all the way and stow it in our vehicle."

Corporal Belakov yanked on the box until it slid out of the compartment, tipped free of the airplane and slammed against his boots. The driver grabbed the other end of the box and together they shuffled with it to the personnel carrier. They lifted the box and rested it on the floor by the back seat.

The Major took a writing pad from his leather map case and scribbled notes. The other soldier handed him the items he'd taken from the pilot. The Major recorded the dead man's name, then tucked everything into the map case and climbed into the personnel carrier. The driver started the engine.

The commissar clambered into the back seat and said he was ready.

The Major shook Belakov's hand. "Corporal, Mother Russia appreciates your diligence and sacrifices."

The personnel carrier accelerated and disappeared into the tree line.

PHANTOM PANTHERS

STAVKA HQ The Kremlin Moscow

The staff car makes its way through the busy streets of Moscow. It then took its place in a long line of vehicles waiting to enter the nerve center of the Russian Military.

The watch guard approaches Colonel Bulganin's staff car, "Good morning Comrade Colonel", your passengers papers, Bulganin's Aid de Camp hands the guard his papers.

The guard salutes, all is in order, you may pass Comrade Colonel.

STAVKA (Soviet General Staff) is a hornets nest of activity, the members that occupied this facility were on a 24 hour status, one could get orders and information on any military matter that the Russian Military was engaged in.

Bulganin makes his way to operations, Ah, comrade Colonel, Stalin has called an impromptu meeting, the entire staff will attend.

The war room was a menagerie of maps and composites of units and where they were deployed.

General Govorov motions for Colonel Bulganin, "Comrade General Vasilesky." I have just arrived from the field and hands the general a folder with the photos that staff had been waiting for. "Our specialists have just analyzed the film from the recon aircraft that was shot down over our Southern Front."

Bulganin offers the general a magnifying glass. "These are the prints with the most telling information."

The general placed the magnifying glass and squinted through the magnifying lens at the photos. He studied one, then another, and a third. He sat the magnifying glass aside and then raised his head, smiling.

Bulganin smiled back. "Comrade Bulganin, the Hun has taken our bait, hook, line and sinker. He has deployed his best armor and troops opposing our Southern Sector."

The general tapped the magnifying glass against the folder. "And these confirm that the German High Command have a far smaller force opposing our strongest forces."

Stalin, the Commander of the Supreme Soviet now enters and chairs the meeting. Tamping a wad of tobacco in his pipe and striking a match on the corner of the table, he takes a deep drag.

Voroshilov, what have you to report?

Comrade Stalin our southern forces have met and overcome strong resistance in Moldova, we should still meet our objective of Bucharest and cut off the German forces protecting Budapest as we approach the fall weather.

Stalin in a seemingly cheerful mood, "Excellent".

Vasilesky, what do you have to report on Bagration?

Vasilesky, we have just received updated reconnaissance photos, "Maskirovka" has exceeded our expectations. Getting this information at this late date gives us less time, but our forces have been placed where they will be victorious.

Comrades, I have commanded that our attack must commence on the June 22nd, to commemorate the Nazi invasion of our Motherland. Radio Zhukov that our attack will take place as scheduled, this will be the beginning of our race to Berlin.

CHAPTER 2

Army Group Center HQ, Western Russia.

The camouflaged netting covered the entrance to the headquarters operation's center. The staff car halted and a cloud of dust swept over its occupants and the receiving party standing at the shoulder of the road.

Ignoring the dust, the men of the receiving party—the headquarter's *Generalmajor* Frankel and his staff officers, plus the sentries—snapped to attention. The staff adjutant stepped forward and opened the rear door of the Mercedes.

Generaloberst Heinrici emerged, followed by his aide-de-camp. Frankel saluted. The sentries presented arms with their rifles. Sweat dripped down everyone's necks and darkened their collars.

Heinrici returned the salute with his general's baton.

Frankel extended his hand. "Welcome *Generaloberst*. The men are eager to meet you."

Heinrici shook his hand. "Likewise."

"A pleasant trip here?"

"As pleasant as possible considering this miserable Russian humidity."

Frankel and Heinrici walked side-by-side into the building. The orderlies and clerks paused from their duties and stood at attention. Heinrici waved his baton. "Carry on."

He removed his hat and gloves and handed them and the baton to his aide-de-camp.

"Your chief of staff arrived earlier with the map overlays and operations orders," Frankel said. "The *Panzertruppen* have been assembled and await your final briefing. Those commanders who cannot attend have sent liaison officers."

They entered a large hall converted into a briefing room. The anxious officers milled about the tables and along the sides of the room.

The two generals halted at the entrance. The adjutant eased around them and bellowed, "Panzertruppen. Achtung!"

As one, the men stood ramrod straight, shoulders back, and snapped their heels together.

Heinrici stepped over the threshold and nodded by acknowledging with "Heil Hitler".

The adjutant said, "Generaloberst Heinrici, Panzertruppen stand down."

The men relaxed and tracked the general as he paced to the large map board at the front of the room. He halted before the map, turned and panned the assembled ranks with a proud smile.

He recognized many of the faces, having served with them throughout the Russian campaign. The once fresh *leutnants* were now battle-tested field commanders. Mustered in this room were decorated veterans of the Wehrmacht's many campaigns. Their victorious rampage across Poland and France that ultimately chased the British back across the English Channel. Men from the Afrika Korps. And of course the survivors of the near continuous combat against the Russian horde since the German invasion of 1941.

At the start of the war, an assembly of such officers would've seen them turn out smartly in their black Panzertruppen uniforms, death head's insignia gleaming, boots polished.

Now the men wore a patchwork of outfits. A few still donned the short black jacket of the Panzertruppen, marking them as elite troops. A gray version for those in the assault guns. The standard field gray uniform for the infantry, artillery, and engineers. Plus camouflaged smocks and jackets in a variety of patterns.

Though the officers appeared fatigued, they were hardly beaten. To a man, the Russians feared them more than they did their revered master, that murderous Bolshevik Stalin.

Heinrici stood before the map. The orders for defense had been issued and the combat units should be in place in anticipation of an imminent attack, his army group poised as a gigantic death machine ready to grind the enemy into pulp.

A colonel shifted nervously. The yellow piping of the signal branch decorated his collar tabs and shoulder insignia.

Heinrici pointed to him.

The colonel stiffened to attention. "Herr general, I am Oberst Rudorffer, communications officer for the 2nd Army Headquarters. We have positioned our forces per your orders... but..."

"But what, Herr Oberst?"

"If you permit me, Herr general." Rudorffer stepped to the map board. "Our standing orders were to oppose the Soviets here." He traced a finger along a river.

The general smiled, showing that he respected the colonel for speaking his mind. Slavish obedience to orders was not a healthy prerequisite for an effective commander. "Oberst Rudorffer, what Berlin says and what Ivan is going to do are two different things." Heinrici pointed to the middle of the map. "Army Group Center's forces have withdrawn from their original positions. Their redeployment will save them from annihilation from the Russian's initial barrage and aerial attack. When Ivan lifts his fire, our forces will move forward to attack positions."

The Oberst gulped. It was more than a rumor of the harsh treatment dealt to officers who defied the Fuehrer's hold-your-ground-to-the-last-man orders. "Herr general, you're sticking your neck out, aren't you…sir?"

The men in the room averted their eyes at the uncomfortable breach of etiquette.

Heinrici tapped his finger against the Iron Cross 2nd Class on the colonel's tunic. "Herr Oberst, to win without risk is to triumph without glory."

The colonel snapped his heels and nodded. "Your point is understood, Herr General."

"Very good." Heinrici surveyed the other officers. "Who is here from the 667th Sturmgeschütz Brigade?"

A colonel and a captain stepped forward. "Herr General, I am Oberst Otto Mader." The colonel was a short man in his mid-thirties with the compact build of a bricklayer. Bright blue eyes beamed from a round face creased with worry lines. Mader pointed to his companion. "This is my operations officer, Hauptmann Hans Krieger."

The captain was a lanky twenty something with the rangy features of a draft horse.

Heinrici squinted at Mader. "Oberst, where do I know you from?"

"Sir, I was the former head of armor training at the tanker school in Grafenwoehr."

The general nodded. He beckoned them to the map and ran his finger along a bend of the Mogilev Road. "Mader, you have one of the key features to protect. This road. The approach to Minsk. This is where Ivan will make his initial thrust."

Mader leaned over the map. His gaze circled the disposition of forces on both sides of the battle line and he no doubt noticed that he was greatly outnumbered.

The death machine worked both ways.

CHAPTER 3

Red Army forward command center, 2nd Belorussian Front

As Marshal Ivan S. Konev enters his operational headquarters he is met by his operational staff officers. He is approached by his Chief of Staff, Major General Semenov Ivanovich Bogdanov.

"Seme, where did you find this?", Marshal Konev inquires. He had not seen a bottle of champagne since he left for the war and as Seme handed him the bottle Konev held it in his hands and stroked the yellow label.

"I have seen nothing but cheap wine and Tushonka for too long. I can't remember what real champagne even tastes like." Konev untwisted the wire keeping the cork in place and peeled back the foil. He held the green bottle in his left hand, and pulled out the cork with his right. All of the officers smiled as the cork popped out of the bottle and foam trickled over the lip and ran down the bottle's side.

Seme filled the Marshal's glass and then those of the officers who had been waiting with extended arms. He left just enough in the bottle so that it would not be empty when he put it back on the table. "We took it from those who would not appreciate it as much as we do. They were keeping it safe until we 'encouraged' them to donate it to us. As he pops the cork, it is captured contraband that I have been keeping it just for this moment."

Seme took a sip and smiled. "The French have their flaws, but who else can make a drink such as this?" as he fills the Marshal's and then the other officers glasses.

"A toast to Operation Bagration and our success," Marshal Konev said to the other Russian officers standing next to him as he raised his glass. "It has been a long and difficult road. All Russians have paid a high price for us to be in a position to win the war. Now, now it is the Hun who will pay, it is our struggle that will make victory taste sweeter, that will give this victory its taste But we, have to wait no longer. Victory will be ours."

The officers roared in agreement and raised their glasses as Marshal Konev spoke. "Your enthusiasm is only fitting. Our attack is on, and the outcome is certain. To the Motherland and our triumph over Germany!" June 22nd is the third anniversary of the Hun invading our Motherland, it will forever be indelibly etched in all of our minds. Salute to our Motherland.

The officers took one last sip of champagne and placed their glasses on the table before facing Marshal Konev and saluting. They swaggered back to their posts, lightheaded from imbibing too much national pride, depart to their posts and waited for the order to fire.

For many of them, the radio silence was unbearable. They stood behind artillery and sat underneath turrets and in cockpits, holding their breath until they heard the order they all knew was coming. Finally, when the tension had spread across the entire Army, the moment the soldiers had been waiting for arrived.

They were only minutes from the start of Operation Bagration— and the annihilation of the Hun before them: Army Group Center. At this moment, kilometers to the east and behind him, forward airfields were hives of activity as the Soviet air armada prepared their Shturmoviks, medium bombers, and fighters for the dawn's aerial onslaught.

Konev to Bogdanov, "Comrade the Hun has spent three years teaching us how to fight." We have paid a high price for our victories, but we have learned our lessons well.

Bogdanov replies, "Our forces are now a giant steamroller."

Konev read his watch, savoring the French libation he had just enjoyed, he anticipated what the dawn would bring.

A woman's voice—one of the headquarter's radio operators—counted from behind the blackout curtain. "Pyat. Chetiri. Dva."

Bogdanov's heart thumped in cadence with the numbers.

"Odin. *Nul*."

The barrage lasting nearly an hour lit up the predawn sky as if it were the noon day hour. The Katyusha recoiled backward and then lurched forward as their rockets fled in an endless precession of fire and smoke. The rockets moaned as they chased one another across the sky. "Oh! Oh!" they seem to say, as if they were attempting to warn the enemy they were attempting to kill. Soldiers flinched when the artillery rattled. They would turn their eyes away from the flashes, which lit up the sky like the sun. A gassy haze billowed across the battlefield and flames from the Katyusha illuminated the clouds.

The Russian rockets and mortars streak toward the German lines. As they complete their arc and race toward their targets, shattering the silence of the eastern front. When the weapons impact the ground, the terrain shudders from the endless carpet of high explosives that devastates the entire landscape. The shells burst into countless pieces and the shrapnel cuts through the air and anything standing in its way.

Now the Russian tank armada rolls forward like a giant tsunami forming in the ocean. Commanders riding the crest of the wave, standing in their turret cupolas and waving their units onward. For each and every one of them, it was more than must a battle. It was a chance to bring pride to the home country and to return the glory they all knew it deserved. They yelled their thoughts into the radio and while you could not hear them speak over the roar of the battle, one could read the words on their lips, "Revenge!" ....Death to the Fascists! "On to Berlin!"

The air armada passes overhead. Every one of these "Stormbirds" is armed with cannons under each wing and destined to kill any enemy of the Motherland.

As the infantry observes their air forces attacking, the artillery barrage subsides after more than an hour. The tankers know their long awaited moment has arrived. The order has finally been broadcast.

Marshal Ivan S. Konev stands in their battlefield headquarters as Operation Bagration comes to life and his veterans of the Great Patriotic struggle carry out the orders they had been so carefully briefed on. Officers intently listen to their radios and update the operational maps on the wall as the Russians advance toward Germany.

"Onward! Onward to final victory!" Konev urges his commanders.

Konev strutted out of his makeshift HQ and folded his arms. The features on his Slavic face seemed to vibrate from the flashes pulsing from all directions.

"Aren't you impressed, Comrade Bogdanov, that we've spared no expense giving this wonderful goodbye present to those Nazi sons-of-bitches?"

"A multi-colored star shell signaled the start of the................ Attack!"

Oberst Mader scrunched low in the cupola of his StuG III assault gun, a headset clamped over his *feldmütze*. He munched a crust of hard bread that he washed down with the swill known as ersatz coffee. At any moment he expected the order for the counter attack.

PHANTOM PANTHERS

Hans puffed on his cigarette and peered through his binoculars. "Nothing yet, Max. Ivan will be here soon. Of that, I have no doubt." Hans now orders his gunner Wolfgang, bore sight your gun, I am sure you will need it. Ja Wohl, Mein Herr. Wolfgang answers back smartly.

Han's driver, Max Koch, wiped grease from the wrench in his left hand and placed the oily rag in his back right pocket.

"As you say, sir. I hope he is prepared for the greeting we are going to give him when he arrives." He reached for another tool to clean, although he had wiped every one of them at least twice since the tank came to a stop. He yawned and thought of taking a nap, but decided against it.

He smiled, removed his hat, and wiped his brow. "Did I ever tell you about the girl who is waiting for me in Berlin?"

"Yes, Max." Hans had heard the story so many times he knew it by rote. It seemed to him Max had no other stories to tell. "But please tell me again."

Hans threw down his cigarette and leaned against the front of the copula. He scanned the horizon and he tried to block out Max's story.

"I was there on leave with three men from my unit. We had just started tanker school. We were walking down the street, and as we passed a bakery, I bumped into."

Hans pulled the binoculars from his eyes, and he strained his ears to the east. "Max, silence." Max stopped his story in midsentence and looked toward his commander.

Hans looked through his binoculars in the direction of where the sound was coming from. He struggled to find any clue of who or what was causing the sound. Finally, he saw a thin plume of dust and diesel smoke on the horizon.

Hans slid into the tank and secured the hatch. "Maintain radio silence.

As Hans spoke, German soldiers scurried to the safety of their tanks. Hatches on dozens of tanks were closed and sealed, and every man focused on the radio in the tank, waiting for their next order.

He watched the smoke and fire subside in the hills and swamp two kilometers in front of his unit. Since early this morning, the Russians had pounded the woods and marshes with tons of artillery shells. Katyusha rockets deluged the countryside. Then at dawn, flocks of medium Ilyushin bombers had dumped more bombs into the inferno.

Mader finished his breakfast, unmoved, unimpressed by what he saw. After all, he'd been fighting these Communist bastards for a year. The Soviets weren't very good shots and they liked to waste their ammunition. General Heinrici's defensive plan had ordered the brigade of assault guns to withdraw to let the Russian fury fall on empty real estate.

A flight of feared Shturmoviks roared overhead but Mader and his men remained unseen beneath the trees. The armored ground attack planes flew straight east, most certainly racing home to refuel and replenish their cannon and rockets.

Mader watched the airplanes disappear. His detachment of six StuG IIIs hid in the shadow of the trees like enormous steel beetles, their crews lounging on the fenders or on the grass close by. Waiting. Sleeping. Banking as much rest as was possible before the impending ordeal of savage combat.

The StuG III was originally an armored self-propelled artillery piece developed to help the infantry blast through enemy fortifications. The vehicle mated a short barreled cannon to the proven hull and engine of the Panzer III medium tank. The gun was mounted directly to the superstructure to give the vehicle a low profile and simplify manufacture and maintenance. On the other hand, it lacked a turret so the crew had to shift the entire vehicle to aim the cannon, a definite disadvantage in a close-in melee.

The StuG III had evolved into the present model that mounted a powerful 75mm antitank gun and helped the vehicle earn the reputation as a deadly tank killer.

To Mader's right waited the six StuG IIIs of Hauptmann Krieger's tank platoon. Between Mader and Krieger's units, they had twelve assault guns to stop the Russian tidal wave that would soon sweep toward them.

Someone banged on the armor skirt of Mader's vehicle. It was Gruber, the detachment supply sergeant.

Mader lifted his headset from one ear. "Yes sergeant?"

Gruber took off his helmet and rubbed the sweaty grime from his face. "Sir, I've distributed the ammunition. Each unit got only 40 rounds for the main guns."

"How about fuel?"

"No one received a full complement." Gruber looked more dour than usual.

"That's all right. We'll make do with what we have."

Gruber put his helmet back on and hustled down a trail through the forest.

A voice buzzed through Mader's headset. He adjusted the earphones and listened carefully. As often as he'd done this, he couldn't help but feel his pulse race at the news.

Mader acknowledged the message. He stood tall in his cupola, cupped his hands around his mouth, and shouted, "Panzertruppen, mount up."

Despite the overwhelming odds, it was time to prepare for the Russian juggernaut.

After being ordered to pull back from the initial Russian barrage, elements of the Third Panzer Army and Ninth Army have now moved into their forward positions and lie in wait from concealed positions to launch their attack.

He watched the smoke and fire subside in the hills and swamp in front of his unit. Since early this morning, the Russians had pounded the woods and marshes with tons of artillery shells. Katyusha rockets deluged the countryside. Then at dawn, flocks of medium Ilyushin bombers had dumped more bombs into the inferno.

Oberstleutnant Mader now stands erect in the cupola of his StuG, gazing through his binoculars observes the Russian onslaught, T-34's race over the landscape in unison with Russian shock troops. The sky overhead is filled with aircraft in aerial combat. Despite the overwhelming odds, it was time prepare for the onslaught that he knew was imminent.

From overhead the 667th StuG brigade now hears the screaming rockets launched from a Nebelwerfer battalion concealed in the landscape. Nebelwerfer, "the poorman's artillery" now rains down a torrent of death upon the advancing Russian units. The mortar shells create a deafening concussion combined with a thin skin, would produce an enormous carpet of shrapnel that would cover a large area. The advancing Russian shock troops not protected, inside an armored vehicle or revetment would be shredded by millions of tiny metal shards designed to eliminate and opponent. As the barrage subsides, the Russian shock infantry disappear and now the Russian armor is attacking without supporting infantry.

Oberst Mader now barks out his orders from his command vehicle, Panzertruppen, engage on my signal, vier, drei, zwo, ein. Now the engines of the 667th turn over in orchestrated coordination, all engines turning over at once would give an enemy forward recon or scout unit the impression of one tank, instead of a platoon of tanks.

PHANTOM PANTHERS

Now settled in, Gerhardt revs his engine and reads his engine gauges. Klaus at his radio, ready to transmit instructions and orders at a moment's notice. Wolfgang, now loading a round into the breech of the high velocity 75mm cannon, slams home the breech bloc and acknowledges, gun ready Herr Oberst.

As the enemy tanks grow larger in Rudolf's gun sight graticule, the crew waits, they wait until their enemy completely fills their gun sight graticule. Mader and Krieger direct their company of tank killers to hold fire until they are in lethal killing range, the orders to all units is to swing into a position that presents the advantage of a naval broadside attack. The StuG's 75mm cannon could only traverse 14 degrees left or right, the commander would give orders for the driver to change position of the StuG to accommodate the best angle of attack. The Russian tank units now fills their guns sights as they enter the kill zone, the order is given, *Fire*.

Rudolf's hand now depresses his gun lanyard. The vehicle lurches as the gun recoils and the round escaping through the muzzle brake and forms a large cloud of dust. The cabin fills with smoke and the smell of black powder permeates the interior of the vehicle.

They engage in a heated battle and destroy a great number of Russian tanks, T-34 now burst into flames, turrets fly into the air and one could hear the screams of the tankers that are trapped in their caskets of steel.

Otto and Hans' tank killers now unleash a formidable hail of armor piercing projectiles that turn the battlefield in front of them into chard masses of burning wreckage. Round after round find their mark, time and again their enemy is rendered mute and the spearhead of the Russian attack has been challenged by this small cadre of German tank killers. Otto constantly on his radio barks out orders to reposition and maintain attacking at all costs. Clouds of black smoke now consume the battlefield.

The sky overhead is filled with Me-109s and Russian Yaks as the engage in aerial battles. Now the soviet Shturmoviks, "Black Death" execute their devastating ground attack. The German tank forces now come under an overwhelming aerial attack, Shturmoviks, circle around behind their targets and attack from the rear, a tanks most vulnerable area.

Deafening noise and giant flashes of flame stream from the Shturmoviks 23mm cannons on each wing as they unleash their deadly cargo when as they find their targets. Otto and Han's units are decimated but they are the only StuG's still continuing to carry on the attack.

Otto barks out a plea on his radio, StuG units report……the only answer to his radio calls is Hans. The voice of his longtime companion is relief.

Otto now order his only remaining Panzersoldat, Hans follow me, Hans replies, Ja Wohl, Mein Herr. Now with reckless abandon Otto and Hans make a suicide charge through the eye of a swirling maelstrom.

Russian mortars now fall around the remnants of the 667th.

They order their gunners to jam their gun lanyard closed as they charge at full speed. Firing their cannon at anything in their killing zone. As their ammunition runs out they are over powered by an onrush of Russian T-34's. In head on attacks the tank killer that had served them so well now is just a burning hulk, in its last death throes.

Hans in desperation grabs the MG-34 machine gun in the loaders position and chambers a round of 7.92 mm and watches as he pulls the trigger, Russian infantry fall under his enfilade of fire.

After a brief respite, he jumps down from his burning tank and grabs a couple of potato mashers, "German Hand Grenades" and grabs an MP-40 from one of his dead comrades.

PHANTOM PANTHERS

As he steps from behind his cover he lobs the grenades and bodies of Russian infantry are decimated in the explosions. He then finishes off the rest of the Russian troops and makes his escape under a hail of bullets.

Otto limping from a flesh wound, finds his way to a drainage ditch near the battlefield, suddenly he makes out another soldier in a German uniform, Hans, he yells out, you made it.

Hans answers back, we survived! You're wounded Otto. Otto responds, it's only a flesh wound.

Hans let Otto lean on his left shoulder and braced him with his left arm. Otto could not place much weight on his leg and the two struggled forward as best as they could. Hans, being a good soldier, did not complain. In his mind, he had been given the opportunity to help a commanding officer with an injury, and he took it as an honor. The fact that it was Otto, someone he considered family, was beside the point. He would have done the same for any officer.

Hans and Otto had gone as far as Hans could carry them without taking a break. Hans lowered Otto onto a flat grassy spot on the side of the road and wished he had remembered to bring a canteen with him. He tried to swallow, but his parched throat felt like he was swallowing sand.

After he had the chance to catch his breath, Hans looked at Otto's blood soaked pants. "It's time to go," he said as he extended his arm for Otto to grab onto. Otto grimaced as he stood on his left leg.

"Sir, perhaps I could help you," Hans heard and he turned to find a brown-haired boy wearing a grease stained Gefreiter's uniform.

Hans nodded. "Of course." Hans looked at the soldier's face. "He cannot be more than sixteen or seventeen," he thought.

As the boy stepped toward them, Hans noticed the canteen hanging from his belt.

"Here, sir, perhaps you would care for a drink." He handed the canteen to Hans, who took a sip and gave the canteen to Otto.

The Gefreiter glanced at the gold insignia on Otto's shoulder and came to attention. "Oberstleutnant!" he blurted out as he saluted. "Gefreiter Franz Kaufman at your service."

Otto saluted back. "Perhaps we could dispense with the formalities and continue marching?"

"Of course." Hans and Franz gathered Otto under their arms and the three of them walked west.

Nearly two hours later, Franz stopped in his tracks. "Sir, do you hear that?"

Hans turned and heard an engine chugging behind him. Moments later, a troop transport truck pulled beside them. Hans waved at the driver, who pulled over to the side of the road.

A number of soldiers were reclined in the back of the truck. The wooden panels at the end of the truck bed had been removed, and Hans and Franz walked Otto behind the truck and propped him near the bumper.

The soldiers in the truck were indifferent to Hans and Franz until they recognized Otto's rank. Then they sprang to their feet and pounced at the chance to help the Oberstleutnant.

After Hans and Franz loaded Otto into the truck, Hans stepped to the driver. "Oberstleutnant Mader is injured. We must take him to the nearest aid station. Do you understand?"

The driver nodded. "Yes, Hauptmann. We will go directly to the aid station, as you ordered."

Hans climbed into the truck, reached through two of the wooden slats, and waved to the driver. The Krupp groaned and moved forward.

Hans slid next to Otto. "We are on our way to get you help, Otto. It will not be much longer."

The medics at the aid station scrambled to get the Oberstleutnant out of the truck and into a field hospital.

One of them stopped to look at the gash on Hans' head. "Let me see that. You may need stitches," he said and reached to tilt Hans' head to get a better view.

"It is nothing. Just a small bump. Surely you have more important things to worry about in the middle of a battlefield." Hans pulled his head back and motioned for the medic to move his hand. "Where have you taken Oberstleutnant Mader?"

The medic pointed to a camouflaged tent. "The doctors are examining him and will decide on what treatment he needs. He is in good hands."

He glanced again at Hans' head. "If you feel lightheaded or nauseous, you need to see a doctor immediately. Do you understand?"

"Yes, yes." Hans was quickly becoming annoyed with the medic's obsession with the bump on his head.

"Our mess tent is right over there. I am sure you must be hungry. Soldiers from the front always are. They can show you where the showers are and where you can take a nap. And over there," he said as he pointed over Hans' left shoulder, "is the motor pool. They can take you to command headquarters when you are ready. You will need to check in there, I suppose."

Hans nodded. "If you hear anything about Oberstleutnant Mader's condition, you will relay that to me, won't you?"

"Of course."

Hans walked to the mess tent and tried to put thoughts about Otto's leg out of his mind. "German doctors are excellent. He is in good hands," he told himself

"Let me help you, Oberstleutnant," Hans said as he opened the rear door of the Kugelwagon. Otto had been lucky in that the bullet passed through the muscle in the leg. No major arteries were hit, and no bones were fractured.

"It looks worse that it is. I can make it on my own." Otto brushed Hans aside and slid into the back seat. Hans sat next to the driver and they headed toward Combat Headquarters. They did not know why they had been summoned to meet with their commander.

As the driver headed away from the front, Otto could not help the wave of despair that came over him. "I failed my men and my country," he thought. "I should expect whatever punishment comes my way."

He and Hans sat in silence. It was not until the Combat Headquarters came into sight, some thirty minutes later, that either of them spoke a word.

"Here were are, sir," the driver nodded as the building came into view.

Hans dared not ask why they were here. Like Otto, he was not sure why he had been called, and he was certain if Otto had known he would have told him. An Oberst had come to the hospital and interviewed him about the tank battle with the Russians, but had left Hans with no idea as to why.

Otto leaned on his crutches and stepped up the stairs toward his uncertain future. A guard opened the door and saluted. Another soldier greeted them in the vestibule and walked them back an office where a Generalmajor sat behind a dark wooden desk and talked on a telephone. A Nazi flag was draped next to the window behind the desk, and a well-stocked bookshelf sat on the wall to his left.

Otto leaned on his crutches and saluted when he entered the doorway. The Generalmajor waived him into the room. Hans entered, saluted, and followed Otto.

"Yes, sir. I understand. Heil Hitler!" he said as he hung up the phone.

"Oberstleutnant Mader and Hauptmann Krieger?" The two men nodded. The Generalmajor closed a file on his desk. "I was just reading about you." He stood and turned to look out the window behind his desk, with his hands clasped together behind him.

"Do you know there are men in Berlin who refuse to fight for Germany? They are given the honor to go to battle for their country and they refuse to serve in the Fuhrer's army."

Otto's heart began to pound.

"Those men who are not brave enough to fight are not brave enough to live. I am told that when they are captured, they are hanged on the spot. There are times when there are no trees left for them, so they must dangle from streetlamps."

Hans resisted the urge to blurt out how they had followed their training and that they had taken every action they could to defeat the Russians.

The Generalmajor turned from the window and sat in his chair. "And that is what makes your bravery so extraordinary. I am proud to know that Germany still has men such as you fighting for her."

He opened the file and flipped though it until he found a page to his liking. "It was quite a battle you had with Ivan. Please tell me about it."

Otto paused to choose his words carefully. "Sir, we were only following orders." He and Hans exchanged a quick glance.

"That is the response I would expect from a true soldier such as you. But looking at the file, it seems you went above and beyond your orders. I am told your tanks were outnumbered by as many as eight to one. Yet you were able to inflict casualties at a rate of at least five to one.

"And even though you were attacked by surprise, you retreated, regrouped, and attacked. You were able to destroy the spearhead of a major advance by our enemy. Had you not fought with such honor and valor, the Russians would have advanced even more quickly than they did." He paused and thought about how quickly the enemy was able to cut through the German lines.

"But the Reich will prevail. When the war is over, it is Germany who will raise her flag with pride."

He looked Otto in the eyes. "Your bravery and gallantry have not gone unnoticed. Actions such as yours have eyes in Berlin looking your direction."

"Sir, I am honored to serve my country. It was my duty to fight, and I was proud to do it."

The Majorgeneral turned his attention to Hans. "And you, Hauptmann Krieger, you displayed equally impressive strength. Not only did you fight alongside Oberstleutnant Mader and inflict major damage to the Russians, but when the battle was over you saved his life and made sure he was taken for medical treatment.

"Such loyalty is sadly lacking these days, even by many men who wear the same uniform that you and I do. Your willingness to stand next to your commander during battle and to preserve his life are exemplary. If only every man in the Reich would act as you did."

"Thank you, sir. But as Oberstleutnant Mader said, we were only following orders. It was my honor to fight."

"Your modesty is refreshing. But I am not the only one who has taken note of you. Your actions have been well received at the highest level. You are both to be awarded the Oak Leaves to Knights Cross of the Iron Cross."

Hans' knees nearly buckled and he fought hide it from the Generalmajor.

PHANTOM PANTHERS

The Generalmajor continued. "As you know, the Oak Leaves is one of the highest awards that can be given to German soldiers for bravery and leadership during battle. I cannot think of a more deserving pair of soldiers to receive it."

CHAPTER 4
Wolfsschanze, Hitler's Eastern Headquarters

The train ride through Eastern Prussia flew by in a quiet haze for Otto. He spent most of the ride reflecting in silence and wondering what it would be like to meet the Fuhrer in person. It seemed that the rest of the Panzertruppen were doing much the same and no one spoke very much at all. He knew that he should be eager, but for some reason he felt a strange feeling of apprehension about the whole ordeal. Even after several hours on a train, he'd come no closer to figuring out what was throwing him off.

Otto didn't know exactly where it was that the train finally stopped, only that it was somewhere he'd never been before. When he and the rest of the small entourage disembarked from the train, they were met by a group of Hitler's own personally appointed bodyguards, the black uniformed SS.

From the platform, the SS officers directed Otto and the rest of the Panzertruppen to a motorcade of black Mercedes which were apparently going to take them the rest of the way into Hitler's top-secret HQ. Otto and Hans got into the back of one such vehicle and soon the duo was being driven through the dark, mossy woodlands that pervaded so much of Eastern Prussia. The air was hot and humid, the thick canopy growth trapping moisture like a sponge. Otto found himself sweating in the back of the luxurious sedan, and he could see that Hans felt the same discomfort.

They passed through Rastenburg, as well as several other small towns, until finally reaching the redoubt known as Wolfsschanze.

It was even more incredible and secretive than Otto could have imagined. Built near the beginning of the war, the Wolf's Lair, as it was known, was Hitler's haven; it was where he strategized, where he ruled, and even where he relaxed. From outside the complex, Otto observed thick concrete walls draped with mossy camouflage. Despite its enormous size, the Wolf's Lair was well hidden and had remained unknown to the Allies even through their ever broadening reconnaissance.

Otto's staff car, which happened to be at the front of the motorcade, pulled up to the main guard gate leading into the military complex. A stoic SS sentry robotically demanded the appropriate papers from the driver before allowing them to pass. Behind them, Otto saw that the same cautious measure was taken with each and every vehicle in the motorcade; security was clearly at its tightest here in the heart of the Reich.

Once through the main gate, Otto and Hans' driver parked them in a small lot and informed them that they'd make the rest of their journey through the fortress on foot. They waited, leaning against the side of their sedan, as the rest of the tank crewmen and officers were checked and admitted through the main gate. When the rest of the Panzertruppen – Otto counted about a dozen in total – were checked in, another SS officer led the group through the first security boundary of Wolfsschanze. This was Otto's first time inside Hitler's Eastern HQ, but he'd heard rumors of its design. He knew that the complex was organized into three zones, or layers, each more tightly guarded than the last. At its center were Hitler's own personal quarters, rumored to contain many secret passages into and out of the camp.

As Otto followed their appointed chauffer through the first zone, he was struck by an ominous air of tense protocol. Wolfsschanze's location deep inside the woodlands of Eastern Prussia was no accident; the entire camp was camouflaged with moss and mud. Nets hung between each building, woven with underbrush from the surrounding forest. Every building was made from enormous stone blocks or concrete – no fragile wood or commercial brick anywhere to be seen. Otto knew that the purpose of all the camouflage was to avoid discovery by air, and he had no doubt that the complex was indistinguishable from above. Even if the Allies or the Communists somehow discovered the location of the Lair, Otto observed multiple concrete bunkers throughout the first zone, and he had no doubt those bunkers were built with thicker and thicker walls the deeper into the Lair they went.

All in all, the Wolf's Lair was well fortified, but extremely depressing. Even in the middle of the afternoon, the filtered rays of the sun through the dense forestry made it feel like twilight. It made for a very ominous experience.

When they made it to the gate leading into the second zone, they were again obligated to display the appropriate paperwork. One at a time, each member of the gathered Panzertruppen was cleared for entry into the second layer.

The second layer of the complex was more tightly packed than the first. Otto noticed multiple high-ranking officers going about their duties as their group made their way towards the third zone. He actually recognized two of the officers from posters he'd seen earlier in the war and he pointed them out to Hans as they walked. This was clearly the residence of many great men.

Outside the gate leading into the third zone, Otto and the rest of the Panzertruppen were instructed to wait in a small anteroom within a guardhouse while some last-minute preparations were made for the awarding ceremony. It was then that Otto noticed just how many high-ranking officers were in their presence; as many if not more than there were Panzertruppen.

Otto took the opportunity during their brief intermission in the anteroom to do a once over of the gathered Panzertruppen.

He knew, or at least knew of, almost every man there. Some he had known from training, others from fighting and still others merely by reputation. As they waited, many of them made small talk amongst themselves. They all wondered what exactly lay in wait for them inside the third zone.

Finally, a man who identified himself as the Officer of the Watch entered the anteroom.

"The Fuhrer is ready to commence with the awards ceremony now," he proclaimed to the gathered Panzertruppen. As one, the Panzertruppen formed up to a single-file line and made their way out of the anteroom. The Officer of the Watch led them to just outside the gate leading into the third zone, then stopped them.

"I'm sure you each understand that security is of the utmost importance at this dire time. Before you can enter any deeper into Wolfsschanze, I'm afraid a body search will be mandatory," the Officer said.

The Officer of the Watch started at the back of the line and did a thorough frisk of each man. Each member of the Panzertruppen was asked to surrender his pistol and any other weapons on his person, even something as small as a pocket knife. Finally, he got to Otto who was at the front of the line with Hans.

"Herr Oberstleutnant, your Luger please," said the Officer of the Watch after performing a full-body frisk.

"No," Otto said flatly.

"Oberst Mader, this is not optional. You will surrender your pistol or you will not enter the third zone."

Otto looked the Officer directly in the eyes. "I don't care. If the Fuhrer can't trust his officers at the front, then who can he trust?"

Otto saw a vein on the Officer's neck begin throbbing as his face turned beet red. "You've been chosen to receive the Oak Leaves, the highest honor any man can earn and you have the gall to…"

"The Fuhrer can shove his Oak Leaves up his ass if he can't trust a man who's already proven willing to give his life – and more – for the Fatherland. I keep my pistol, or I leave right now."

Before the officer could say anything else, Hitler's Commander der Panzertruppen, Oberst Nicolaus von Below, stepped out from the anteroom where he'd been watching the confrontation. "Excuse us for a moment, gentlemen," he said as he took the Officer of the Watch by the elbow and led him back into the anteroom.

Otto could feel the tension build in the air around the gathering as they waited for the Officer to return. Suddenly he found himself feeling extremely anxious about the award he was about to receive. More than anything, he just wanted this day to be over.

Finally, after what felt like an hour but was in fact only a couple minutes, Oberst Bellow came back out of the anteroom followed by the Officer of the Watch. Oberst Bellow addressed the gathered Panzertruppen.

"Fellow patriots of the Reich, given your uniquely proven dedication to your country and our cause, it has been decided that you shall all be allowed to enter the third zone with your side arms in tow. Please appreciate the depth of our trust demonstrated by this allowance; it is entirely unprecedented. But, then again, this is an unprecedented time for the Fatherland, so special exceptions must be made."

The announcement did nothing to make Otto or Hans feel any better about their situation. Nonetheless, they followed along as they were led into the third zone, side arms still in place. Past the steel wall, they were led to Hitler's personal bunker and then into the conference chamber inside. It was a small auditorium with a map table at the center, the only decorations being multiple flags bearing the swastika and eagle of the Reich.

Once the Panzertruppen were seated around the room, along with several other generals and high-ranking officers, one of

Hitler's personal aides entered the room and announced that the Fuhrer would join them momentarily. However, 'momentarily' soon became 15, then 30 minutes as the Panzertruppen anxiously awaited their Fuhrer. The air inside the chamber felt painfully intense, even for men trained and bred to face down Germany's enemies from inside the hellish bowels of a tank.

Finally, Otto could hear voices approaching from the corridor adjoining the side of the room opposite from which they'd entered. As one, the gathered Panzertruppen and officers stood at attention. As the voices drew closer, it became clear that one of the voices was louder than all the rest. Near to shouting, in fact.

"What do you suppose has the Fuhrer so upset this time?" Otto heard a general he recognized as his former commander, General Warlimont, whisper loudly to one of the other officers next to him.

"Most likely another reminder from Fraulein Braun," the other whispered back. "She's been badgering him nonstop for more generous rations in Berlin and to lift the ban on women's permanent waves."

The voices were growing closer and closer to the auditorium and now Otto could actually make out the contents of the tirade from the voice that could only be Hitler's. "… My front line generals do not share the fervor of a true National Socialist! Goebbels was right, they are all weak and ignore my wisdom in the art of war. I must constantly remind them that I'm responsible for the economics of the German people – as important to our victory as any battle." At that, the door opened and Hitler burst into the room, red-faced and bespectacled, one of his hands shaking violently. He seemed surprised to find the group of Panzertruppen and other officers waiting for him.

One of the aides near the back of the room quickly made his way over to Hitler and whispered something in his ear. His eyes widened in recognition, and he scanned the room with new awareness. He took a deep breath to compose himself, adjusted his glasses, straightened his jacket, and then let a somewhat forced chuckle tumble out of his mouth.

"Gentlemen, forgive me for raising my voice. The frustrations of wartime have taken their toll on us all, it seems," he said warmly.

As Otto beheld his Fuhrer up close and personal, he had to agree. Hitler looked weary, as if he hadn't had a good night's sleep in years. His shoulders were slouched, and his eyes had dark rings around them. He wasn't skinny or malnourished, but somehow he looked gaunt. Little beads of sweat dotted his brow. Otto felt bad for the man; he reminded him of Atlas, the Greek titan forever condemned to bear the weight of the world.

The Fuhrer continued his introductory remarks. "Today we are here to acknowledge and glorify the courage and prowess of our most remarkable Aryan warriors. Don't let my complaints distract you from this wonderful day; I deal too much with politicians and high officers, a task even more frightening than Ivan's invasion." He let out another chuckle at that, and the rest of the room joined him. Otto knew that several such generals and politicians were in the room even now, but none showed any sign of offense.

"In a different time, it would be right to dedicate an entire day – nay, an entire week – to the glorious feats that each and every one of you have accomplished. Were it up to me, we'd have parades in your honor and all of Germany would celebrate with us. Unfortunately, the constraints of wartime don't allow such frivolity, so this private ceremony will have to do. I won't keep you long, as I know you've all traveled far to be here today." He turned to the Officer of the Watch, who was still pouting near the back of the room. "Bring me the Leaves!"

The Officer of the Watch walked up the front of the room bearing a small wooden box, which he then handed off to the

Fuhrer. Then he turned to the Panzertruppen. "Achtung!" he barked, and the awardees straightened into proper form – heels together, backs and arms straight with eyes pointed forward.

The 'awards ceremony' turned out to be rather casual in nature. Hitler made his way around the room deliberately, stopping in front of each man as his aide announced the recipient's name and accomplishments to the room. Hitler would then shake his hand and personally pin the Oak Leaves to his collar, meanwhile making smart remarks and attempting to harness the charisma that Otto knew had once come so easily. Now it just seemed forced and insincere.

Finally, Hitler came to Hans and Otto. After he heard their names announced, Otto noticed a distinct spark of recognition in his eyes. "General Warlimont," he called to the other side of the room, "Are these the two officers you had told me were under your command?"

"Ja Wohl, Mein Fuhrer," Warlimont said as he marched up beside the Fuhrer. "These were the only two survivors from their unit – they were tank commanders from the 667th StuG unit that effectively slowed the Russian's armored forces from advancing on Western Russia. They faced insurmountable odds and lived to tell the tale." Otto noticed the use of the word *were* and wondered what, if anything, it meant.

"Ahhh," Hitler said, "So you killed a lot of Russians then?"

Hans didn't seem sure whether or not the question was rhetorical, so Otto answered for him. "Yes, we certainly did, Mein Fuhrer."

"Most excellent!" the Fuhrer said as he clapped each man on the shoulder. "An Oberst and his faithful Hauptmann; it does my heart good to know we have men like you guarding the Reich against the Red rats of the East. If Stalin had any compassion at all he'd take mercy on his men and spare them the wrath of

Panzertruppen such as you. You have my personal thanks for your deeds!"

The Fuhrer extended a handshake to each man. Otto noticed that his grip was tight, but clammy. Otto stared straight forward as Hitler pinned the Oak Leaves to his collar. But, the Fuhrer noticed something else as he was attaching the award.

"I see you bear a Golden Wound," he said pointing to another badge on Mader's uniform. "When did you earn that?"

"It was the battle at Smolensk back in '41," he explained, "It was the same fight that earned me my Knight's Cross."

"Truly amazing!" Hitler said, before turning to the rest of the gathering. "This is exactly the type of man that the Reich needs more of." He turned back to Otto. "The Reich always pays its debts and you Oberst, have done much to deserve our gratitude. Rest assured that you and your family will be richly rewarded when the war is over." At that, he gave Otto another tight, clammy handshake before making his way back up to the front of the room.

Reich's Leader Bormann will direct you to your departure quarters. Martin, show my loyals to Master of the Order Baron Rudolf Von Sebottendorff.

As if on cue, all of the aides and non-officers quickly made their way out of the room. All that was left were the high-ranking officers near the front of the room and the Panzertruppen still standing at attention around the perimeter.

Gentlemen, my associate, SS Standartenfuhrer Franz Sonnenlightner, on behalf of Reichsfuhrer Heinrich Himmler, high priestess of the Vril Society, "Panzersoldaten, the Fatherland already owes you more than can be repaid for your courage and gallantry in the face of our enemies. And yet, there is more work to be done… In fact, it is the most important work that has ever been given to any man of the Wehrmacht." You men, through your demonstration of mettle and military prowess, are to be the cornerstone of that work. He looked around the room, meeting the eyes of each and every Panzertruppen gathered there.

Standartenfuhrer Sonnenlightner continues. "At this moment, I am personally detaching you from your respective commands and placing you under my personal supervision for the remainder of the war. This is a special assignment, Panzertruppen; only you can fulfill the needs of the Reich. Each of you will play a direct part in our victory over the Allies and the Bolsheviks, even more so than you already have."

He paused for a moment to take a breath.

"At this time, if any one of you is not prepared to give your life for the Reich, I ask you to leave this room. You will not be punished or looked down upon in any way, however, we cannot have anything less than full dedication to the task which I am about to set before you."

He paused again, waiting for any of the Panzertruppen to object. "Excellent," he said when no one left. Around the room, Otto heard quiet murmurs as the Panzertruppen exchanged nervous glances with each other. Every man among them was anxious to hear what exactly their 'special assignment' would entail.

"Panzertruppen, I'm sure that your reassignment under my command comes as a stark surprise. I'm sure that many of you were expecting this to be a conventional awards ceremony, one from which you would return to your normal units with your normal men." The Baron looked around the room solemnly, as if he could read the minds of the awardees. "I'm here to tell you that 'normal' will not be enough to win us this war. We need something… Supernatural." "We are in a time of dire need, brothers, and we need the weapons – the power – to match that need. Each of you have been chosen to be the anointed by which we will harness that power and strike the finishing blow against our enemies.

And what a blow it will be!" The Baron said as he slammed his fist into his open palm.

The Baron was excited now, almost giddy. His glee was infectious, and Otto found himself smiling. He had suspected from the beginning that they wouldn't have been called all the way to the Wolf's Lair just for a routine awards ceremony... Now, his hunch had been proven right.

"When I dismiss you from this room, you will be immediately transported to Wewelsberg Castle." The murmurs spread around the room at that. Wewelsberg was the symbolic heart of the SS. What could the Panzertruppen be needed for there? "Arrangements have already been made with your former superiors so that they won't expect you back in their ranks. Your personal effects have also been taken care of; you will find them waiting for you at Wewelsburg."

One of the awarded Panzertruppen voiced what all of them were thinking. "What's at Wewelsberg? Shouldn't we head straight to the front?"

The Baron smiled at that. "I applaud your eagerness to face our enemies, comrade and rest assured that they will feel your wrath again in due time. However, we have new weapons for you – superior weapons – and there is a certain... Let's call it a training process... That you must complete before you can properly put those weapons to use."

"Well, now," once the Baron finished, "what do you all think of that?" The room was silent now. No murmurs, no nothing.

Slowly, Otto raised his hand.

"Herr Oberst Mader?" von Sebottendorff acknowledges.

"Mein Herr von Sebottendorff, you know that I would give my life for the Reich. I always have and always will do whatever is asked of me, as would any man in this room," Otto prefaced, "But I also know of every armored training ground throughout Germany.

I know of no such facilities at Wewelsberg. What training could we possibly do in an old castle that we couldn't more effectively do at Grafenwohr, or somewhere else even closer to the front?"

The Master of the Order smiled once Otto had finished his question. "I can see that we have truly chosen the greatest warriors that Germany has to offer. Would that all of our soldiers shared the fervor and dedication possessed by each and every one of you in this room! We'd need no new weapons to win this war." von Sebottendorff now looked directly at Otto. "You will understand everything in due time, Herr Oberst. Right now, all I ask is that you trust your Fuhrer and the mission he has given me. Can you do that?"

"Ja Wohl, Mein Herr. 'Til the day I die." Otto said and he meant it.

"There are things which even I am not permitted to speak of," von Sebottendorff said, now addressing the rest of the Panzertruppen, "At least, not now. Not in this room. As I've asked Oberst Mader, I ask each of you – trust me. Trust our mission and follow your instructions. Do not worry about anything else. If you can do that, then I promise you that the war is taking a different course. Things have been put in motion and you are each about to play a pivotal part. Throughout the trials that await you, remember what you're fighting for. You're not just fighting for our Fuhrer. You're fighting for our country, for your families, for your comrades and for your children. You've already earned my thanks, gentlemen, but when you've completed the task set before you, all of the Fatherland will thank you too."

He let that final statement hang in the air for several moments as the Panzertruppen took in all that he had said. Then, once he was satisfied that there were no more questions, he said, "That will be all," and let his hands fall to his sides.

As one, the Panzertruppen reactively raised their right arms into the air, palms down in salute. "Heil Hitler!" they shouted. "And may the Reich last a thousand years!", as they departed from the Wolf's lair.

CHAPTER 5

Wewelsburg Castle, Symbolic Heart of the SS

Otto was thoroughly exhausted by the time he, Hans and the rest of the awarded Panzertruppen de-trained in the Village of Wewelsburg. They had been on a train all night and then all the next day, so that the sun was already setting by the time they arrived in the village. Despite his best attempts, the seasoned tank commander hadn't managed more than a couple hours of scattered dozing on the train. He wasn't the only one, either; the assembled soldiers were unanimously groggy as they filtered into the motorcade that would take them from the village to the Castle proper.

Fortunately, their SS chauffeurs were patient. Otto couldn't help but notice the stark contrast between the stoic attitude they'd encountered from the SS in Wolfsschanze and the almost reverential one they were greeted with here. It felt as if each of their SS handlers knew some deep secret that he and the rest of the Panzertruppen were yet to discover. Or maybe it was some inside joke, or some sense of sympathy. It was hard to tell.

As they approached Wewelsburg, the Castle eclipsed the setting sun forming a black silhouette against the twilight sky. The sun created shimmering lines of light around the edges of the castle's silhouette, deep red and magenta clouds blended into gold across the evening sky. It was as if Mother Nature herself were giving them royal treatment.

"Beautiful, isn't it?" Hans said from his seat next to Otto. The two had stuck together and ridden in the same car, as per usual.

Otto had no reply. Seeing Wewelsburg Castle for the first time hadn't done anything to assuage Otto's unease.

Finally, the dozen awarded Panzertruppen arrived in the motor pool outside Wewelsburg Castle. They entered the Castle proper through the East wing, their SS chauffeurs showing them across the bridge that spanned the Renaissance-era moat.

The sun had set completely by the time they'd entered the Castle proper, but even in the moonlight Otto was struck by the enormity of the establishment. He could see that Hans was too; the younger man's jaw hung open as he looked up at the walls around them. The castle was built as a triangle, with a tower on each corner and an enormous triangular courtyard at its center. From the courtyard it seemed that you could access each of the towers, as well as several other rooms and stairways leading up to higher levels. In the darkness, Otto couldn't accurately count exactly how many floors high the Castle went, but he estimated that its walls rose at least 15 meters, possibly even 20. Some of the rooms were lit, but most of them were dark.

"This place must be ancient," Hans remarked as they made their way across the courtyard.

One of their SS escorts near the front of the party heard Hans and confirmed his guess. He looked back over his shoulder as he said, "Ja, the castle dates back to the ninth century. It fell into Himmler's possession in 1934." The man looked forward again as he continued, "This is the location and is the center of the Ahnenerbe under the Third Reich, but the Fuhrer has put a hold on all non-essential construction until the final victory."

Just as the SS officer finished explaining the Castle's history and purpose, they arrived at the North tower. It was the largest of the three, both the thickest in diameter and the tallest. Two enormous wooden doors stood as the entrance into the tower from the courtyard. The leading SS officer turned to address them once more.

"Once you enter through these doors, you will not be able to leave until the ceremony is complete. Any man without the courage to continue had best leave now," the officer said, standing in front of the thick wooden doors.

"Ceremony? We weren't told anything about a ceremony…" Hans subtly whispered into Otto's ear. But, nobody made a move to leave, so the officer opened the doors to the tower and strode in. As one, the Panzertruppen followed him inside. Only the leading SS officer accompanied them inside the tower; the rest that'd been in their escort party waited outside.

Inside the tower, they were led up a spiral staircase. The climb left Otto surprisingly winded, but he supposed that a good night's sleep would fix that. *Plenty of time to sleep when I'm dead*, he thought.

Finally, they reached what had to be the top of the tower. The stairs led them directly into an enormous circular chamber with a massive roundtable at its center. The scent of fresh baked bread filled the air, and Otto soon saw why. The table was set with several loaves of bread and just as many stoneware carafes.

The whole scene reminded Otto of a fairytale he'd heard as a child, the one about King Arthur and the Knights of the Round Table. The table he saw here even had twelve seats, just like the one in the story. At each seat was set a stoneware plate and chalice, and the room was lit with thick, well-used candles. The only thing that separated this particular table from the one Otto had always imagined in the stories was that this one had a swastika engraved across its enormous surface. Except that the swastika one the table had twelve spokes instead of four, one extending out to each seat.

"Please, sit down," a mousy voice said from the opposite side of the room. The voice took Otto completely by surprise, for he hadn't seen the small, fat man who'd been standing in the shadows, apparently waiting for them. "You must be famished from your journey," he said, now making his way fully into the candlelight. "Eat, drink," he said jovially, "we've been waiting for you."

"And who exactly is 'we'?" one of the other Panzertruppen asked.

The horn rimmed glass man smiled, "I am Heinrich Himmler and the men you've already met are my Black Guard. They are the best and brightest that the SS has to offer and without their help, the ritual that is to take place tonight would not be possible." He looked around at the clearly skeptical soldiers. "But, please! Eat something first. You will need your energy for what's to come.

The Panzertruppen made their way uneasily around the table, each man finding a seat. The loaves of bread were passed around and each man tore himself off a piece. The carafes were filled with red wine, and the SS officer and Himmler went around filling each soldier's chalice.

"I hope you will forgive me for preparing such a modest meal," the pudgy man who called himself Himmler said, "but I thought it fitting given the circumstances. A 'last supper' of sorts, a parting meal before each of you are resurrected as true Aryan warriors."

This was getting a little bit too strange for Otto and he didn't think that wine would do anything to help his nerves. So, he politely refused when Himmler went to fill his chalice.

"Do you have water? I'm too tired for wine," Otto stated, trying to be polite but too exhausted to care if he failed.

Himmler smiled, which only made his double chin more noticeable. "Ah, I think you will find this particular wine more… *Rejuvenating*… Than most," he urged gently. "Plus, a little inebriation will help you to relax."

Otto had to admit that he had a point there; he was anything but relaxed. Perhaps the wine wasn't such a bad idea after all. He didn't make another objection as Himmler filled his chalice.

PHANTOM PANTHERS

The tankers ate their meal in silence, too fatigued to make any sort of conversation. Himmler, however, seemed almost giddy at their presence. He strode around the table as the twelve men ate, regaling them with tales of the Castle's history. He told them of past kings and conquerors; some of the tales sounded historical, but most of them sounded like they were taken from folklore. He spoke of ancient magic and of Germany's 'ancestral inheritance', and of witch hunts and ancient Gothic artifacts.

As Otto drank his wine and ate his bread, he found himself feeling substantially more intoxicated than he'd expected from a single glass. The wine was sweeter than any he'd ever tasted, but it had a strange thickness to it and a slight metallic taste, as if something else had been mixed into the drink. Otto found himself staring blankly at the table as the world swam around him; Himmler's words began blurring together and the black lines on the table looked as if they were slithering back and forth like snakes.

Otto blinked and rubbed his eyes. Everything was normal again. Otto looked at Hans next to him and saw that his younger companion was just as wobbly as he was. His head bobbed up and down slowly, his eyes half shut. Otto nudged him and he too snapped back to reality.

"Now that you've eaten your fill, the ritual can begin! Please, follow me," Himmler said, walking over to stand in front of the stairway up which they'd come. It took the Panzertruppen a moment to respond, their wits slowed by both the wine and the hour. It was full nighttime now and the moon was well into the sky. It cast a deep orange glow into the room; the moon seemed almost bloated from its position suspended above the horizon. *A harvest moon*, Otto thought idly as he stood. *What are the odds?*

From the room with the round table, Himmler led them slowly back down the staircase. He took his time to make sure that none of the men missed a step in their inebriated state. Otto and Hans tagged along at the back of the procession.

"You okay?" Otto whispered to Hans.

"I think so, just a bit tipsy. That wine was strong."

Otto had to agree with him on that. He focused intently on the stairs in front of them, taking each step deliberately in order to keep his footing.

At the bottom of the stairs, Himmler led the Panzertruppen across the chamber that formed the tower's ground floor. They went across the room to an unmarked wooden door on the opposite side. Himmler pulled out a ring of keys from his robes and gingerly selected an old, iron key. It was worn and rusty, but the door opened easily when the small man gently twisted it into the lock.

Beyond the door was another stairwell, but this one was narrower and pitch black, and it led down instead of up.

Himmler turned to address the Panzertruppen. "Are you ready, Panzertruppen?" He looked around at each soldier. "You entered this castle as men. You've eaten the holy sacrament; you've cleansed your mind of inhibition. Now, you're ready to unlock the power of the immortal Reich. The next time you see this room," he motioned to the chamber around them, "you will be gods, not men. You will possess the power to liberate the Reich and usher in a new world!"

The retarding effects of the wine seemed to be fading, and Otto found himself beginning to feel excited for the first time since his arrival at Wolfsschanze. He could feel the power of this place and it energized him. Power… That was what he wanted. He would be the one to save the Reich; he and each of the other men gathered here.

"Heil Hitler!" he found himself shouting, though such fervid patriotism was outside his normal behavior.

"Heil Hitler!" the rest of the Panzertruppen cried together. Their call echoed around the tower chamber, and it was apparent that Otto wasn't the only one buzzing with the anticipation of new power.

Himmler smiled and grabbed a torch from the tower wall. Then he turned around, and led the way down the narrow staircase that descended beneath the tower, torch held above his head. The Panzertruppen followed in single file, the walls too narrow for any other arrangement. There were no lights in the stairwell other than the torch Himmler held in hand, and the ceiling stooped low overhead.

The lack of illumination combined with the twists and turns of the stairwell made the going slow, but after several minutes of blind groping a distinct red glow could be seen ahead. Around another corner the procession finally made their way down onto flat ground. The stairwell opened up into a crypt of some sort. It was much wider than the stairwell down which they'd come, but the ceiling was still low enough to touch. The walls were lined with iron sconces holding strange black candles lit with rich, red flames.

At the other side of the crypt was a set of thick wooden double doors, much like the ones at the tower's entrance. Above the doors was inscribed a single line of old German text. As nearly as Otto could translate, the inscription read "Hall of the Dead".

A shudder ran down Otto's spine. He tried to gather his thoughts to focus on the task at hand, but he felt so strange... Even now, he had to concentrate to keep the walls from swimming.

Himmler led them through the crypt and as they neared the double doors on the opposite side, Otto could have sworn that he heard voices. Some sort of foreign chant was rumbling from the room beyond.

"Do you hear that?" Otto whispered to Hans, but his younger friend was clearly also under the effect of the wine, his eyes only half open, and he didn't respond.

Outside the double doors, Himmler stopped and turned to address the Panzertruppen once more. "Walk carefully comrades, for through these doors is holy ground," he declared. "Take your boots off, take your uniforms off; these robes will be all that you wear into the Hall of the Dead." Otto wasn't sure where the robes had come from, but he now saw that Himmler had a number of plain burlap robes draped over the arm that wasn't holding the torch. Slowly, the Panzertruppen drunkenly disrobed their uniforms and donned the simple brown robes.

Finally, once every man was properly dressed, Himmler opened the doors and proceeded into the chamber beyond. It was an enormous circular chamber, much like the one at the top of the tower. Except, there were no windows in this one and no table. Instead, it was lit with the same strange, red-glowing candles as had been in the crypt. Twelve figures in black robes were lined around the perimeter of the room. As Otto looked closer, he realized that they were the ones he'd heard chanting in the hall, but even now that he was in the room with them, he couldn't understand what they were saying. They were chanting in some sort of foreign tongue. Or maybe Otto was just too drunk to make out their mumbled words; either way, he soon forgot the figures as he absorbed the rest of the room.

Positioned around the room were twelve stone plinths. The floor bore the same black, twelve-spoked swastika-like design as had been on the table where they'd eaten their 'last supper'. Each plinth was positioned on one of the points. There were several objects lying on each of the plinths, but from the entrance to the room Otto couldn't make out exactly what they were. But, perhaps most peculiar of all was the statue that rose from the center of the room, right at the black sun design's center. It was a statue of some sort of archaic beast, a dragon or hydra of some sort, and it looked as if it held a babe in its mouth.

"Each of you, find a pedestal. The ceremony is about to begin," Himmler said. His voice seemed distant now, as if the room itself were swallowing sound.

Hans looked even more intoxicated than Otto felt, so the older Oberst helped guide the younger Hauptmann to one of the plinths, and then picked his own right next to Hans. Around him, the rest of the Panzertruppen did the same.

Now that he stood over the pedestal, he could more clearly make out to the objects lying on the plinth. There were three of them – a strange ring that bore a type of sunburst insignia, a thin, metal-capped rod that bore runic etchings along its shaft, and a sort of medal not so dissimilar from the Oak Leaves he'd received just… 24 hours ago? He couldn't remember how long it had been since he'd been in Wolfsschanze. Time didn't seem to flow normally in this place.

Now one of the robed figures stopped chanting and stepped out from the perimeter of the room. When he pulled back his hood, Otto recognized him as the Baron. Behind him, another man stepped forward and pulled back his hood, but this man Otto didn't recognize.

"Panzertruppen, I see you've already met our heir and leader, Reichsfuhrer Heinrich Himmler. This man is Hauptsturmfuhrer Wolfram Sievers," the Baron said, indicating the robed man next to him. "Together, we three will induct you into the ancient order of the Teutonic Knights, or the Black Knights as they were known of old."

"Panzertruppen," Sievers began, "through your blood, sweat and courage, you've brought glory to the Reich. You've proven your dedication to the destruction of our enemies and any who oppose our true Aryan heritage. This ceremony is nothing more than the realization of the sacrifices you've already made."

The chanting around the room grew slightly louder and Himmler continued after Sievers. "Panzertruppen, I am Reichsfuhrer, the reincarnation of the Great Heinrich the First, the Germanic king of old. Great warriors of the Reich; as I am the resurrection of a once-great king, now you shall become the resurrection of once-great conquerors."

Again, the volume of the chanting grew louder. It became hard to hear the words that the three men at the center of the room spoke. Now, the Baron spoke, "Placed in front of you are three totems of power: the holy Spear of Longinus, shattered and re-formed into the batons you see before you. The Luciferian Crown, which you shall wear always on your right, middle finger. And the Emblem of the Teutonic Knights, an award befitting the greatness of your new stations."

Otto's eyes widened as he realized the trueness of the power that hummed in this ancient tomb. These were relics only whispered of in legends; could this really be the true Spear of Longinus, the same spear that once pierced the side of Christ? Could the balding spectacled man that stood in the middle of the robed trio at the center of the room really be the reincarnation of Germany's first king, Heinrich I?

Otto knew that at a different time, in a different place, he would laugh at the notion. But the wine he'd drunk – if it were really wine at all – had dulled his senses beyond the bounds of normal alcohol, and he was exhausted on top of that. Now, through drowsy eyes and ears, the entire scene seemed hauntingly real, divinely orchestrated.

Now, another man broke from the black figures that chanted along the perimeter of the chamber. This one, however, seemed more out of place than anything. Awkwardly, he began, "I am Dr. Hermann Schreck Grand Master of the Order of the Coven, the man who uncovered and deciphered this ancient ritual. Now, it is I who will lead you in your induction into the Order of the Teutonic Knights." He looked around the room, his eyes beady behind his thin glasses. "Each of you will now extend your right hand over your plinths, palm open and facing upwards."

As one, the Panzertruppen obeyed.

"Now, do not flinch. Do not pull away. Only blood can pay for blood, and blood is what we seek. The blood of our enemies." Otto watched, hand outstretched, as the man who called himself Sievers brandished a jagged bronze dagger from his robes, as if on cue. Its hilt was carved into the likeness of a ram, although there was something otherworldly about the depiction. From this place at the center of the room, Sievers strode forward to stand in front of Otto's plinth first.

Otto's heart was beating madly in his chest. He struggled to keep his outstretched arm from shaking as Sievers reached up and gingerly grabbed his wrist. He looked at Otto directly in the eyes.

"Otto Mader, former Oberstleutnant of the 667th StuG Brigade, repeat after me…" Otto looked at him, forcing himself to maintain his composure. "I, Otto Mader…"

"I, Otto Mader…" Otto repeated.

"A trueborn warrior of the Reich…"

"*A trueborn warrior of the Reich…*"

"…Pledge to seek the glory of the Aryan race and to forever guard the heritage of the Fatherland." Otto struggled to repeat the words properly.

"I swear this in the name of the Fuhrer and by mine own blood it shall be true."

"*I swear this in the name of the Fuhrer and by mine own blood it shall be true.*"

At that, Sievers raised the jagged knife and swiftly slashed it across Otto's outstretched palm, tearing a deep gash across it. Otto instinctively tried to recoil, but Sievers held his wrist tight.

Blood spilled out of the wound and onto the three objects on the plinth below. Blood pooled around and beneath the three objects, until it slowly began dribbling off the side of the pedestal. Only then did Sievers release his grip on Otto's wrist.

The wound on Otto's hand burned intensely. It felt as if the knife had burned him in addition to creating a laceration. He cradled his wound against his chest as Sievers moved adjacent to him, now in front of Hans' pedestal. Sievers began repeating the same ritual with Hans, but Otto was too distracted by the pain in his hand to pay attention. He felt tears welling up in his eyes, but when he used his unwounded hand to wipe them away, he found his hand sticky and red; he was crying blood.

As Otto looked down at the pedestal in front of him, he saw that the objects that had once been inanimate now seem to have a life of their own. The etchings along the rod, the Spear of Longinus as they'd called it, now pulsed with a gentle glow, as if it thrived on his blood. The ring that bore the Luciferian Crown seemed to twitch in place, as if it were itching to adorn his finger. The multi-faceted Teutonic Cross also had a slight glow to it, but nowhere near as intense as that from the baton.

Sievers had finished the liturgy with Hans and had now moved onto the next soldier at the next pedestal over. As Otto looked at his friend, he saw that the younger man also somehow wept tears of blood. Dark lines streamed down his face as he held his hand against his chest. He realized that the chanting had grown louder now too and it continued to crescendo as Sievers made his way around the room, completing the blood rites with each soldier in turn. Finally, Sievers rejoined the Baron, Himmler and Schreck at the center of the chamber, all of them standing beneath the statue of the beast at the chamber's center.

Himmler raised his hands over his head now and had to shout to be heard over the chanting of the dark figures around the perimeter of the room.

"What has been said cannot be undone," he proclaimed, "and what has bled cannot be healed. You shall bear the scars of this rite for as long as you live and in turn you shall seek the blood of our enemies until the day you die." He looked around the room now, arms still raised, examining each of the Panzertruppen in turn. "Each of the relics before you contains the power of our ancestors; taken together, they will pass that power on to you. For so long as you bear this ring, the Teutonic Cross and the Spear, you shall experience the true might of the Aryan race. In your hands, you hold the power of the gods themselves!"

The chanting continued to grow louder and the candles around the room flared brighter in their sconces. Himmler stretched to raise his arms even higher.

"My treasured Panzertruppen, the ritual is complete! You will sleep now, and when you wake you will no longer be men, but messiahs come to deliver Germany from her enemies." Himmler looked around the room one more time, smiling. "Now... Sleep!"

With that, he threw his arms down to his sides, and as one the Panzertruppen collapsed on the ground behind their pedestals, each and every one struck unconscious.

⁂

When Otto awoke, it was daytime. He was sleeping in a bed, although he couldn't remember how or when he got into it.

He looked around the room, rubbing the sleep from his eyes. The floor and the walls were made from stone... The sun shone in through a single, large window in the room. With some effort, he realized that he was still in Wewelsburg Castle.

On the table next to his bed, Otto found a plate of bread and fruit already prepared for him. Next to it were the ring, the baton and the Cross he remembered from… Somewhere.

He rubbed his temples, struggling to remember what had happened the night before. As he pressed his fingers against his head, he felt a searing pain shoot through his right hand. Then he remembered the gash and it all came flooding back. The blood, the chanting, the invocation… It all seemed so far away.

In the light of day, the three relics looked rather ordinary. A simple iron ring with a sort of sunburst design, a hand crafted steel rod with intricate etchings and the multi-faceted he'd been told was a Teutonic Knight's Cross. He couldn't remember why or how he'd ever detected any sort of intelligence in the objects. He donned the ring on his right, middle finger, just as he'd been told.

The Officer of the watch now enters the chamber and an "Achtung" could be heard. *I will now give you your new unit assignments. Newly ordained Knights, you will proceed to Northern France and detrain at the Caen railhead. After you have rested you will proceed to your new units.*

Hauptmann Hans Krieger, your new unit is the 654th Panzerjager, 12 SS Panzer Group.

He reads off the units to the other Teutonic Knights.

Herr Oberst Mader you will test your new powers serving with the Panzer Lehr of the 1st SS Panzer, LAH.

Early the next morning Hans awoke anticipating their journey home and then on to Northern France. Rubbing his neck, he noticed he felt no sensation where the dagger of the ritual had taken place. He examined his hand with great care. There was no sign of any cut.

He looked at Otto now awake and examining his hand he found no cut, nothing that would leave anyone to believe that they had participated in a ritual that caused pools of blood to puddle during the ritual.

PHANTOM PANTHERS

Otto now made a comment to his comrade, Hans, I feel no ache in my leg, I feel in perfect health, how do you feel?

Hans replied, I feel refreshed, but I have an eerie sensation………..

Otto and Hans were consumed with a strange and mystical phenomenon, they were compelled to blindly obey the ritual that they had participated in the Hall of the Dead.

CHAPTER 6
Bad Helmstedt, Germany

Otto recognized much of the countryside as they made their way into Bad Helmstedt, the place he'd always called home. After being dispatched from Wewelsburg that morning, the holy Panzertruppen had traveled by armored vehicle to nearby Munster, about two hours north of the castle. From there, each Teutonic Knight had been sent their separate ways, Otto Mader and Hans Krieger both boarding the same train to Bad Helmstedt. They'd ridden several hours, and the sun was well past its apex as the train finally screeched into the Bad Helmstedt train station.

The station was small, but surprisingly busy. It appeared that they weren't the only soldiers stopping into town for some brief respite between duties. Multiple families crowded the platform, and it was surprisingly difficult to get through the throng of people while maintaining a firm hold on their heavy, military-issue duffels.

They finally made it out of the train station and into the courtyard beyond the station's entrance.

Outside the bustle of the station, Otto took a moment to absorb the sight of his hometown. Nostalgia washed over him like a soothing, hot bath. "It feels good to be home," he said with a smile. He looked at Hans, but the younger man's attention was clearly somewhere else.

"Do you think that Inga will be glad to see me? I've been thinking about her so much, and yet I haven't seen her in… Eight months now? What if she's become accustomed to my absence?"

Otto smiled. He remembered Hans' wedding just two short years ago. It was a humble affair due to the economics of wartime, but an unforgettable one nonetheless. He had been so happy to see his Hauptmann finally married to a woman deserving of his affections. But, as a relative newly-wed, Otto knew that Hans didn't share the same kind of seasoned confidence in a woman that Otto himself had developed over nearly twenty years of marriage. That made him think of Magda, and suddenly it felt like an eternity since he'd held her in his arms. Only a little while longer...

"I promise that she still loves you, Hans, you have nothing to worry about."

"Of course... You're right," Hans said, but Otto could tell that his friend was still a bundle of nerves.

It was easy to find a taxi; a busy train station is like a gold mine for cabdrivers, and they swarmed the street like ants. It took them several minutes to get out of the congestion of the streets around the train station, but before long they were gliding through the quiet township of Bad Helmstedt. Otto recognized each and every street corner, and his excitement began bubbling to the surface as they drew closer and closer to his home.

When at last they pulled up to his house, Otto could see Magda waiting for him at the window. He could also hear Maximillian barking, the white Labrador somehow recognizing his master even before he'd exited the taxi. He couldn't have kept the smile from his lips if he'd tried. But he didn't try – this was his home, his wife, his family. It felt good.

As Otto dismounted from the taxi and pulled his duffel from the trunk, Magda ran out from the house to greet him. But, Max got to him first, almost knocking him over as the immense dog got up on two legs and licked his face. Otto dropped his bag to ruffle the dog's jowls, giving the dog exactly the warm greeting it was after. Then he turned his attention to his wife.

"Magda…" Otto looked deep into his wife's kind, gentle eyes before taking her in his embrace. "I've missed you so much," he whispered into her ear. Her soft, chestnut-colored hair smelled of flowers, her round and rosy cheeks glistened with tears. Her arms around him felt more like home than the house that stood behind them. This was love; this was what he was fighting for.

The slam of a car door broke the loving couple from their romantic reverie. Hans was standing outside the cab now, waiting to give his greetings to Magda. Otto let his wife go from his embrace and smiled as she wiped the tears from her face. Composure regained, she made her way over to Krieger.

"Hans, it has been too long," she said as Hans kissed her on the cheek.

"Aye, that it has," Hans said. He waited for a moment, clearly expecting something.

Fortunately, Magda knew exactly what he wanted. "I think you'll find Inga down the street at the Knobelsdorff's. You remember the way?"

Hans nodded, and was running down the street before anyone could say another word.

Otto turned back to pay their driver, and realized that Hans had forgotten his duffel in his haste. Otto let out a small chuckle as he shared his friend's forgetfulness with his wife.

"Well, it doesn't really matter; I already talked to Inga and they'll be over for dinner tonight. We'll just have to remember to give it to him then," Magda said. Otto nodded in agreement and began hauling both his and his friend's duffels inside.

"In the meantime, the kids won't be home from school for another hour…" Magda's mischievous suggestion hung in the air, and Otto hurried all the faster to get the luggage inside. There were more important things to attend to.

Even as Magda watched Otto make his way inside their home, she could tell he had changed. Something about him was different, but not in a bad way. Somehow he felt more... Commanding. More powerful. And yet there was a darkness to him too. The war had obviously changed him, but she still loved the man inside. He had never been more attractive to her than he was in that moment, and their love making was as passionate as it had been on their wedding night.

As they lay in bed recuperating from their intense romantic endeavor, they heard the voices of kids coming through the front door.

"That'll be the kids home from school," Magda said, "You'd better get dressed before they find us indecent!"

Otto smiled and roused himself from the bed, naked. He found his uniform and considered it for a moment, then opted for a more casual knit shirt and canvas pants – civilian clothing.

Sure enough, the children had seen their father's duffel bag in the entryway, and Otto had barely gotten dressed when they burst into the master bedroom and swamped their father in hugs and kisses. All except Kurt, who at 15 years of age was a bit too old for running to papa. Instead, Otto shook his oldest son's hand heartily and asked, "Have you been taking good care of your mother, son?"

"Yes father, of course." Otto beamed with pride; it was good to have another man in the family.

The Maders had four children in total... Three boys and one girl. Kurt was the oldest by several years, and the most like his father. He was dutiful, disciplined, one could almost say humorless, just like Otto. Peter and Johann were 14 and 12 respectively, but couldn't be more different from each other. Peter was an academic, clearly the creative type, while Johann was a little troublemaker, poorly suited for the indoors. Their youngest child and only daughter, Petra, had just turned four years old earlier that month, and she was truly the apple of Otto's eye.

Otto had always wanted a daughter, but after many years without children, he'd begun to resign himself to the fact that a daughter was out of the picture. When Magda became pregnant, he'd prayed many nights for a little girl. He was the first one to hold Petra when she finally made her way into the world, and he would never forget how she felt cradled in his arms... So tiny and gentle, whimpering ever so softly. It was one of the happiest days of his life, second only to his wedding day.

The family spent the afternoon in the living room, all chatting and having a good time. Otto spoke to each son in turn, inquiring into their endeavors and making sure they were behaving well and keeping up in school. He let Petra sit on his lap as she showed him her newest toys... A little wooden doll was her favorite one, and Otto delighted in watching his little girl play make believe as the rest of the family conversed. It had been almost a year since Otto had been together with his family, and he cherished every single moment of the afternoon.

Later that night, Otto, Hans and both men's respective families gathered at the Mader's home for a homecoming feast. Magda and Inga had done a magnificent job of stockpiling rations for the night's festivities, and everyone got seconds that asked for them. The Mader house was loud with laughter that night as the men shared stories and the kids made jokes.

After the meal, Inga brought out her own specialty spiced wine she'd saved for the occasion. Otto toasted, "To family, love and the fatherland!" The wine's sweet warmth made the evening all that much more relaxing as the sun dipped below the horizon and evening fell on Bad Helmstedt.

Eventually, all the children except Kurt retired to their rooms while the adults remained in the living room catching up with each other and talking about the war. The women had heard much gossip all around the town, and the two soldiers did what they could to enlighten their mates as to how the war effort was really going. Kurt listened quietly and soberly, absorbing everything he heard like a sponge.

"Say, Otto, what happened to your Knight's Cross? I noticed Hans was missing his earlier, but now that I see you both bearing the same new decorations. That doesn't look like normal SS insignia, so I have to ask…"

Otto smiled at the question. "Hans, your wife is very perceptive!" He turned to Inga, "I'm pleased to inform you that this," he indicated the Teutonic Cross, "is the decoration of a new unit of 'Teutonic Knights'." When Inga looked confused, he went on, "To tell you the truth, we still don't know exactly what we're doing in this new unit, but we were personally appointed by the Fuhrer himself, so we know it's important."

Magda was flabbergasted, "So you actually met the Fuhrer?! What was he like?"

Hans cut in. "Well, I wouldn't really call it 'meeting'. He addressed a group of us as one and bestowed us each our new insignia, but we didn't personally converse with him at any point. Not in the way you're thinking."

Otto nodded in agreement. "To tell you the truth, the Fuhrer has been taxed as much as his country. It's been a long war, and the hardest part is just beginning. Hitler bears the burden for us all, and that burden has taken its toll. Nonetheless, he remains hopeful, as do we all, and this new unit we're a part of is to be the answer to our nation's prayers."

Magda and Inga both looked like they were waiting to hear more.

"Sadly, we can't say much more than that. All I can tell you is that we now have the means to defeat our enemies."

"And defeat them we will!" Hans exclaimed, and the group toasted another glass of wine to that.

<hr />

Hans and Inga departed the Mader residence around 5:30 to make it back to their home down the street. The little hand on Otto's watch had just hit 10 when Magda called Otto to the living room to have him look outside.

"Who could that be?" She asked. Otto looked out the front window at what his wife beheld; it was a large black sedan, and it was parked right outside their front gate. Even as Otto watched, three suited, official-looking men exited the vehicle and began walking towards their house. Otto, fearing they would wake his children, went out to meet them before they could knock.

"Greetings gentlemen, how can I help you?"

One of the men spoke. "We're here to speak to Oberst Otto Mader, would that be you, sir?"

Otto saluted, "Oberst Otto Mader of the 12th SS Panzer, at your service. May I ask what brings you to my humble home at this hour?" He didn't like the feeling of this, but he didn't let his suspicion tarnish his courtesy.

The man in the middle spoke now. "Nothing more than the simple pleasure of conversation, Herr Oberst. Is it safe to assume we're speaking privately here?"

Otto looked back to make sure his wife was still inside, then replied deliberately, "We should be safe here, especially at this hour."

The man in the middle waited for a moment, as if he expected Otto to invite him inside. When he didn't, the man somewhat awkwardly proposed that they converse in his Mercedes-Benz. Not seeing any choice in the matter, Otto agreed.

When the doors to the Benz closed behind them, the man that had been in the middle, the one Otto assumed was in charge, sat in the back seat with him. The other two men sat in front, silent.

"I understand that you've been gone from Bad Helmstedt for almost 9 months now, which would explain why you don't know who I am."

Otto stared at him, waiting to be enlightened.

"I am the new mayor of Helmstedt, Manfred Bonhoeffer. My two associates are Bernhard Niemollar," he said indicating the man in the driver's seat, "and Gustav Hohne," indicating the other man in the passenger's seat. "You may trust that their ears are closed and their mouths will remain silent. What's said in this car will never leave this car, understood?"

Otto nodded.

"Excellent," he said. "Now, am I safe in making the assumption that you are intimately knowledgeable about the state of the war?"

Otto nodded again, more slowly this time.

"Then you are no doubt aware that the Allies have successfully invaded Normandy, yes?" The mayor paused to make sure Otto was following along. "And tales of your valiant confrontation with the Russians have already spread to our small town."

Otto knew that the compliment was a hollow one.

"While I applaud your tenacity, I'm sure you know better than most that our fight with Ivan is a losing one. We should have never invaded Red soil."

Otto didn't nod this time, he just stared, waiting for the mayor to get to the point. As the mayor looked at him, Otto could tell he wasn't getting the reaction he'd hoped for. Nonetheless, he continued...

"Like a foolish bear, we've stirred the Reds from their hive. It's only a matter of time until their swarm successfully fights back.

Deutschland can only take so many more stings." The statement hung in the air for a moment. The mayor decided to take a different tact.

"Tell me, Otto, what do you think it would take to appease our enemies and abate their respective invasions?"

"Do you really believe we should sue for peace?" Otto asked, his irritation getting the better of him. "Have you already forgotten Versailles, mayor? Another 'peace treaty' would be the end of Germany as we know it. Our only route to peace is victory, and that is exactly the route I intend to take."

"Ah, but what if there was an alternative? What if we could convincingly demonstrate our peaceful intentions to both the Allies and the Reds at the same time? All without any more senseless bloodshed?"

Otto was skeptical. "There's no way."

"What if I told you that plans are being set in motion that could end the war with just one more casualty?"

Now Otto understood.

"What you speak of is treason, good sir, and I want no part of it." Otto made to get out of the car, but before he could open the door, the mayor reached across and stopped him.

"Just hear me out, Herr Oberst. The war is lost. Our people – your people – are suffering. It's only a matter of time until the clamp set in place by the Allies and the Reds tightens on our nation; a military victory is out of the question. Our only option is to show our enemies the contention of the German people against their leader, that they may have mercy on us after the war is over."

This man was weak, Otto realized. And Otto had no appetite for gutless cowards.

"If you mean what I believe you mean," Otto said menacingly, "Then consider yourself lucky that I don't personally turn you in to the Fuhrer myself."

The mayor sighed. "Turn me in if you wish, Mader, but this madman you call a Fuhrer will die regardless of my indictment. An assassination is not so easily interrupted. All I hoped for was your cooperation, that the task may be ever so slightly easier when the time comes to take action."

"I say again: I want nothing to do with your spineless plot," Otto said flatly.

Niemollar turned from the driver's seat. "Think of your family, Oberst Mader, isn't their well-being more important than your Fuhrer's life, or your honor?

"On that you are correct, sir, and as it happens you've put me and my family in danger by coming here tonight. You don't even realize that Germany's greatest weapons have yet to come to bear; these weapons will descend on Normandy within the month, and within the year we will have beaten the Allies *and* the Reds back into their holes. The only thing that could possibly interfere is little cockroaches like you."

The mayor looked shocked, but Otto continued anyways. "If you care for your lives, you will never speak of this again. If I hear so much as a whisper of this treason – from *anyone* – I will personally inform the Fuhrer of our little conversation here tonight."

At that, Otto got out of the car and slammed the door. The window rolled down, and the mayor looked up at him one last time.

"We may be cockroaches to you, Herr Oberst, but you forget that cockroaches live on where others die. Just think about it. You'll know what to do when the time comes." Heil Hitler, the window rolled back up and by the time Otto was back in his home, there was no sign of the black Mercedes.

"Who was that?" Magda asked.

"Just some pests," Otto said, "nothing a beautiful woman like you needs to worry about." By the time they made it back into the bedroom, Otto had put the encounter completely out of his mind.

CHAPTER 7
Operation Goodwood the Battle for Caen

The next day, Otto and Hans had made their way back to the train station before the sun breached the horizon, but not before saying goodbye to their respective families. Saying goodbye was both painful and exciting – on the one hand, it always hurts to leave those you love, but on the other hand, both men were anxious to put their supposed powers to use for the Reich. Otto promised Petra that he'd bring her back flowers from his 'trip'; she'd been giddy to hear that, even despite her grogginess.

The train from Bad Helmstedt was nearly empty and it had taken them quickly through Köln to the German headquarters in Bad Münstereifel. From Münstereifel, they'd taken a military train to rendezvous with the rest of the Teutonic Knights. From there they'd taken yet another armored transport train west to the outpost just south of Caen. Their travels had taken all day; the sun was looming low in the French sky as they pulled into their final destination.

As soon as they disembarked onto the dimly lit train platform, an SS Standartenfuhrer was waiting for them. Otto, Hans and the rest of the Panzertruppen formed a line in front of the officer and saluted in silence, awaiting instruction.

The Standartenfuhrer's voice was stern, as to be expected from a German officer. "Panzertruppen, your equipment will be unloaded during the night to ensure that they remain unseen by Allied surveillance. In the meantime, you will all follow me to command

HQ for your attack briefing." He paused for a moment before saluting the troop, "It is good that you've arrived, Panzertruppen, your aid will surely secure us this victory."

As the group arranged themselves into two single-file lines, Otto and Hans shared a look that belied their skepticism, but neither man said a word as the group made their way out of the station and into the small stone-built house that served as division HQ.

Inside, they were met by another high-ranking officer. "Greetings, Teutonic Knights." The man bowed low, an uncustomary salute. "For those of you who don't know, I am Standartenfuhrer Ernst Krag, and it is my responsibility to serve as a liaison for this 'special' group of Panzertruppen." He looked around the room, surveying each Knight in turn. "Each and every one of you has been chosen for your superior bravery, loyalty and battle-savvy. Let me make this explicitly clear – you are our last hope to win this war."

The room was silent at that, all joviality gone from the Standartenfuhrer's voice. He directed the troop's attention to an enormous detailed map of Europe at the back of the makeshift HQ.

"As I'm sure that all of you are aware, our enemies are very close to holding a dangerous and decisive strategic advantage over our army. The Russians close in from the East, and now the Allies seek to cut us off from the North and West. We are in a vise, gentlemen, and there is only one way to break it – here, Caen. This is the lynchpin that holds the Allies' strategy together. If we can wrench Caen from Allied control, then we can also take control of the Orne River. If we control the Orne River, then we can easily beat our enemies out of Normandy and defend our territory against the English Channel."

"Any questions so far?" Krag paused a moment and looked around the room to make sure that the Panzertruppen were paying attention.

"Each of you to stand in this room right now will be key to our victory in the battle ahead. As you know, you've each been bestowed with The Spear of Destiny, which is entombed in your batons. As long as you have your baton in tune with the powers of the ritual you've partaken of, you'll experience a limitless source of energy that will radiate through it. Do you all understand this?"

As one, the Panzertruppen respond, "Ja Wohl, Mein Herr."

"Very good. Now G2 has warned us that the British intend to make an attack stemming from the Orne bridgehead on July 17. That's tomorrow. They intend to move through Caen, and it's likely that they intend to push southeast towards Paris in an effort to permanently liberate France from our control. That cannot and shall not happen."

Krag paused a moment to let the severity of the situation sink into the room.

"What the British don't know is that our forces – primarily made up of your Panzers– will be ready to greet them in Caen." Krag smiled mischievously at that. "No doubt you've heard that British air forces make daily bombing runs across Caen to ensure that it remains out of our control. We now intend to use this strategy against them."

The curiosity felt by every officer – Otto included – was palpable.

"You see, gentlemen, our compliment of Panzertruppen will be ready and waiting around the wooded perimeter of Caen. Bombings typically commence between 0600 and 0900. After the bombings, all our Panzertruppen will use the fog of war created by British heavy ordinance to move into position on the Eastern side of the Orne bridgehead. Well, almost all..." He paused to look around the room.

"Who here is with the 654th Panzerjager company?" Krag asked. Hans and three other officers stepped forward, saluting. Looking back to the map, Krag continued, "You, along with the Tiger Schwere Abteilung 503 and the 12th SS Panzer Group will position yourselves in flank position along the southwestern side of the bridgehead. Together, our two groups of forces will catch the British in a vice of our own. We shall crush them and send them scurrying back across the English Channel with their tails tucked in between their legs."

A cheer went up around the room at that, but both Otto and Hans remained somber. Even the most foolish of strategies could be made to sound impervious on paper, but everything can change in the thick of battle. Unlike Otto, Hans felt obligated to voice his concern.

"Are we the only members of the 654th Panzerjagers?"

Krag's smile almost instantly evaporated. "General Eberbach has ordered our units into action as soon as they arrive and are ready for battle. The other members of your company will be deployed as they arrive. Is that understood?"

So our forces will be spread out... Vulnerable and unorganized? Otto thought. Hans was clearly thinking the same thing as Otto, but he could see that his younger friend wasn't going to press his point further. "Ja Wohl, Herr Standartenfuhrer," he echoed.

Krag continued. "Your position will be about 2.5 kilometers from our current location. The rest of you will be grouped together with the Panzer Lehr Division under the command of the 1st SS Panzer LAH, here," Krag indicated a spot on the map. "After the bombings, you will skirt the town to the West and follow this road until you see the Ardenne Abbey tower. Due to the recurring bombings, you'll probably only be able to reach your objective through the intersection of these two roads, here," he said, indicating another spot on the map near the middle of Caen. "There you will receive your final orders from our OP, Meyer and his group. Understood?"

As on, the room responded, "Ja Wohl, Mein Herr."

"Excellent. You are all dismissed; you are to rendezvous with the rest of your units immediately. Your new weapons are ready and waiting. We have less than 12 hours until the bombings begin."

From the stone command hut, Otto and the rest of the Teutonic Knights proceeded to rendezvous with their respective divisions, and to finally lay eyes on their new tanks. Each fighting unit was manned with experienced Panzertruppen from a number of Panzer Divisions to give it an elite status, and each man had been anointed with an honorary Teutonic Knights' Cross to symbolize his position.

Sure enough, the new Panther G's and Jagdpanthers had been unloaded while they were meeting, and their crews were ready and waiting for their commanders' arrivals.

Immediately, Otto was struck by the omnipresence he felt emanating from this new and imposing weapon of destruction that stood before him. His Panther G was brand-new and fully armed. He slowly walked around the tank, examining every inch. He ran his hand along the slopes glacial plate on one side of the tank, and let his fingers trail along the metal as he walked around to the front glacial. His new driver beamingly told him that what he felt was 100 mm thick of the best steel Germany could produce.

Let's just hope 100 mm is good enough, Otto thought to himself.

Looking up from the glacial plating, Otto then examined the long gun barrel. It was a high velocity 75mm cannon, which his new gunner informed him was capable of destroying a target from twice the distance of his old StuG.

"Impressive," Otto said.

His driver piped up again, "There are always a couple quirks with a new tank, especially with these new Maybach engines, but we've already worked everything out of this one. She runs smooth as butter."

After Otto finished circling his new tank twice, he turned to his crew. "Men, it would be my preference to spend several weeks training with each other and learning how to fight together. Unfortunately, our enemies lie just over the horizon; we don't have time for familiarity. So, instead, I'm just going to trust you, and in return I ask that you trust me. Together, we will kill many British tomorrow."

His men hooped and hollered at that.

"Make your final preparations men; we depart in exactly two hours."

Finally with his division, Hans had also been introduced to his own new tank, one of the newly developed Jagdpanthers. Otherwise known as Hitler's "Hunting Panther", Hans knew the Jagdpanther was the premier tank killer in existence anywhere in the world. Built on the same chassis as the normal Panther, it was fitted with a gargantuan 88mm cannon capable of obliterating a target from nearly a mile away with accuracy.

After examining the tank's exterior, Hans proceeded to climb into the commander's seat. The power he felt sitting inside the tank was tangible and he instinctively ran his fingers across the Cross of the Teutonic Knights that hung around his collar. As his fingers made contact with the metal decoration, he felt a surge of energy pulse through his body. It was simultaneously mystifying and intriguing and it only made Hans that much more eager to take this and new weapon into battle. The hesitance he'd felt in the briefing had melted away; where he sat, he knew he held power. He spent the time remaining until their scheduled departure chatting with his crew, sharing war stories and talking strategy is.

※

It was still dark outside when the first bombers hit Caen. It was early… Too early. Otto's division of Panzertruppen hadn't disembarked from the outpost, but they began rushing into position at the first sound of explosions. Otto and his crew quickly mounted up inside their Panther and began to move out away from the outpost and into the northern line of trees, towards Caen.

Others weren't so prepared.

Otto had no idea why the Allies were breaking routine until the first row of bombs was laid across the outpost. In an instant, darkness gave way to fire; rabble gave way to screams. All at once the outpost was in ruin. Even as Otto watched through his copula sight glass, one of the aircraft scored a direct hit on the stone-built commander's hut he'd been briefed in earlier that night. The building was there one moment, and the next it was gone.

The bombings continued for what seemed like an eternity. They made one, two, three, then four more passes over the outpost, letting row after row of terror wreak havoc across the camp. Finally, the bombings stopped, and Otto let out a long breath as he heard the enemy retreat into the distance.

Quickly, Otto moved his tank out of the tree line and tried to locate the rest of the Panzertruppen. He felt an immense wave of relief when he identified Hans' Jagdpanther, still in one piece and seemingly unharmed. He was one of few, though – there was no sign of the stone hut or the railroad platform, and the groans of dying men filled the air. Several non-tank military vehicles had been completely destroyed, and even some of the tanks had sustained heavy damage.

Otto and his crew slowly made their way over the now-uneven terrain to assess the damage and determine who might have been injured by this bombing raid. As they drew closer, a few survivors straggled out of the demolished command building. Everyone has been injured or killed except one Jagdpanther commander and two of the other officers in Otto's group. It appeared that Hans and Otto were the only remaining Teutonic Knights.

Just as Otto was ready to dismiss the possibility of any other survivors, Krag stumbled out of the command hut, bloodied and glassy-eyed. When Otto saw him, he dismounted his tank and ran over to the injured liaison officer. As he drew closer, he saw that the man's left arm was badly injured. Krag collapsed to the ground just as Otto arrived. Hans had followed suit, and was within earshot when Krag issued his final command.

Otto kneeled next to Krag to inspect his wounds. "Herr Oberst, you must..." the injured commander took a long, rasping breath, "carry out our plan." The man was dying, it was obvious.

Krag's eyes snapped open and narrowed in on Otto. "Do your duty as a Teutonic Knight" The Standartenfuhrer took another labored breath, and closed his eyes. " He reached up with his good arm and tapped Otto's Teutonic Cross. "Use your power, Herr Oberst. You and the Knights are Germany's last hope." After that last command, Krag slipped into unconsciousness, and Otto knew they had neither the time nor the resources to bring him back from the brink of death. But, with this last command, Otto could feel his doubt transforming into resolve. He stood, feeling like a tank commander once more.

"Get the remnants of our armored troop underway," he said to Hans. "We leave for our attack positions immediately." As he climbed back up onto his Panther, he barked out an order loud enough for all the remaining survivors to hear: "Panzertruppen, follow my lead. Today we show the Brits the meaning of Blood Magic."

Even as he took command of the troop, his crew couldn't help but notice that their commander's new Panther G began emanating an undeniable aura of power.

※

Otto, Hans and what remained of the Panzertruppen meandered through a city that was once a serene and peaceful French community. They were somber as they delved further and further into what was now the ruins of constant bombing. There fighting force was rather meager now, but nonetheless, they made their way to their attack positions. There was no evidence that they'd been spotted by Allied forces, although Otto never let that particular paranoia slip from his mind… He didn't intend to be caught off guard again.

Finally, they made it into the tree line that surrounded Caen. Otto could rest a little bit easier with the trees overhead – that meant that they were protected from the wandering eyes of an aerial patrol. Once undercover, Otto, Hans and the remaining commanders all convened to discuss their battle plan, along with another high ranking German Panzer commander that had been waiting for them in a camouflaged revetment just inside the tree line. He informed them that several other units were in position and that despite their heavy and unexpected losses, the counter-attack was still to unfold as planned. Apparently an observer was able to maintain his position in a tall church steeple, Ardenne Abbey, which offered them a panoramic view of the terrain around Caen. This allowed them constant updates on the Allied movements; they were preparing for an imminent attack.

After a quick briefing, Otto, Hans and the rest of the Panzersoldaten serving as Teutonic Knights mounted up with their new weapons and as they readied for battle an ominous confidence seemed to settle over the group. It was all or nothing now

– either the two remaining Teutonic Knights would harness the power of their rituals and the meager German forces would claim victory, or the rituals would prove to be a hoax and every man among them would die.

With that mentality, Otto and Hans and their remaining units took up battle positions as laid out in their plan. Even without the observer, the spearhead of Allied forces were drawing close enough to maintain visibility.

Finally, when Otto was sure that they'd be spotted if the Allies drew any closer, the order came over the radio that they'd all been waiting for: "Attack!"

As one, Panthers and Hans lone Jagdpanther now lurched forward into battle. Otto clutched his Spear of Longinus in his left hand, and the baton felt hot in his hands. Somehow, he felt as one with his Panther. He wasn't looking through the sight anymore – his eyes *were* the sight. But it was more than that... The tank responded to his every command, even before he spoke it. The crew inside was moving strangely, almost robotically, as they each manned their respective portion of the Panther. And he was moving fast – much faster than any tank he'd ever commanded.

With reckless abandon, Otto and Hans sped towards the enemy forces. Round after round exploded against the side of their tanks, but nothing was felt within. Not so much as a shudder.

Then, once Otto's 'eyes' locked onto a target, his mind issued the command – "Fire!"

A bolt of energy exploded out of the tank, unlike any high explosive Otto had ever experienced. The normal piercing round seemed to have been supernaturally enhanced; as Otto watched, it pierced straight through an enemy tank as easily as a toothpick pierces through butter. Together, Otto and Hans led the charge against their now-desperate British and Canadian opponents..

From the smoke and dust which enveloped the battlefield spurted huge flashes of flame as ammunition exploded aboard stricken tanks, sending their turrets wheeling through the air as they separated from shattered hulls. German tanks collided with Allied ones, ramming against each other and remaining locked together in a tangled embrace of death. The battle spun around them like a vast whirlpool, flattening orchards and churning wheat fields in a confusion of blazing vehicles and charred corpses. They made short work of the initial British forces, but more lay in the field beyond, waiting to be squashed like grapes in a wine churn.

Otto felt a fire burning inside him now and he wouldn't have stopped the attack even if he'd been ordered to stand down. The enemy's blood called to him. Despite being a soldier, he had never considered himself a violent man, but in this moment he wanted one thing – the death of those that opposed him.

What was left of Tiger Company 503 located to their west and the 12th SS Panzer now closed in on the remaining British forces. They forced them into a tight-knit gauntlet on the other side of the Orne River that Otto, Hans and the rest of his Teutonic corps now charged into head-first, the Teutonic warriors leading the charge.

The British forces beyond the bridge had time to prepare; they weren't caught unaware like their massacred advance forces had been. As Otto and Hans Panthers roamed onto the battlefield beyond the river shooting at anything that moved, the British Armed Forces returned with an offense of their own.

Unfortunately, they had no knowledge about the Tiger Company and the antitank units that had flanked them even before the battle begun. The other group of Germans and their weapons were cunningly concealed in the surrounding terrain and as the allied forces attacked towards Caen, the fields, hedges and farm buildings came alive with a sustained German barrage. The fire that they laid down reverberated like thunder through the air.

Truth be told, it was a one-sided battle. The British and Canadian tank forces were proving no match for the foes that now bore down on them. From within his tank, Otto smiled as he watched supernatural and normal German tanks alike score hit after hit on the enemy. The combination of Teutonic Knights, the Tiger Company 503 units, the Mark IV Panzers and the antitank units of the 12th SS Panzer Division were too much for the Allied ground forces to handle.

Everything was going smoothly until their Ardenne Alley observer spotted another group of Allied tanks moving towards the melee. Otto could guess what the Allies were trying to accomplish: they were trying to beat the Germans at their own game. Otto issued the command to divide their unit into two forces; one would stay and continue engaging the Allies, while the other would retreat to advantageous terrain to counter-ambush the Allied reinforcements. There is only one man Otto trusted for the job, and that was Hans.

He commanded Hans over the radio, "Hans, take three of our tanks to the Western edge of the battlefield and find suitable camouflage. Your objective is simple: when the Allied reinforcements show face, destroy the first and last vehicles in the attacking force. The remaining units in between will be trapped and helpless – easy pickings."

"Ja Wohl," came the faithful reply over the radio.

Hans did as he was ordered, and soon spotted the Allied reinforcements through his Jagdpanther's sight. His crew responded to his commands even before he spoke them. His Jagdpanther turned slightly right… then stopped. The Allied tank units grew larger in his gunners sight graticule and when they entered the kill zone. His gunner watched as his loader slammed the breech block closed with and APC round and readied the gun for a 1200 meter shot. Then… "Fire!"

The blood round hurled out of the Jagdpanther's 88mm cannon streaked across the battlefield. Thunder echoed in its wake and the explosion the shot created when it hit was enormous. Hans had only intended to eliminate the leading vehicle of the of the opposing tank force, but with rapid fire he destroyed the first three. Two tanks and a jeep were engulfed in flame as the APC rounds found their mark, leaving a crater where there'd been plated steel just a couple seconds before.

The three tanks that had accompanied Hans followed suit and while their rounds weren't quite as destructive, the havoc they wrought on the Allied armored units was effective enough. What had once been the organized armored spearhead was now a piecemeal force of trucks, jeeps and tanks, all scattered and ablaze.

From what Hans could see, the British and Canadian forces employed American M4 Sherman tanks, as well as several British Churchills. The M4's were particularly easy prey – their engine used high octane fuel, which was extremely volatile. In addition, they were lightly armored and had a high profile. To a Panzerjager like the Jagdpanther, even a non-Teutonic tank killer, the enemy forces may as well have been driving large, squishy water balloons just waiting to be popped. And pop them they did. Round after round of "Blood Magic" was hurled from his Jagdpanther, each hit yielding at least one kill.

The battle wasn't over, but it *was* already won. The allies were outgunned, outmaneuvered and outsmarted. Where the M4 needed to be within 800 meters to score a lethal hit, the long-barreled Panthers and the massive Jagdpanthers could do the same at over twice the distance. Together with the supernatural firepower brought by the two living Teutonic Knights, it was more than enough to ensure an Allied slaughter.

PHANTOM PANTHERS

Hans laughed with gleeful bloodlust as round after round of destruction burst from his Jagdpanther. He was so drawn into his bloodlust that he heard nothing of the world around him. All he wanted – all he could do – was kill, kill, kill. The Jagdpanther constantly rocked back and forth and smoke filled the cabin as each round echoed from its massive 88mm cannon. Hans could almost feel the tank laughing with him as his ball gunner laid down a field of enfilade fire at the advancing infantry. They stumbled as they died, forming a mound of corpses in front of his Jagdpanther.

In the end, any opposition not under cover or protection was caught in an endless blizzard of red hot projectiles coming from all directions. It truly was a massacre, and by the time the sun had reached its apex, there was no sign of any living Allied forces. Every one of them to a man was dead.

When Hans finally pulled himself from his lustful trance and came back to the world inside his tank, he found himself surprisingly tired. He was bodily exhausted. He was sure that his tank was in ruins, out of commission for any future battles.

And yet…

When Hans and his crew dismounted the Jagdpanther to examine the damage it had taken during the battle, they were startled to see that there was no sign that any enemy projectile had scored a hit. The gouges created by enemy heavy ordnance were nowhere to be seen. In fact, the front glacial – which should have sustained the most damage – looked as if it had just come off the factory floor. It gleamed in the sunlight, and the way the light reflected off the tank almost made it seem like the machine was satisfied, content.

Hans didn't know what to think that he and his Panzerjager were impervious to harm, but he did know one thing – the super real power of the Teutonic Knights was very, very real.

Situated on the only high ground north of Caen, a British Liaison Officer stood upright in his command vehicle overlooking the carnage of the battle. As he raised his binoculars from his chest to view the progress of his armored spearhead, he was dismayed as he surveyed the terrain in front of him.

"It's not possible..." he muttered under his breath. "G-2 had missed the mark again about the German force they faced"

The officer's aide piped up, "What's that, sir?"

"We've been tricked, lad. The Germans have beaten us to the punch again. Their superior armor was too much for us on an open field, as we knew it would be. That's why we'd gone to such great lengths to avoid this kind of confrontation in the first place. The liaison officer lowered his field glasses back to his chest and thought for a moment.

"Dammit!" He shouted. The aide jumped at the outburst. "We're going to need some help cleaning up this mess. Our air forces are our only hope."

Within minutes, the liaison officer was comforted by the sound of British Hawker Typhoons and American P-47 Thunderbolts streaking by overhead. As he watched through his field glasses, their air forces unleashed a torrent of destruction on the ruined battlefield. RP-3 rockets streamed off the wings of the Typhoons, each one carrying a deadly payload of destruction. Meanwhile, the P-47's strafed the battlefield with armor-penetrating rounds, carving out a path of destruction through the Nazi forces. The German Wehrmacht in northern France had become trapped, to breakout was their only alternative.

The liaison officer smiled. We may have lost the ground battle, but the slaughter will be repaid by air. No doubt that the Germans' precious "Fortress Europe" was now a house without a roof; this victory was messy, but it ensured that Allied air forces had full control of the air and the battlefield alike. The battle for Caen

PHANTOM PANTHERS

was over and the overwhelming advantage in Allied resources had proven to be the deciding factor.

Having been ordered to form a rear guard for the retreating Wehrmacht, Otto and Hans with their Phantom Panthers disappear into the landscape, to reappear nobody would know.

CHAPTER 8

Otto knew that the British had bombed the majority of north-central Germany; even if word hadn't passed through the ranks, the numerous ruined cities that he, Hans and the rest of the rearguard passed through were evidence enough. Still, he'd held out hope that his hometown of Bad Helmstedt might've somehow remained immune to the traumas of war. That hope quickly evaporated as their caravan crested a hilltop a couple kilometers west of the town, only to see huge portions of it in smoldering ruin. There were pockmarks of destruction across the cityscape where the British bombers had laid their fiery carpet.

The morning was dark grey and drizzly, a bitter cold autumn day. Still, even in the poor visibility, Otto conservatively guessed that more than half of the small town lay in wreckage. They were approaching off-road, since all of the main roads leading into town from the west had been destroyed. The mood of their meager and depleted ranks were somber as they made their way down the hillside and towards the town.

❧❀❧

It had been six months since the Panzertruppen made their epic stand in the battle of Caen. Otto still remembered how sweet their victory had tasted; to realize their power as Teutonic Knights and avenge their fallen brethren so decisively had been nothing short of miraculous. But, the elation was short-lived; the Brits' airborne retaliation had quickly turned their victory into full-fledged retreat. Just as quickly as the war effort had regained hope, it was snatched away again.

The majority of the Teutonic Knights had been slain in the unexpected bombings at Caen. That day had proven that while the imbued men were nothing short of invincible inside their empowered tanks, while outside they remained flesh and blood just like any other human being. Otto didn't know what had happened to the rest of the Knights, but as far as anyone had heard, he and Hans were the remnants of a once mighty force.

Predictably, what started as a retreat from Caen had soon turned into a retreat from all of France. With their sly victory at Caen, the Allies foothold in France grew impenetrable and they pressed their advantage ferociously. The Wehrmacht was chased incessantly out of France, then out of Belgium. All the while, Hans and Otto remained in the back lines as the only rearguard for the German army, always ready to defend against their pursuers. There had been two separate occasions where they would have sustained heavy losses from an ambush, had the two men with their holy Panthers not been there to stop it.

Ultimately, Otto reflected, that was a pretty good summary of why the Teutonic Knights would never have been able to deliver Germany. No matter what, numbers always win. Each of the German Panthers was easily worth 10 of the Allies' M4s and Churchills. Better still, each of the Teutonic Knights' supernatural Panthers was worth a great number of enemy tanks. But, when you're outgunned by a ratio of 20 to one, having two indestructible weapons just doesn't mean enough. Otto questioned whether even a hundred such weapons would've been enough to salvage the war effort.

Nonetheless, Otto and the rest of the Wehrmacht trudged eastwards. Their mission was no longer one of victory, but of survival. They'd successfully evaded the jaws of the Allies, but the Russians had crossed German borders to the East.

The Fatherland was under invasion.

Now, Otto, Hans and all the remaining Panzertruppen were en route through central Germany to make a last stand against the Russians knocking at their door. They'd come to Bad Helmstedt hoping to find a functional railhead, which would expedite their journey to the front lines. Judging by the wreckage they'd seen from their vantage point outside of town, they'd be lucky to find a passable road, much less a functioning railroad.

Sure enough, as they made their way through what used to be the Western edge of Bad Helmstedt, it was clear that there would be no railroad transport to be had. When Otto and Hans spotted the remains of the train station, they knew that their only choice would be to continue on foot (or on tread, as the case may be).

After thinking for a few moments outside the ruined train station, Otto shouted out an order from within his Panther. "Panzertruppen, we may not find a train here, but we won't leave empty-handed. You have the afternoon to seek supplies, rations, anything you can find to sustain our journey eastward. We reconvene our march at the eastern edge of town at precisely 1500."

"Ja Wohl," came the echoed replies. The tone of their situation was overwhelmingly dismal, just like the dreary weather.

Otto's intent with his order had actually been two-pronged; it was true that they desperately needed supplies, but he also wanted time for he and Hans to privately investigate the welfare of their respective families.

Together, they'd left their Panthers with their respective crews, then negotiated the use of a jeep through the wreckage of western Helmstedt. Finally, they found their neighborhood; or rather, what used to be their neighborhood. Nearly every house had been leveled and the old-fashioned cobblestone that had served as pavement was completely impassable. Enormous craters dotted the road as well as several of the lots where Otto distinctly remembered there being houses.

Otto slowed the jeep to a stop at the corner of their street, but before he could even engage the parking brake, Hans burst from the vehicle and sprinted down the block, frantic.

"Wait! Hans, wait for me!" Otto ran after him and watched as his younger friend tripped over a piece of rubble, only to bounce back up again, completely unfazed.

Hans was still 50 paces in front of Otto when he finally stopped and collapsed to the ground. Otto recognized the pathway leading up to the crumbled foundation of what used to be Hans' home. It was completely gone. A few lots down the street, Otto could see that his own home had shared a similar fate – only one wall still stood of his old abode. There was no sign of any living thing anywhere on the street.

"Inga… Oh, my sweet Inga…" Hans was rocking back and forth, head buried in his hands. "What have they done?"

Otto struggled to maintain his own composure as he sunk down beside his friend. He put one arm around his shaking shoulders in a comforting embrace. "Come now, Hans, you don't know that she's gone. I'm sure that she made it out alive."

Hans paused his sobbing for a moment and looked up, "Really?"

Otto gave Hans' shoulders a light squeeze. "Of course! Remember how good they were about warning civilians? I'm sure they all got out. Hell, her, Magda and the kids are all probably sitting down to lunch somewhere even now… We just have to find them."

Hans didn't say anything; Otto couldn't tell whether he was comforted or not, but he stood up and followed Otto back to the jeep regardless.

"Let's head over to the missing persons bureau. That was on the eastern side of town, remember? So there's a good chance it's still standing. With any luck, they'll be able to tell us where our families are."

Hans nodded, and together the two men trekked back through the bumpy wreckage towards the inhabited side of town.

Otto's assumption had been right; the missing person's bureau remained standing, although it had taken the two men several tries to locate the building. It wasn't a place that either man had ever visited before, so they ended up driving up and down several different streets in their search.

Finally, though, they did find it, and with it a surprising amount of civilians in a similar search for loved ones. There was a line of people crowded outside the doors leading in. Depression filled the air. Due to the crowd, Otto actually ended up parking nearly a block away from the building's entrance.

"Wait here," Otto said, turning to Hans in the passenger seat. "It will be easier for one of us to get in than both. Meanwhile, I think I saw an open soup kitchen across the street; why don't you find us something to eat?"

"I'm not hungry," Hans said, flatly.

Otto slapped Hans on the knee in an attempt to lighten the mood. "Well look at it this way: by the time you have our food, I'll know where to find your wife!" Hans didn't reply, but Otto knew that he'd been heard. Truthfully, he wasn't hungry either – the possibility of his family being dead had left his stomach clenched since their arrival in Bad Helmstedt – but he didn't want Hans sitting idle with his thoughts if he could help it.

Using his military status to his advantage wasn't normally something that Otto did, but he wasn't about to wait at the end of the excruciatingly long line of people outside the bureau. Instead, he shoved his way to the front, stating his business as 'classified' to anyone who asked. Finally, he made it through the surprisingly small wooden double doors that served as the main entrance to the building.

Once inside, Otto quickly made his way to one of the four news boards that had been drawn up around the room. Each board was covered with a long list of names, each one belonging to a recently missing and/or deceased person in the town. He pushed his way to the board titled "J – M" and ran his finger down the list.

Dammit, he thought as his finger found a line in the K's.

Krieger, Inga....................Deceased, November 17th, 1944

His heart sunk in his chest. Tears began to well up in his eyes as he became all but certain of his own family's fate. After all, Inga would've been just a few houses away from his. But, determined to know for sure, he wiped his eyes and kept scanning the list...

He felt something die inside when he found the names he never wanted to see. They were the first names listed in the M's:

Mader, Johann....................Deceased, December 17th, 1944
Mader, Kurt......................Deceased, December 18th, 1944
Mader, Magda....................Deceased, December 17th, 1944
Mader, Peter.....................Deceased, December 17th, 1944
Mader, Petra...........Missing, Last seen December 17th, 1944

Otto felt his knees buckle, and his vision tunneled in on the names in front of him. He felt himself fall as the world went black around him.

<hr />

Otto awoke in a small office room. As his vision cleared, he took stock of his surroundings.

He was slumped in an uncomfortable wooden chair across from a cluttered desk. A bespectacled man sat behind the desk... *I guess this is his office,* Otto thought. Another man stood behind the desk next to the bespectacled fellow; he looked ragged and hard, but his eyes were very kind. He was wearing overalls and a thick, wool shirt. Otto guessed that he was a farmer or some other type of manual laborer.

For a moment, Otto didn't notice the man sitting in the chair next to his own. The man was dead silent and white as a ghost. It took him a double take to realize that the man sitting next to him was, in fact, Hans.

"Herr Oberst, you and your companion have our deepest condolences for your loss," the office man said as soon as he noticed Otto awake.

"Where am I?"

"You lost consciousness, Herr Oberst. Mr. Kline here found you collapsed on the ground," the man with the glasses motioned to the ragged man standing next to him, "so we brought you back here while you recovered." The man glanced at Hans, "Hauptmann Krieger came in to look for you just a few minutes ago."

"How do you know who I am?" Otto asked.

"We haven't had high ranking officers in Bad Helmstedt for some time. To say you stood out would be an understatement, especially after the scene you caused coming in." The man was being polite, but his tone told Otto he was being more dutiful than truly empathetic.

Otto wasn't in the mood. "Hans, come, let's go to the rendezvous."

Just as he was turned to leave, the office worker stood up. "Wait! Mr. Kline here is something that might interest you."

Otto stopped and turned to face Kline. "What is it?"

Kline glanced at the office worker before stepping out from behind the desk, hesitantly. "Herr Oberst, my name is Dietrich Kline. My family owns a small farm south of town. We've been lucky enough to avoid any damage from the bombing."

Otto was getting impatient. He just wanted to be left alone. "And?"

"Herr Oberst, is your daughter's name Petra, by any chance?"

Otto's voice caught in his throat. Now that he thought about it, he realized that Petra's name hadn't been listed as *'Deceased'* on the news board... In his grief, he'd simply assumed that she was dead.

The man could see the answer to his question written across Otto's face. "Would you like to see her?"

Otto could barely nod, the tears were freely flowing down his face.

"I'll take you – she'll be in your arms before the clock strikes one, if we leave now."

"Yes... Yes, let's go." Otto began to follow Kline out of the office before remembering Hans. He turned, but Hans interjected before he could say anything.

"You go. Reunite with your daughter. I wish to mourn my wife alone."

Otto knew that the two hours or so they had before needing to leave Bad Helmstedt would be far from enough to truly mourn a woman such as Inga, but that sort of thing didn't need to be said. Instead, he grimaced, nodded, and left the office with Kline.

༺✦༻

As the two men made their way through the un-bombed southern portion of Bad Helmstedt, Otto was struck by the sheer number of people huddling on the streets. They all looked defeated, beaten down. Otto was reminded of his impression of Hitler all those months ago in Wewelsburg Castle... *It seems our country finally bears the burden of its master.*

The two men made small talk as they rode Dietrich's tractor out of town. Otto learned that the farm had been in the Kline family for three generations. They were a family with deep Lutheran roots and Dietrich reassured Otto that someday he'd see his family again. "They're waiting for you in a better place," he'd said. Otto had never considered himself a particularly godly man, but that thought was comforting, and he held onto it.

Dietrich went on to share that he'd lost his only two sons to the war effort.

He told Otto how they'd found Petra three days after the bombings… Apparently their church had put together a group of volunteers to scour the wreckage for survivors, and Petra was one of two people they'd found alive. She'd been sleeping under the only wall that stood of Otto's former home when they found her. She hadn't been trapped; she just didn't know where else to go, so she stayed. Dietrich and his family couldn't bear the thought of shipping her off to some orphanage, so they took her into their home instead. She'd been living with them ever since. Apparently, his own daughters had taken her in as a sister, and his wife was happy to have another child in the home after the loss of their two sons.

"When I heard that a military detachment had come into town, I had this strange feeling that I'd find you. I can't explain it," he said as the tractor puttered along. "So, I drove into town straight to the place where I knew I'd go if *my* family were missing."

"You were lucky to find me," Otto said.

"Lucky? Maybe. I'd like to think it was something more divine than that. Either way, your daughter will be very happy to see you. In fact, I think that's her now…"

Otto could see what must be the Kline farm about half a kilometer down the road. A tiny figure was running out from the homestead to meet them. Otto recognized his daughter's distinctly child-like canter even from a distance.

"Stop," Otto said as soon as they reached the dirt driveway. When Dietrich complied, he jumped out from the tractor's bucket seat and sprinted out to meet his daughter.

"Papa! Papa!" She cried out as she ran.

When they met, she flung herself into his arms.

"Oh, Petra, my darling, I'm so happy to see you." He hugged her tight, cherishing the feeling of his daughter's arms around him.

After the longest hug he'd ever had from his daughter, he finally pulled her away to examine her. "Are you hurt, Pet?"

"Ja, I've got a really big bruise and lots of cuts," she said nonchalantly, showing him a grapefruit-sized bruise on her ribs and all the different cuts on her arms and legs. "But I think I'm okay."

Otto was overwhelmed with emotion as he witnessed his daughter's wounds and he quickly pulled her into another embrace.

"Are you here to stay, Papa?" She asked. The question broke his heart. He took a long time to answer, preferring to enjoy his daughter's embrace as long as he could.

"Papa?" She prodded him again.

"I'm sorry, my love, I have to leave just one more time. But this is my last time I'll be gone! We'll get to stay together soon."

Petra pouted at that.

"Well, did you at least bring me any flowers like you promised?"

Otto had almost forgotten his pledge to his daughter all those months ago; he was surprised that she remembered. Her question made him smile.

"I'm sorry, not this time, Pet. But I tell you what…"

"What?"

"I'll bring you three times as many flowers next time I see you! Is that okay?"

Petra pouted her lip out a tiny bit further. "Fiiiiine," she said, "but they better be the prettiest, most colorful flowers I've ever seen!"

Otto chuckled and swooped Petra up into the air like he'd always done when she was a baby. She giggled merrily, her lack of flowers completely forgotten.

Otto spent the next hour with his daughter and the Kline family. He consoled his daughter and they cried together about their lost family. The time flew as they talked and played games and drank hot tea; it was almost enough to make Otto forget his duty. But, the time finally came for him to leave.

When the time came, Petra walked with him and Dietrich out to the Kline family's tractor.

"Tell me again when you'll be back, Papa?"

"Soon," Otto said, "with all the flowers you could ever want."

"Ja Papa!" Petra exclaimed, clapping her hands together in glee.

"Now come here and give Papa a goodbye kiss!" Petra ran at him and jumped up into his arms one last time. She planted a big kiss on his cheek and he held her tightly against his chest.

"You're going to stay with Dietrich and his family for a while, is that okay?" Otto asked.

"Yes, Papa."

"And you'll be good, and listen to Mr. Kline just like if he were me?"

"Yes, Papa."

"Good. Now run along back inside to play with the girls." Otto said, smiling.

At that, Petra whirled around and ran back to the homestead where Mrs. Kline was outside waiting for her to come in.

Under his breath Otto whispers, *Aufweidersehen, Mein Susse*

As Otto and Dietrich began the drive back into Bad Helmstedt, Otto asked Dietrich once more...

"You're sure you can take care of her?"

"Aye, Herr Oberst, she will be as one of our own for as long as she stays with us. One month, one year, it doesn't matter. You do what you need to do and we'll care for your daughter until your return."

"Thank you, Dietrich. All I want is for her to be happy. You have a good family, you're a good man; she'll be happy with you."

"And when you come back, you can be happy together!" Dietrich said encouragingly, clapping him on the back.

"Yes, when I come back." Otto said, gazing off into the distance.

In his mind, though, he knew that his final mission had only one possible outcome. His orders were simple: fight to the death and take as many Reds with you as possible. With Petra's care accounted for, he was fully prepared to do exactly that. In fact, ready wasn't the right word… He was *eager* to show the Bolsheviks the wrath of an armored German with nothing to lose.

Otto and Hans began the last leg of their journey, knowing it would be their last battle, where it would end, no one knew.

CHAPTER 9

Somewhere in Rural North-Central Germany

"We must be getting close," Otto said, "I'd guess we'll catch up to them within a few hours."

Hans nodded in grim determination, gazing off to the north as he listened. The younger of the two remaining Teutonic Knights had been distant and cold since the news of his wife's death in Bad Helmstedt.

Understandably so, Otto thought. Of course, Otto had his own wife and children to mourn, but he also had one living treasure left in the form of his daughter… Hans had nothing; no family, no wife, no children, no home. Nothing. Everything he'd held dear was now gone.

It had been two weeks since the rag-tag Panzertruppen made the depressing trek through the ruins of Otto and Hans' former home. For the past three days, they'd been following the trail of a Russian armored force. Their first evidence of the Russian army hadn't come from any military intelligence, but from the smoldering ruins of what used to be a small farm-town, not so different from Bad Helmstedt. Then, they passed through another pillaged town. And another. Each time, the wreckage was noticeably more 'fresh'… They were closing in.

Fortunately – or unfortunately, for the towns in their way – the Russians seemed to be on a brutish warpath with no regard for surveillance. Likely they made the mistake of assuming the Wehrmacht had no more fight left in it. As far as either Hans or

Otto could tell, their meager force had yet to be spotted by their enemies. That, at least, was good news.

As they continued in pursuit of the Russian column, Otto couldn't help but question exactly how much of an impact he and his troop would be able to make on the uncountable Russian army. They had Otto's imbued Panther G, Hans' similarly imbued Jagdpanther and then a number of remaining 'normal' Panthers, all showing obvious signs of wear. He wasn't worried about himself or Hans doing enough damage, but the rest of the tanks in his unit would be lucky to fire two shots before the Russians obliterated each non-Teutonic tanker.

But now wasn't the time for second guesses or doubts; Otto knew that too. Each and every man remaining with them had lost family. Most of them had lost *all* of their family, just like Hans. Not all of them lost their loved ones at the hands of the Russians, but at this point the Allies were Red and the Reds were Allies. When you're stuck between a rock and a hard place, all you want to do is break something... You don't much care what it is you're breaking.

Otto grimaced. He intended to break a whole lot of Russians before the day was over.

At that exact moment, as if the gods themselves felt his bloodlust, Otto's radio buzzed... It was his outrider. "Herr Oberst, we've spotted the Russians. Approximately a kilometer north of your current location. They're heading for a river; it looks as if they mean to cross."

Otto thought for a moment. Fighting his enemies with their backs to a body of water would certainly give them a strategic advantage. But he needed more information. "Have they begun fording across yet?"

"That's a negative, commander, it looks as if they're seeking a suitable place to cross."

"Excellent," Otto replied, lost in thought. There is a slight hill to the North, Otto guessed that the river must lie on the other side. That meant they'd have the advantage of elevation and position. He was convinced; the time to strike had finally come.

"All units, prepare for battle. Our enemies are in sight and we have them cornered." Otto barked into the radio-comm. "This is it boys; time to make the Russians bleed Red."

"Oberst?" The outrider buzzed in again.

"What is it?" Otto inquired.

"What I'm seeing can't be the full Russian force… I only count approximately 20 armored units."

Otto smiled. This was even better than he'd hoped; that could only mean that the force they'd spotted was the Russian armored rearguard. Otto guessed that the main Russian force had likely already crossed the river, but that left the rearguard vulnerable and out of position. A rookie mistake, but not totally unexpected from the likes of Ivan.

"Our enemies have misplayed their hand," Otto relayed to his unit. "Hauptmann Krieger and I will lead the charge; the rest of you will be on cleanup duty. If we want to maintain our element of surprise, we must ensure that no Russians escape this engagement alive."

"Ja Wohl, Mein Herr," came the unanimous, typical reply.

Otto quickly outlined the rest of his battle plan, and within minutes Germany's last remaining Panzertruppen were ready to engage the enemy. Otto's plan was simple: they would form a half-circle perimeter just outside of Russian vision, right below the crest of the hill leading down to the river. Then, with their enemies trapped, he and Hans would rush over the hill and down towards the rearguard, drawing as much fire as possible in the process. Finally, with the enemy distracted trying to kill the two indestructible tanks, his remaining units would rain hellfire down from the hilltop.

The only problem was distance. Ideally, Otto would have liked to take advantage of the German tanks' superior range, but only 500 meters lay between the hilltop and the river's edge. That meant that both sides would have equal opportunity to score direct hits. Otto didn't like it, but he didn't see any other choice. They weren't going to get a better engagement than this one.

"Is everyone in position and ready to fire?" Otto asked over the radio.

"Ja Wohl."

"Follow my lead," Otto buzzed out.

He double-checked to ensure that his Spear of Longinus was properly inserted into his Panther's console. As he watched, the strange baton seemed to pulse with energy, and he felt a tingling around his neck where his Teutonic Knight's cross dangled against his collar. He felt energized; ready.

With that, he and Hans revved their tanks over the hilltop and began descending towards their enemies. Otto smiled as he saw the sudden shock spread through the ranks of the Russian rearguard as they scrambled to mount a defense.

"Look at that," Otto cackled, "They're all clumped together like a bunch of ripe grapes waiting to be popped. Fire at will!"

Hot lead spewed from the Panther's auxiliary coaxial machine gun, looking more like a solid line of molten fire than any kind of normal munition. But his Panther's 75mm cannon wasn't to be left out of the party – thunder echoed across the hillside as a supernaturally enhanced HE round turned a defenseless Russian armored transport into a blackened crater.

Hans' Jagdpanther had a similar thirst for Red. His first target was a Russian antitank, which his larger 88mm cannon turned into slag metal with a single armor-penetrating shot.

With reckless abandon, the two sole-surviving Teutonic Knights spearheaded the attack on the Russian rearguard. Even over the sound of his Panther's Maybach engine, Otto could hear explosions all across the hillside around them. Numerous direct hits against his tank did nothing more send slight vibrations into the tank's interior. There was nothing the Russians could do to stop the wrath of the holy Panzertruppen.

Otto only saw red as he and Hans together tore a swath through the Russian rearguard. In those moments, as he was filled with the bloodlust of battle, he felt as if he could take on the entire Russian Army and come out on top.

It took Otto several minutes to shake the violence out of his system after the skirmish was over. He'd never felt that kind of bloodlust before... Normally, he prided himself on his ability to remain cool and calculated in the heat of battle. But it didn't particularly matter; their victory had been completely one-sided.

Or so he thought, until he realized just how poorly their plan had panned out.

It was true that he and Hans had completely obliterated the Russian rearguard. Not a single Russian survived the attack. However, it wasn't until he tried to radio his fellow Panzertruppen that he realized the extent of their own losses. While he and Hans had charged in, blinded by bloodlust, it seemed that the Russians' counter-attack was more potent than he'd thought. Despite being on lower ground, the Reds had successfully destroyed every single non-Teutonic tank on the hillside.

It was just Otto and Hans now. But that didn't mean they were done fighting.

"The main Russian force can't be more than a few kilometers north of the river," Hans said as they and their remaining crews regrouped to discuss the next step. "I think our course is simple. We've come this far, why stop now?"

Otto was inclined to agree. He knew that destroying one armored force wouldn't be enough to halt the Russian onslaught. There were still Bolsheviks to be dealt a death blow.

Hans continued. "We may not be able to single-handedly destroy our enemies, but that doesn't mean we can't cripple them. I say we take on one final battle. We've escaped death so many times; this time I say we chase it." Otto saw a morbid glint in his Hauptmann's eye, and he had no doubt of Hans' sincerity. This was a man with nothing to lose and those are the most dangerous kind. Combined with the power of their two tanks, it wasn't inconceivable that they'd be able to take down a surprising number of enemy units with their two alone.

It would be a tale for the ages – two men against an army.

Otto had decided.

"You're right, as you always are, old friend. But just one problem – how do we get to them? There's a river there, and we don't have the equipment to safely ford it."

He and Hans walked over to the river's edge to examine the shoreline. They could see the other side; the river couldn't have been more than a hundred meters from shore to shore. It wouldn't have been the largest river he'd crossed…

Hans cut into his thoughts. "Clearly the Russians have already made it across. If it was safe for them, why shouldn't it be safe for us?"

He made a good point.

"Look, you can even see the bottom… There, look there." Otto followed Hans' finger and saw that, sure enough, there appeared to be a sort of sandbar extending across most of the river.

"What do you all think?" Otto said, now turning to his crew. "You've been with these tanks just as long as we have… Is this a river we can ford?"

Hans' driver was one to answer. "With all due respect, Herr Oberst, I've seen these tanks through battles that no man has a right to live through. They're indestructible! What harm could a bit of water do when even the most fearsome armored weapons in the world can't make a scratch in the Zimmerit?"

Otto's gunner chimed in, "It's as Hauptmann Krieger said: the Russians already did it with their inferior tanks; surely, we can too with ours."

"Then it's settled!" Otto exclaimed. "Mount up, boys, there are Russians waiting for us on the other side. Let's make them regret ever setting foot in the Fatherland."

Progress across the river was slow and tentative at first. Despite the crews' confidence in the tanks, every man among them was prudent enough not to blindly rush into an unknown body of water. When they'd gotten 25 meters or so out with no sign of difficulty, there was a collective sigh of relief among crew and commander alike.

"See?" Hans said over his radio, "I told you there'd be a sand bar. I could see it from the shore. We've got nothing to worry about."

Otto wasn't quite ready to celebrate just yet... He'd do that when they made it to the other side. "Let's just go slow and steady," Otto said, "no need to take any unnecessary risks."

Otto could see Hans smirking face in his mind's eye as he said that. His younger protégé had always been somewhat of a daredevil.

"I tell you what," Hans buzzed, "you can go slow and steady; I'm going to go find me some Reds." With that, Otto saw Hans Jagdpanther lurch forward in the water as he no doubt ordered his driver to accelerate.

PHANTOM PANTHERS

Hans' Jagdpanther was over halfway across the river – about 15 meters in front of Otto's Panther – when he slowed down. For a moment, Otto thought his friend had finally taken his caution to heart. His radio crackled to life.

"Uh, Otto?" Hans said, "I think we might be stuck."

Now Otto looked closer at Hans' tank. He could see its treads spinning, but Hans was right; the tank wasn't moving forward at all. In fact, it almost looked as if the Jagdpanther was moving backwards.

"Hold tight, I'll get in front of you and clear a wake for you to follow in," Otto buzzed over. "Looks like the tortoise *does* beat the hare," he jibed over the radio.

"Ja, Ja, just get us across," Hans said. Otto could tell he was irritated by the sound of his voice.

But, as Otto came closer to the other tank, his own Panther's progress began to slow.

"Herr Oberst, we're losing traction," his driver informed him. Then, before Otto could reply, "I think we're stuck, sir."

"Shit!"

This wasn't good. The one rule of fording a river, especially with a 45 ton tank, was: never stop moving. If you stop moving, you'll sink. Otto knew that. Every man among them knew that.

"Keep trying – don't spin the tracks too fast though. Slow, slow, slow." Otto urged. But even as he said that, he kept moving… Backwards. Some sort of undercurrent was pulling them back towards the middle of the body of water and upstream too.

Frantically, Otto scrambled to open the hatch. He had to get better vision of their surroundings. Apparently, Hans had the same idea.

"We're stuck!" Otto shouted across to Hans poking out of the Jagdpanther.

"I know! And we're moving – look!" Hans pointed to the shoreline just 50 meters away. What auto had felt inside the tank was clearly true... Their movement was obvious when measured against the stationary shoreline. Not only were they moving backwards, they were being pulled sideways. It almost seemed as if they were sinking too.

"Uh oh..." Hans said. Otto turned to see what he was looking at, but it was something on the opposite side of his tank.

"What is it?" Otto called.

Hans didn't explain. "We have to get out. Now! Right now!" Hans was shouting down to his crew, still in the cabin below. Then, even as Otto watched he saw the far half of Hans' Jagdpanther suddenly dip into the water, as if the ground below it had suddenly fallen away.

"The sand bar..." Otto realized.

"Sir, we're taking on water!" His driver's call from below broke him from his reverie. Hans was right – they had to get out. Now. The mysterious watery force was pulling them off them even further out and down.

"Get out!" Otto shouted down to his crew. He climbed back down into his commander's seat to grab his enchanted baton from its slot, but he had to pull his hand away as soon as he touched it. The runic etchings around it were glowing orange and it was searing hot to the touch. Something about it struck Otto as malicious, as if the baton wanted to stay in the tank, but he didn't have time to ponder that now. He quickly ditched the baton and turned his attention to his crew.

"What are you waiting for?" Otto asked, urgency lacing his voice. "We're being pulled down – we have to get out right now!" The water was lapping at his feet now.

"Oberst... Sir... We're stuck!" That was his gunner.

"What do you mean you're stuck?

Otto could feel the adrenaline pumping through his veins as the water was now up to his shins. Then, suddenly, the floor fell out from underneath him and he stumbled to the down to the ground. Except, down was sideways and the ground was the wall.

That must be the edge of the lake shelf, Otto thought.

"Oberst... Help!"

Otto scrambled down into the hull to help his crew, but it was exactly as they said. In an instant the crew members in the lower quarters were being buried in a watery grave.

The water was rushing in through all the hatches now and the cabin was filling fast. His crew was desperate now. His driver was screaming, but that scream turned into a gurgle as water covered his head. The cabin was almost completely full of water and filling fast. Otto felt his tank sinking, and he knew they must have been pulled fully off the sandbar now.

I have to get out, Otto thought as he took one final breath. His gunner was clutching onto his sleeve, but he tore his arm away. He made one last attempt to save his companion before mouthing the words, "I'm sorry," and made a swim for the hatch.

Looking back, he watched as the last gasps of life escaped from his brave companion.

Glancing over his shoulder he saw that his longtime friend was in the same predicament, both vehicles were sinking fast and Han's crew was trapped in their Jagdpanther and now their invincible monster was going to be in their last resting place, a soldier's tomb.

Otto had never been a good swimmer and he considered it a miracle when he crawled onto the shore. He collapsed on the ground, but quickly got back up again as his stomach expunged itself of river water. The world went black around him as he fell, unconscious, into a mixture of mud, sand and vomit.

"Otto..." The voice was distant, hazy. But familiar. "Otto... Wake up..."

He recognized it now; that was Hans.

"Get your friend up now or we'll shoot him and throw his body in the lake."

That nasally voice, Otto didn't recognize. But he was conscious enough to recognize a threat. When he opened his eyes, Hans was kneeling over him. His normally well-kept blonde hair was wet and matted. Upon further inspection, Otto noticed blood running down one of his arms.

"Where are...?" Otto began to ask, but the words made his throat hurt and he hacked up a coughing fit. "Where are we?" He asked again once he'd recovered.

"Where you are doesn't matter!" The unrecognized voice shouted. Now that Otto was becoming more alert, he noticed the thick Russian accent of the voice.

Before Otto could reply, two sets of hands grabbed him by his shoulders and hoisted him off the ground. He didn't even try to walk as his captors dragged him into the back of an armored transport. Hans climbed in after him, hands on his head.

"If it vere my choice, I'd shoot you both right here." Otto now saw the man who the sharp, nasally Russian voice belonged to. He was short and gaunt. His sharp cheekbones and arched nose made him look distinctly avian. "Lucky for you, Colonel values information over blood. But that doesn't mean I von't shoot you if given half a chance." The man smiled now, patronizingly. "You two'd best behave," he clucked.

At that, the man slammed shut the grate on the back of the transport and they lurched in their seat as the vehicle began moving, stopping near what seemed like and endless precession of prisoners.

PHANTOM PANTHERS

"Commissar Romanenko, more German prisoners for your interrogation." The nasally man had led them inside a tent and he now presented them to what was clearly a high-ranking officer. Colonel Romanenko wore a thick fur Ushanka and he had deep-set eyes with thick bushy eyebrows and a mustache to match. His dark eyes narrowed as he took in the two prisoners set before him. He took a deep drag of his cigarette – it was that horrible Russian mahorka by the smell – and considered the men for a moment.

"Ve found these papers on them; they're vet but readable," the nasally man said, presenting Romanenko with his findings. Romanenko took the papers from them and turned them over in his hands.

"Is that all?" The commissar's voice was gruff, scratchy from years of smoking such harsh Russian tobacco.

The nasally man nodded.

Romanenko tossed the papers on the table behind them. "Then what are you still doing here?"

The nasally man was clearly perturbed, but he said nothing. Instead, he about-faced and marched out of the tent.

Otto and Hans were standing side-by-side, hands bound behind their backs. Romanenko walked in a circle around them, inspecting them from head to toe. He stopped in front of Otto.

"Herr Oberst, the war is over for two of you." He blew a puff of smoke into Otto's face. "It says in your papers that you were a commander of some merit. Tell me, what was your unit?"

Otto stared straight ahead, silent. The commissar waited for a few moments, then turned around to face away from Otto. He walked slowly over to the table at the front of the tent and picked something up. He held it behind his back as he walked back up to Otto. With one hand, he reached out and grabbed Otto's chin, forcing him to meet his eyes.

"Well Herr Oberst, I will ask once more. What was your unit?"

Hans began to say something, but a glare from Romanenko silenced him. Otto stared ahead in silence once more and again the commissar waited a few moments. But, this time, he whipped his hand out from behind his back and struck Otto across the jaw with a heavy truncheon. Otto felt the full force of Romanenko's hand switch. He struggled to right himself after reeling from the thrashing. The splitting pain in his jaw led him to believe it was partially fractured.

Otto looked straight ahead once more, but this time he answered. "I was attached to the 17th SS Panzer Grenadier Division."

"Ah, tankers, eh? Romanenko bellows. "I bet you destroyed a lot of good Russian men in your tanks, eh?"

"Yes."

The commissar turned to Hans, arching an eyebrow as he took another drag of Mahorka, truncheon still in his other hand. "And what about you? Same unit?"

"Yes," Hans said.

"You know, that's funny, because we've already captured other members of your 17th SS Unit… Except they didn't say anything about any living commanders."

Otto was silent.

Suddenly, Colonel Romanenko was screaming. "You are lying! Don't lie to me, you German swine! I'll have your heads mounted outside my…" He paused mid-sentence as he noticed something on the ground at Otto's feet. He knelt down and picked it up, holding it in his hand.

"This is a Bravery decoration that I haven't seen before…" then Romanenko says after several moments. He looked up to Otto, raising his truncheon menacingly. "You will tell me what this means, Oberst."

Otto paused before he answered. "We were… Part of a special unit."

"You are lying!" He used the butt of his truncheon to slam Otto in the solar plexus. "No special units existed! We would know! Tell me the truth right now, or I'll have your tongue."

As Otto tried to recover his breath, he gasped out, "Look, my comrade has one too, we were part of a new unit and we were given new awards to revitalize our courage. Our unit has since been destroyed."

The commissar walked over in front of Hans and ripped the Teutonic cross from his neck. He eyed Hans suspiciously, looking back and forth between the two men.

"You are both liars. More likely that you're deserters running like frightened dogs to the mercy of your enemies. You wouldn't be the first we'd caught trying to make it to the American lines."

"No, we told you…" Otto began.

"I don't care what you told me! You are lying!" Otto thought the man's head would explode if he screamed any louder. Romanenko took several deep breaths and then took another deep drag of Mahorka to calm himself. "Let me remind you that in the Soviet Army it takes a brave man to be a coward; I could have you all shot for the lies you have told me." He turned to look towards the entrance of the tent. Stepanovich! Get in here!"

The nasally man walked back in.

"Make sure these get to G2," handing Lt. Bersudsky the Teutonic crosses. "Perhaps they will be able to uncover the truth that these two so desperately want to hide." He now turned back to Otto and Hans. "As for these two, brand them and put them with the other scum. But make sure they're not in the same cell… I don't trust either one of them."

Lt. Bersudsky roughly grabbed each captive by the arm and led them out of the tent. "Looks like you're mine now," he said menacingly. "I was denied the honor of squashing you Germans at the front, but on days like these I'm glad I get to take care of the leftovers."

Hans climbed back into an armored transport, a different one than the one they'd arrived in. "Say goodbye to your friend!" He said to Otto with a chuckle. But before Otto could say anything, he slammed the transport's door shut and the truck – and Hans – sped off.

"You'll get to stay with me," Bersudsky yells. "But I warn you, we don't have any blankets here. In fact, we don't have any food either. I hope you like eating worms, Oberst." As Otto was herded towards the Russian's makeshift prison camp, the smell of death filled his nostrils. He wondered just how long he'd have to live in this cold, hell of a place. At the same time, he wasn't sure that he wanted to know the answer.

I hope Petra will be happy and safe… was his last thought before he was thrown into the gated pen with the rest of the German POWs.

Commanders of the Phantom Panthers disappeared into a sea of the unknown.

CHAPTER 10

29 Years Later, Somewhere in Central Germany

"Hurry up Private, we're running late!"

Colonel Donavan MaClosky was on his way to oversee his division's routine training maneuvers at the nearby tank firing range. It was all too rare that his 2nd armored division – otherwise known as "Hell on Wheels" – got to use live fire, and he'd been looking forward to this session for several weeks. It was a beautiful summer day, and the sky was crystal clear.

Perfect weather for training maneuvers.

Unfortunately, this incompetent driver was going to make him miss it; they only had a five-hour window to finish their exercises, so every minute counted.

MaClosky understood *why* he needed a driver, but the suits above him insisted on it as a matter of protocol. He knew that his begrudging attitude towards the whole situation only increased his frustration, but he couldn't help it.

"I swear to God, Private, if we're not there in the next two minutes, you'll be working graveyard shifts for a month!" Spit flew from his mouth as he shouted.

The Private was visibly shaken. "I'm trying, sir, but this thing can't go any faster."

"Oh yes it can; just watch!" At that, the Colonel reached over and physically pressed on the Private's knee, forcing his foot harder on the gas pedal.

Sure enough, the command jeep did go faster, just like MaClosky had said it would.

Unfortunately, the Colonel had chosen the worst possible moment to lose his temper; the Private was so distracted by keeping the gas on an even keel that he didn't notice the sharp turn right in front of them. Before either man could react, the jeep went careening off of the shoulder of the road and into the lake beyond.

As soon as the jeep crashed into the water. Fortunately, both men retained their consciousness. Cursing at the top of his lungs, McCloskey and his driver managed to save themselves as the vehicle slowly but surely filled with water and began sinking.

Both men were absolutely filthy by the time they staggered onto the shore. The lake was murky and muddy, and globs of muck hung from their uniforms.

"God damn idiot for brains! What the hell were you thinking?!" MaClosky yelled as he tried to fleck some of the muddy goop from his clothes. "If you'd been gettin' us there on time, none of this would've happened!"

"Yes sir, I'm sorry sir," was the private's subdued reply.

"Shit! Now we'll never get there!" MaClosky screamed. He went on like that for several minutes until, fortunately for the Private, a trailing recon unit came down the road, pulled up and stopped. The driver, a recon officer, looked amused as he dismounted his vehicle.

"What happened here, Colonel? Where's your jeep?"

"That'll be 'Where's your jeep, *sir*,' to you, soldier. And what the hell does it look like you imbecile? This idiot," he said motioning to the Private, "drove us into the lake."

The recon officer laughed out loud at that, as did his partner who remained in the passenger's seat.

"Ha, ha, it's so funny, is it?" MaClosky said, his voice dripping with malice, "Well guess what? I've just decided who's going to dive down and hook a chain up to pull that jeep out. You." MaClosky smiled, victorious. "Better strip down; wouldn't want your nice uniform to get all wet, would we?"

The recon officer frowned as he realized exactly what his punishment would entail. Nonetheless, he did as he was ordered and, once down to his skivvies, began wading into the lake, tow cable in hand.

"How's the water, soldier?" MaClosky called out to him. "Oh that's right, I remember – it's freezing." Now MaClosky was the one laughing out loud. It seemed that the other man's discomfort was just the thing to lighten his mood.

It took the recon officer several dives to both scope out the jeep and determine how best to tow it out. Meanwhile, MaClosky notified the rest of his unit that they'd be postponing their training maneuvers for another day. Finally, the recon officer came out of the lake with thumbs up. "We're all set," he called out between deep breaths. "But, sir, there's something else down there!"

"Something else down there?" MaClosky inquired, once the recon officer was on shore. The former feud between the two men evaporated with the new discovery. "What do you mean?"

"Well, sir, I couldn't be sure, but it looks like some sort of giant machine. Maybe even two of them! Looks like the lake is only about 30 feet deep, but it's dirty as all hell… I couldn't make out exactly what they were."

As the Private and the other, dry recon officer slowly began towing the jeep out of the water, MaClosky decided he'd personally go down and take a look. "This better be good, soldier," he called out as he waded back out into the lake, this time absent his wet clothes. He was thankful that it was so hot outside, otherwise the temperature of the water would be unbearable. He swam out to where the recon officer had indicated to look, then took a deep breath and dove down.

What he thought he saw – for it was almost too much to believe – was incredible.

When he came back on shore, still in awe, he ordered the Private to fetch him a field phone.

"Major Ramchek, com unit.

This is Colonel MaClowsky. I need you to contact the local authorities and get me a local dive team and send them over to the South end of Old Baden See Lake, ASAP. Got that?"

"Yes sir," came the voice on the other end, "What should I tell them this is for?"

"Tell them we've found two tanks buried under water, and we need their help before we can haul them out."

As a rescue diver, Walter Rudel prided himself on his sense of adventure. He was also one of those few lucky men who truly enjoyed what he did for a living. As such, he was the first to volunteer when their unit was informed that a nearby US military unit needed local assistance with some sort of diving project. He was antsy with excitement by the time he and the two other volunteers from his unit finally made it onto the now-bustling scene at Baden See Lake.

Along with his two partners, it seems that the military had called in several other helping hands. Numerous military personnel moved along the shoreline like ants, and

Rudel spotted several other units from the local authorities.

A gruff looking, barrel chested man made his way over to them as soon as the dive team arrived. He was wearing a US military uniform, although it was almost indiscernible beneath the thick layer of mud that had crusted over it.

"You must be Walter Rudel," the man said, extending a muddy hand, "I'm Colonel MaClowsky – the one who called y'all out here." If his uniform hadn't given him away as an American, his dialect certainly did. Walter gave the man a firm, albeit dirty, handshake.

"Do you know why you're here?" The Colonel asked.

"We'd been told that you guys needed help with a dive… You found some sort of tanks or something?"

"That's correct."

"Well," Rudel began, "how can we help? Do you want to pull them out, or just get a better look at them?"

The Colonel puckered his lips as he thought for a moment. "I'm thinking we'll have you go scope things out first. From what we can tell, they're pretty well buried down there. That reminds me – did y'all bring digging tools?"

Rudel bag at his side, which contained all of his scuba gear. "Yes sir, we've got enough oxygen to last the whole day, and we brought the equipment to dig out whatever's buried out there."

"Excellent," MaClosky said, "then let's have you go ahead and start digging right away. Once you deem 'em ready to haul, we can get a couple caterpillars down here to tow 'em out." MaClosky went around and shook the other two divers' hands. "We really appreciate your help, fellas, couldn't do this without you."

Rudel's curiosity only grew as he donned his double-hose diving gear. He retrieved his aquatic shovel-pick from his duffel and, along with his two partners, made his way out into the lake, anxious to uncover the buried behemoths.

Beneath the surface of the Lake, the water was certainly muddy, but not unbearably so. Rudel's large goggles gave him the visibility he needed to navigate around the ghostly tomb. As he approached the adjoining mud-mounds that housed the war machines, he took a moment just to stare. The machines had clearly been preserved well; they seemed to emanate some sickly glow beneath the water, like their metallic coating was catching the sunlight from above.

They made relatively short work of the excavation – the mud and sediment surrounding the tanks proved easy to remove, only the sheer volume made the project time consuming.

As he and his partners set to their task, more and more of the tanks became visible. The three divers all shared a look of disbelief when they finished excavating one side of one tank to uncover a distinct German cross. They took a break from their digging to surface and share the discovery.

Rudel excitedly informed Colonel MaClosky of their find. "I'm telling you – it's a Nazi cross we saw down there. That means these tanks must be from World War 2… They've been submerged down here for at least 30 years!"

"Amazing…" the Colonel murmured. "Good work, diver, keep me updated as you learn more."

It was late in the afternoon by the time they were done digging. But, they had gathered enough information to determine the origin and model of both tanks. One was an old German Panther G, the other was the infamous tank-killer of Nazi Germany, a Jagdpanther. Both were clearly from World War 2 and had likely sunk at the same time. They'd even determined a unit number on the Panther G's turret: I-02.

MaClosky was thrilled with this new information. "You and your team have done excellent work, Major Rudel."

"Thank you! Honestly, it was my pleasure. Coming out here and uncovering old relics certainly beats a boring day at the office."

"I'm glad you feel that way," MaClosky said, "we've got a couple caterpillars on their way out right now. If you've got nowhere to be, we'd like you to personally make sure each tank gets out in one piece."

"That's fine," Rudel replied, "I just need to be home when the sun goes down or my wife'll have my head."

About half an hour later, Rudel saw two huge bulldozers cresting the hill down the road. In the time it'd taken the bulldozers the military had requisitioned to arrive, their aquatic find had garnered more local attention, even from the media. Rudel watched as a cute female journalist and cameraman interviewed a handsome military official.

Major Rudel found MaClosky. "Who's that?" he asked, indicating the man being interviewed. The Colonel scoffed loudly, letting him know what he thought of the man in question.

"That's Major Jonathan Duvall," MaClosky said, "He's our liaisons officer to the Munster Military Museum. I guess he's some history buff, so they wanted to interview him about the tanks."

Rudel could tell that the Colonel was at least slightly jealous that he hadn't been the one interviewed. He quickly changed the subject. "Is there anything else you'd like us to know before we go down and hook up the tanks?"

The Colonel pulled himself out of his envious reverie. "What? No... No, just be careful. And be quick – we're paying these construction folks by the hour for their 'dozers."

Several minutes later, the two bulldozers were in position with their butts facing the shoreline, ready to tow. Due to the size of the tanks, each one would need both caterpillars in order to be hauled out. Rudel took the chain from on caterpillar and one of his partners took the other. The third went down with them to help supervise and double check that everything was hooked up properly. They decided they'd start with the smaller of the two tanks – the Panther G.

Finally, once his dive team had ensured a secure connection underwater, Rudel watched as the two caterpillars revved their engines and began moving forward in unison. For a split second, it looked as if the giant construction machines wouldn't be enough to move even the smaller Panther G. Rudel let out a sigh of relief when the caterpillars finally inched forward. Slowly at first, then faster.

Rudel kept a careful eye on the surface of the water, making sure that both chains remained taught. At long last, the hull of the first Panther breached the surface. Then the barrel appeared. Then the treads, then the turret, and before long the entire tank was on the shore. Water streamed out of it like a cup with holes.

"Incredible…" Walter whispered under his breath. Out of the corner of his eye he saw the news team panning their camera between the Major and the scene in front of them, capturing the entire ordeal.

Once the first tank was on shore, Rudel and his crew made short work of hooking up the second one. However, hauling out the Jagdpanther proved much more difficult. There were multiple times where the bulldozers had to stop while Walter's dive team did further excavation to assist the tow. Then, they'd tentatively begin moving forward again, slowly but surely dislodging the enormous tank from its watery prison.

When the Jagdpanther was finally pulled all the way out of the water, it stood even more impressive than the Panther G. Its huge cannon loomed fearsomely over the gathering on the shore, as if it knew that even after three decades it still held immense destructive power. There was no doubt in Rudel's mind that the tank in front of him was the most devastating weapon of its time.

It was then that Rudel noticed something peculiar… Both tanks appeared to be in pristine condition. He was no history buff like the handsome Major undoubtedly was, but as far as he could tell both tanks looked like they'd just rolled off the factory floor. As an avid diver, he'd seen his fair share of underwater artifacts. Without exception, they always exhibited clear signs of aquatic erosion. But these tanks…

It was like thirty years of underwater entombment had never happened.

CHAPTER 11

Small town, central Germany

It had been a challenging day for Petra at the Medizinische Hochschule Hannover and arriving home for some time off was a welcome relief. Petra appreciated the feeling that came after a hard day of work, but nonetheless, the mini-vacation that she'd scheduled for herself was a welcome relief. She'd worked her way through university, she had acquired an education and her shoulder-length blond hair, perfect complexion and toned figure revealed a confident, well-groomed woman. She knew that Otto wanted her to find a suitor, but she was content to remain single.

She'd begun her employ at the Medizinische Hochschule Hannover as a nurse, and she often found herself wishing she hadn't pushed herself so hard to climb the executive ranks. But, she was a Mader... And Maders couldn't do anything less than their very best. It just wasn't in their blood.

As she entered the foyer of her modest townhome, she heard the only other remaining Mader in the living room, "Is that you Pet? You're home early."

"I'm off the rest of today and tomorrow, remember? I told you yesterday how excited I was for my four-day weekend." She called to him as she took off her shoes. "I thought we would spend the afternoon tomorrow with the Ostermanns so that Peter and I can share some time together." Peter was a man she knew her father liked, one of the 'suitors' he so wanted her to take.

"Just a second," Otto made his way into the kitchen to brew their routine post-work tea. It was a fragrantly soothing chamomile, their favorite. Petra was catching the afternoon news on the tele' as a Special News report from America interrupted the newscast.

"From the NBC news room, this is David Brinkley and we are broadcasting live the resignation of our President Richard M. Nixon."

"Good evening, fellow Americans, this is the 37th time I have spoken to you from this office, where so many decisions have been made that shaped the history of this Nation. Each time I have done so to discuss with you some matter than I believe affected the national interest." The news broadcast reveals that the US President has just resigned.

"I knew the Yanks would kick him out of office sooner or later," Otto mumbled as he watched. Petra listened to the President's address as she sat down...

"...I would have preferred to carry through to the finish whatever the personal agony it would have involved and my family unanimously urged me to do so. But the interest of the Nation must always come before any personal considerations..."

She quickly tuned out the disgraced president. She was never one to really care about politics, especially those in other countries. Instead, she began telling Otto about her day.

"I never thought I'd spent so much time in meetings," she complained as the president went on in the background, "the hospital apparently went over budget again this last fiscal quarter, so now we have to cut costs in one of our units. It's looking like it'll be Psych that gets the cut, even though they're already understaffed as is. Makes no sense to me."

"Oh really?" Otto asked, "You're right, that doesn't make sense." Petra could see her father was distracted by the president's address, but she went on venting anyways.

"I tell you, sometimes I honestly think about quitting the hospital to work at the group home full-time. I just don't feel like I'm making a difference where I'm at... All anyone there cares about is money, money, money. No one cares about actually *helping* people."

Petra spent her weekends volunteering at a local group home for orphaned children, a passion she'd had ever since she could remember. Perhaps it was because her own past was filled with abandonment, but she felt obligated to do everything in her power to improve the lives of children in need. And she enjoyed it; she'd been volunteering at one orphanage or another since her teens.

As Otto listened to his daughter complain about her day, his mind wandered back to his days after the war. Otto had suffered as a POW in the Russian prison camps for five whole years after the war ended.

The first year was the hardest. In the months after his capture, he was interrogated every single day. He was beaten, starved, bound, and beaten again. The questions were always the same: who are you, what was the purpose of your unit, and what happened to your tanks?

Otto had told them everything he knew, except the specific location of the tanks. He also kept everything about the ritual at Wewelsburg Castle a secret, fearing that the Russians may have been able to mimic the powers that had been bestowed on him and the other Teutonic Knights.

As time went on and Otto was shuffled from prison camp to prison camp, the interrogations slowly became less frequent, as did the beatings. By the time three years had passed, he knew that he'd been fully forgotten, even to his enemies. He had given up all hope of ever being released, doomed to death in imprisonment. But, in 1949 the US pressed Russia to release all of their remaining POWs, and Otto was finally allowed back into the real world.

Unfortunately, no one was alive to greet him. The world outside felt even lonelier than the one he'd been released from.

Of course, no amount of loneliness could quench the hope that Otto had for finding his daughter.

It took Otto a full month to scrounge together enough money to find work and a place to stay; he barely eked out a living. He spent many days doing odd jobs for anyone that would hire him, desperate for any source of income.

Finally, he saved up enough for a train ticket. But, when he arrived in Bad Helmstedt (the railroad having been repaired after the war), he found that the Kline farm was no longer there. Apparently, it and the rest of the town had been bombed again after he left with the Panzertruppen all those years ago. He remembered how he'd collapsed in agony when he learned of the Kline's – and his daughter's – alleged demise. It was more painful than any torture the Russians had ever inflicted, and he spent many months mourning his lost daughter.

Eventually, Otto pulled himself together and settled down in a small city near Hanover. He used his mechanical experience to land a job with an engineering firm and he worked there for 15 years before retiring and moving outside the city. He had saved well and lived comfortably, but nothing could take away the loneliness. He never remarried; the thought just didn't appeal to him. He'd always known he could never love another woman besides Magda.

Through the years, Otto had always felt a lack of closure regarding his daughter. After retiring, he finally decided that he had to know; was his daughter dead and if not, where was she? Searching through the records of missing persons, schools and local and provincial government access, he finally found a solid lead from local employment records that would take him to Hamburg.

Immediately he made the drive to Hamburg and spent the next two days tracking down his daughter. He'd finally found her as she was leaving work – she was still a nurse at the time – at the Albertinen-Krankenhaus Hamburg.

PHANTOM PANTHERS

She actually didn't believe him when he first told her who he was, but when he gave her a bouquet of flowers and said, 'I hope this makes up for last time,' she burst into tears and gave him the hug he'd longed for all the years since the war.

After going out to dinner together to talk and catch up, she agreed to come live with him in Hanover. They both wanted to make up for lost time. Otto couldn't have been happier and that night in the restaurant he decided exactly what he wanted to do for the rest of his life: he wanted to make sure that his precious daughter was happy. That's all that mattered then, and it was all that mattered now.

⋆❖⋆

"Well, I'm going to take a shower real quick," Petra said to her father. "Want me to make you dinner, papa?"

"No thanks sweetheart," Otto said, snapping back to reality, "I had some soup before you got here. There should be some left for you on the stove, if you'd like."

"Ooooh, that sounds good," she said. Her father had always been a surprisingly good cook. But, she supposed that five years on prison rations would make anyone value fine cuisine, which her father certainly did.

When she got out of the shower, Otto was still watching the news. She ladled herself a bowl of soup from the kitchen and sat down in the living room to eat with her father. She had just gotten comfortable as the anchor was introducing a new story.

"And now we have a unique story about two war relics which have apparently been discovered right here in central Germany. Our remote correspondent, Helga, is on the scene with the full story. Over to you, Helga." The camera switched over from the news studio to an outdoor scene next to a lake. On the scene, Petra saw military personnel, what looked like scuba divers, and even a construction

crew in the background. The news correspondent was standing next to a very handsome, dark haired man in military uniform.

Petra paused mid-bite to admire the man on the screen. He was tall and broad-shouldered, with an angular jaw and deep, ice-blue eyes. He had a slight, mischievous smirk on his face as the correspondent began speaking. Something about him was extremely alluring; almost as if he was looking right at her through the TV. Petra listened intently as the correspondent began.

"Thanks Tanja," the correspondent, Helga, said, "We're here with US Army Major Jonathan Duvall right next to Old Baden See Lake. As you said, the US Military has just uncovered what they believe to be two relics of World War 2. Major, why don't you start by telling us a little about yourself."

"Thanks, Helga. As you said, my name is Major Jonathan Duvall, and I'm the US Army Liaison Officer to the Munster Military Museum. I'm here to oversee the excavation and transport of this unique historic find."

"And why don't you tell us more about what exactly it is that you've found in this lake, and how you found it."

The Major smiled now, showing off a pearly white set of teeth. "Well, how we found them is actually an amusing story in itself. One of our Colonels was en route to some live training maneuvers north of here, but he was unfortunate enough to miss a turn coming around the lakeshore. He ended up crash-landing in the lake." The Major let out a lighthearted chuckle at that. "Normally, we would frown on this kind of embarrassing press-exposure, but in this case the Colonel's mistake has led to an extremely intriguing discovery."

Helen laughed as the Major finished his story. "It sounds like one man's wet uniform is another man's treasure, right Major?"

Major Duvall laughed out loud. "Yes, I suppose you're right on that one, Helga."

PHANTOM PANTHERS

"But, back to this discovery – it includes two buried tanks, is that right?"

"That's correct, when our Colonel's men dove into the lake – which is actually surprisingly shallow – to attach a tow cable to the jeep, they found what appeared to be a single large machine buried on the lake's floor. Upon closer inspection, we determined that it was not one, but two separate military tanks."

"So, let me ask you this Major: what's so special about these tanks? What makes this such an important find?"

"Well, first of all, you can probably guess that finding any tank underwater is a bit of a surprise. But, these two tanks are particularly special. According to the information we've gathered from the divers performing the excavation, what we have here are two German tanks from World War 2. The first appears to be a 'G' Model Panther, which was one of the best tanks of the war on either side. The second is a Jagdpanther, or Panzerjager as they're also known, which was the feared German tank-killer. According to everything we know about Hitler's military strategy, both models were instrumental in much of the Reich's success throughout the middle of the war. And what's so peculiar about this particular find is that these tanks appear to be in near-perfect condition."

As Petra listened to the story and more importantly, to the handsome Major, she noticed that Otto had moved forward in his seat. His elbows were resting on his knees as he watched the interview, soaking up every word. He had a slight scowl on his face.

"Wow. Amazing," Helga said. "And it looks like you're actually bringing one out now!" The camera panned over to the surface of the lake, where two bulldozers were slowly but surely hauling something enormous out of the water. First, the hull of the tank crested the surface. Then, the barrel of the Panther's main cannon. Then the turret, which had I-02 emblazoned across its side.

Petra heard Otto gasp beside her.

Once the tank was halfway out of the water, the camera panned back to Helga and the Major. "Ok Major, while your crew finishes hauling the tanks out of the water, why don't you tell us a bit more about what happens now?"

"Of course. We've got a couple flatbed lowboys you can see back there," Major Duvall said, motioning behind him, "we're going to load the tanks onto the trucks and transport them back to the Munster Military Museum, where we can study them, open them up and hopefully learn more about exactly how they got onto the bottom of this lake. If we're lucky, we may even be able to rev one up for a test-run!"

"Well, there you have it," Helga said, "two awesome tanks in the last place you'd expect to find them. Stay tuned for more local news after this quick commercial break."

Otto had a bad feeling as soon as the news correspondent first introduced the Major. Something about the scene seemed all too familiar to him, although he couldn't quite put his finger on why. Then, as Major Duvall described the tanks they'd found – the same exact models as he and Hans had lost so long ago – that 'bad feeling' had turned into dark foreboding. When the Panther G finally breached the surface of the water to reveal its unit number, I-02, Otto's worst fears were realized.

He listened intently as Helga wrapped up the story, taking in every word. When it was over, he stood up and went to a picture on the mantel. Pulling the picture from the frame and handing it to Petra, she now realized that this picture was of her father and the vehicle he had commanded.

"Petra, my sweet daughter, do you trust me?"

Petra paused for a moment, taken aback. "Yes... Yes, of course I do, papa."

"I wish it weren't true, but it is an undeniable fact; they have uncovered a monster waiting to be unleashed. The museum must be warned."

"I have something very important to do," Otto began, but Petra interrupted him, "How can I help?"

"I must find Hans and together we must convince the museum of the gravity of their find. They may be in grave danger," Otto began to explain. "If I can locate Hans, we should arrive at the museum tomorrow before the tanks are unloaded. Once you leave, I'll call and setup a meeting for us with the Major tomorrow morning."

Now looking into his daughter's eyes, Otto continued, "In the meantime, I need you to take this photo to the Munster Military Museum," he said, as he found a big yellow envelope for the photo to go in. "Deliver it to this 'Major Duvall' personally. Trust it to no one else."

"I just don't understand what's going on. What's so bad about a couple old tanks?"

"Just promise me, Petra. Please. It'll make sense soon enough."

"Okay, I promise. Just give me a few minutes to get my stuff together and I'll leave. Hopefully I can get there before the museum closes tonight."

Otto, with both hands, gently embraces his daughter, tenderly kisses her and in a whisper, tells her, *"Aufweidersehen, Mein Susse"*.

CHAPTER 12

Petra shifted into fourth gear and sped up the entrance ramp, thoroughly confused and distracted by her father's behavior. He had always been such a precise man, a reason for everything he did and always an explanation offered if she questioned anything.

Not this time.

For the first time in her life, she felt he was hiding something from her.

Of course, there were many things about his experiences during the war that he never shared; that was similar to the relationships her friends had with their fathers who had served, and perfectly understandable. Petra knew perfectly well that war is a tough business and men of her father's generation were often reticent to share the brutal realities of what happened with their children. It was a protective mechanism for all parties, she presumed.

This was different, however. All he wanted was a simple errand, it seemed to her, but when she had asked for more details, he had grown quiet and almost defensive. It was clear to her that he placed great importance on her help, but for whatever reason he would not tell her why he needed it. It was all very puzzling, and not at all like her father.

She looked down at the envelope she was to hand-deliver to the museum in Munster. Not just to the museum, but to the man they'd seen on the television.

"*Trust it to no one else,*" he'd warned solemnly, almost as if there was some ancient curse that might be revived if his directions were not followed to the letter.

PHANTOM PANTHERS

She was making good time, and with any luck she'd be in Munster by late afternoon and could take a look around the museum before meeting with the handsome American officer from the television.

Otto hated keeping things from Petra, but he figured the less he told her, the better. He hated involving her at all, but those tanks were too dangerous to be trifled with and he needed time to find Hans. With any luck, the contents of the envelope would delay anyone doing something that might unleash the dark powers of the tanks until Otto, and hopefully Hans, could get there.

They might very well be the only two men on earth who could stop the tanks if they were fired up again. The only men who could stop World War III.

Otto shook his head. The very thought of those monstrous machines being fired up again made his blood run cold. He'd often dreamed of them. Of what would have happened if he and Hans hadn't sunk them in those murky waters so long ago.

What else would they have destroyed? How far would they have taken their original, cursed mission?

"Get a hold of yourself," Otto muttered to himself, running his finger down the list of government ministries and phone numbers.

"Ah. As they say in America, bingo."

Just before he picked up the receiver, the phone rang.

"Hello?"

"*I can't wait all day, my friend.*"

The voice on the other end of the line was unmistakable even though Otto had not heard it for almost thirty years. He was shocked at the emotion that momentarily flooded his consciousness, and had no words.

"*I can see you now, Otto, sitting at your kitchen table with a cup of tea, painstakingly calling various offices looking for my information.*"

Otto laughed. His tea was brewing, but otherwise Hans was correct. Hans could always get a laugh out of him. He realized at that moment that he had wasted far too many years outside the company of his best friend. The scars of war that bound them together had also driven them apart, and that was a shame.

"Why is it that only grave danger has brought us together?"

"Grave danger? Let's not put the cart before the horse, Otto."

"Of course, you're right. Nothing has happened, yet."

Each of them had seen the news reports on the tanks, and of course knew what it meant. They both understood that the power of those beasts could never again be unleashed on the world. Otto's fears that Hans might be hard to find were, fortunately, unfounded.

They made plans to meet at Duvall's office at the museum in Munster the following day and chatted a bit before ending the call to make their travel arrangements.

Hans had been reclusive these past years, but not a recluse. He lived a varied and vibrant existence on a small farm he'd inherited from the parents of his beloved Inga.

He had never remarried, but as Hans put it, he'd never been without the companionship of a woman if he so desired. Hans had been perfectly content with his dogs and his life on the farm, with his pension and his memories.

"*The one thing I never wanted was this,*" Hans had said before hanging up the phone, and Otto could not agree more.

It would be good to see his old friend. Even better if they survived.

PHANTOM PANTHERS

Petra arrived in Munster in the late afternoon and went straight to the museum. She had only gotten more curious about her father's behavior on the drive, alone with just her music and her thoughts, and decided to take a look around to see if there were any clues as to what was so important about the newly discovered tanks.

It was all so mysterious. Had she not seen the look on her father's eyes, she would have thought it all a bit clichéd and silly, like something out of a spy novel. But she would follow his instructions and maybe then he'd tell her more about why he looked so worried.

Petra paid the entrance fee and walked inside, just beating the five o'clock cut off for admissions. She walked past the cafeteria and down a long hall on the way to the first exhibit. Several people passed her going the other way, looking at her quizzically, perhaps wondering why anyone would buy a ticket when there was barely an hour left to explore.

After passing a door marked *Do Not Enter*, she turned down a second hall, never noticing the eyes following her as the forbidden door opened behind her.

Petra walked briskly through the museum, pausing only briefly to study the history of the German armies of the 20th Century. She was looking for something, anything, that might give her a clue as to her father's intentions, but nothing stood out. The exhibits were mostly bright and airy, with windows on either side of the large room devoted to the various armored tanks and other vehicles that had seen action in the first and second world wars.

She stopped to examine a particularly nasty-looking anti-tank rifle mounted on a three-wheeled trailer, which appeared capable of doing quite a bit of damage in its day.

"You like 'em big, eh?"

Petra turned at the sound of the male voice, startled, and saw that she was looking into the eyes of the American James Bond himself, the dashing officer from the television report, the man her father had sent her to see.

Major Jonathan Duvall.

Petra's shock must have registered clearly on her face, because Jonathan immediately broke into a silly grin and apologized for his double entendre.

"I was joking, of course," he continued, this time in perfect German. "My apologies."

He gave a slight bow and walked away, obviously chagrinned, but Petra called out to him in English, stopping the American in his tracks.

"Doesn't everyone?" she asked, and immediately wondered what had gotten into her. *Shameless flirt!*

Duvall turned around, smiling. He walked towards her slowly, as if he was sizing her up for a proper response. When they were about a foot away from each other, they both burst into laughter.

"I've no idea why I said that," Petra said, and truer words were never spoken. Well, of course she knew *why*, the Major was very attractive. But *how* those words came out of her mouth, that was the question.

He laughed again. It was a deep, infectious laugh, the laugh of a man comfortable in his own skin, and it immediately put her at ease.

"I feel the same way," he said. "It just popped out."

Petra's eyes reflexively moved towards the gun, and that made them both laugh again, this time even harder. Petra was giggling like a schoolgirl, which only made her more giddy.

Get hold of yourself, Petra!

When they finally settled down, there was a momentary silence in the hall. They were the last two people there and it was obvious the museum was closing. He looked in her eyes, this time more deeply than before and smiled warmly. The smaller silence, the one between the two of them, was not at all uncomfortable, but almost familiar.

"I'm Jonathan Duvall," he said, offering his hand.

She took it and smiled. His hand was warm and strong, yet his grip was gentle. The thought briefly flitted through her brain that he would know how to handle a woman.

Petra blushed and pulled away. "Yes, I know."

"Really?" he asked, a twinkle in his eye. "How so?"

Petra briefly considered getting right down to business and telling him about the sealed envelope in her car, but instead decided to extend the flirtatious moment between them.

"Your nametag, silly," she said.

"Ah, right."

She looked down at his nametag for the first time, grateful that he had one. His uniform was crisp and sharp, but she imagined he cut an equally dashing figure in street clothes.

Almost as if he'd read her mind, he said, "Listen, I was just about to change in my office and get a drink. Would you…"

Petra smiled. "Sure."

Marlene's was a popular pub near the harbor, and by the time they found a table and ordered the first round, it was clear there was definite chemistry between them.

Unfortunately, between the alcohol and the infatuation she felt, Petra never found the right time to tell Jonathan about the meeting tomorrow morning with her father. The longer she waited to tell him, the more fun they had, the more charming he was, and the more electricity was felt between them.

Jonathan was, as they say, sweeping her off her feet.

Her effect on Jonathan was much the same. Had they been mind-readers, they would have been astonished at the similarity of their feelings.

Both of them had been without a significant other for some period of time that had begun to feel unnatural. Jonathan because his duties split between the base and the museum added up to over sixty hours a week and Petra because she lived with a man whose very presence constantly reminded her of the inadequacies of her suitors.

Until Jonathan.

There was something about this man that turned Petra weak in the knees and she could tell that he felt the same. He reminded her of Otto quite a bit in the way he carried himself, in the bright blue eyes that twinkled with wisdom beyond their years.

As a matter of fact, had he been a little shorter and blonde instead of dark-haired, he could have passed for Otto as a much younger man.

After several rounds and several dances, they were both hot and bothered and extremely comfortable and despite Petra never imagining she would accept in such circumstances and despite Jonathan never imagining he would ask, Petra accompanied him back to the small apartment on the water the Army rented for him when he was in Munster.

By the time he unlocked the door and stepped aside to allow her to enter, it was obvious to them both that they had placed themselves in a dangerously heated circumstance, one whose draw was as old as time and as inevitable as the sunrise.

He entered after her and closed the door behind them, causing the room to go completely dark. He reached for the switch on the wall, but found her hand already there.

"Kiss me," she said in the darkness, and he forgot all about the light.

PHANTOM PANTHERS

Afterwards, they lay in each other's arms, their skin shining in the moonlight that streamed through his bedroom window, half-covered by a single cotton sheet that could hide neither of their lithe, toned bodies. Neither spoke, they merely held each other, both of them surprised at the turn of events.

After several minutes, he turned to her and said, "You know, this isn't something I normally do," he said, almost shyly.

She nodded and smiled. "Me, neither."

"But I'm…I'm really glad we…that…the night ended this way, Petra."

At that moment, he realized for the first time since they'd met at the museum that she'd never told him her last name.

Petra, who was also conscious of that omission, slowly removed the sheet to reveal the rest of her body, naked and glistening.

"Who says it's ended?" she asked demurely.

CHAPTER 13

Early the next morning, as Petra and Jonathan were engaged in a final embrace of lust and Otto and Hans were racing to Munster to make their morning meeting with the American liaison officer at the Deutsches Panzermuseum, the two metal behemoths retrieved from the bottom of the lake were finishing the remainder of their overnight journey to Munster.

"What the hell is going on?" the driver of the first flatbed asked to no one in particular as he slowed to a stop. His partner in the passenger seat, who'd been dozing through a particularly pleasant dream, awoke with a start to the sound of the air brakes.

"What is it?"

The driver, a large man whose belly nearly enveloped the lower section of the steering wheel, turned to his co-driver with a sarcastic sneer, and then pointed to the front, where a late model Mercedes had apparently stopped in the middle of the road after clipping a panel van. "Use your eyes, you idiot!"

"Don't call me an idiot," the co-driver responded. "The idiot is in the Mercedes!"

The fat man had to admit that was likely the case. Neither car appeared to be damaged in the slightest and yet the drivers felt the need to block the entire road so no traffic could pass in either direction. Not that there were many cars on the road at this time of night. The route had been chosen specifically for its low amount of traffic since the wide load of the tanks could lead to problems, such as the one they had just encountered but not caused.

He laid on his horn. "Move it!" he shouted. He was worried the man in the second flatbed would not appreciate it if they didn't make their schedule.

He honked again.

"Would you mind very much not doing that?" a deep voice from outside his window asked, and when the driver turned to look down it was straight up the barrel of a semi-automatic rifle.

<hr />

Jonathan and Petra got dressed, he in his uniform and she in the clothes she'd worn the night before. Her car was still in the parking lot of the museum with her suitcase, as she'd never in a million years believed she'd be spending the night with a man she'd only just met.

Still, there was something reassuring about Jonathan that made her decision not at all subject to daytime regrets. He seemed solid and true, sure of himself and still solicitous. Not necessarily careless or impetuous, in spite of what had transpired between them the night before. Jonathan, to her, seemed to be a man who knew what he wanted and went after it when he found it. Which was exactly how she felt. It had been years since a real man had entered her life and yet she had been dreaming of such a man for so long that when he'd appeared in the guise of Major Jonathan Duvall, she had felt immediately at ease.

Obviously, she thought, and giggled.

He looked over at her, smiling before turning back to the mirror to finish his tie.

The silence as they readied themselves didn't seem uncomfortable at all, it was almost as if they were old friends who'd simply run into each other and decided to make love.

"You know, you still haven't told me your last name," he said.

After the men in both trucks had been forcibly removed from the vehicles, the gangster looking man with the deep voice ordered them bound, which several other men, the ones who carried the semi-automatic rifles, quickly did.

Some of the museum crew had been roughed up; two in particular had resisted and been beaten for their efforts and the gang leader with the deep voice had no intention of booking any more discussion from anyone about what was going to happen.

He was in charge of these magnificent metal beasts now.

"Who do you think you are?" shouted the fat driver, the first time he'd spoken since being roughly pulled from the lead flatbed truck moments after realizing the accident in the road had been faked. He was being bound, and apparently wanted to say his piece before being gagged.

The man with the deep voice turned, smiling beneficently at the big man like he was an errant pup who didn't understand his mistake but would be punished, nonetheless.

"My name is Gunther. I'm the man with the tanks," he said.

Another man, one who'd been pulled from the second flatbed and who the hijackers assumed, correctly, had been in charge of the convoy said, "You'll never be able to operate them."

The man with the deep voice sneered. "We have our ways," he replied, reaching out to touch the cold iron of the monster once operated by Otto during the war. He felt an electrical charge and quickly pulled his hand back as if he'd been burned.

The flatbed driver, his mouth now gagged, stared at Gunther with eyes that said *I told you so*.

"We have our ways!" Gunther shouted.

PHANTOM PANTHERS

"You will talk!" the brutish enforcer said, and hit the old man again, this time breaking a rib. The old man, bound to a chair beneath a hot interrogation lamp, finally nodded, signaling *no more*. His face and body were bruised and bloody.

The brute stepped back, and out of the darkness emerged a tall, distinguished Russian who looked almost as old as his prisoner, but in much better shape.

"You are ready to talk about the "Ritual of Resurrection", Herr Doctor Schreck?"

The old man in the chair nodded weakly.

The tall man smiled. "Good boy, Herman."

✦

Otto and Hans pulled into the parking lot of the museum a half hour before it was to open. The parking lot was empty, save for a single sporty sedan near the entrance. A car that Otto found very familiar.

Jonathan pulled in beside Petra's car and turned to kiss her goodbye, but she'd already leapt out, frantically opening her door.

"What's the rush?" he asked, and shut off his motor. Before he could get out, she was back in the car with a very serious look on her face.

"I should have given this to you last night," she said. "I'm sorry I didn't."

Jonathan took the sealed envelope from her, puzzled. "What's the matter, Pet?"

She noticed what he'd called her, the diminutive version of her name she'd only heard from her father, momentarily blushing before she explained.

"I'm Oberst Otto Mader's daughter," she said. "Mader is my last name."

Jonathan just looked at her. "The man that called me last night? The one I'm meeting with this morning?"

"Yes," Petra said. She looked over his shoulder at her father's car, which was conspicuously parked a few spaces away.

"So…I'm not sure why you suddenly seem so upset."

"I'm not upset, it's just… He wanted me to give that to you, and his car is over there which means he saw my car, and…"

Jonathan leaned in and kissed her, cutting off her manic diatribe. "Don't worry, Pet. I'm sure it's fine."

He opened the envelope and looked at its contents.

"Holy shit."

The tractor-trailers carrying the tanks disappeared into the back roads of central Germany, the dangerous tanks now in the hands of mysterious hijackers. Left behind was the original crew, mostly civilians working for the military, save for one man, the transport leader, who was able to escape fairly quickly from the ties that bound him.

As he ran towards the road, the rest of the crew were left wondering exactly who the man was and why he'd left them bound and gagged in the woods near the roadside without bothering to release them.

Jonathan was practically dragging Petra down the hall towards his office, gripping her wrist in one hand and the envelope in the other.

"What's the matter, Jonathan?" she asked as they arrived at his office door, but he ignored her and barreled inside, not even holding the door for her.

"I thought you were a gentleman," she said angrily, and then turned to see her father and Hans sitting in two chairs behind her, patiently waiting for their meeting. They must have got into the museum while Petra and Jonathan were still in his car, which meant they definitely saw her.

"Papa – "

Otto gave her a quick smile as he and Hans stood up.

"I see you've already met Major Duvall," he said, "And you remember Hans?"

Petra got hold of herself. "Yes, of course." She embraced the old friend of her father's, before they all turned to look at Jonathan, who was clearly upset.

"Now that we've gotten this little reunion out of the way, would someone like to explain this?" he demanded, holding up the envelope.

Otto stepped forward. "Major Duvall, my name is Otto Mader, as I said on the phone, and this is Hans Krieger."

The men all shook hands somewhat awkwardly.

"And apparently, you've already met my daughter, Petra."

That took a little wind out of Jonathan's sails, for sure and he exchanged a quick look with Petra, which was a mixture of embarrassment and apology, a look not unlike she'd just shown her father.

Hans, always the facilitator, decided to step in. "Why don't we all sit down and discuss things."

The flatbed trucks emerged from the forest road and into a clearing that had seemingly been carved into the wooded valley from nothing and turned into the parking lot of a large warehouse. Several support vehicles followed and parked near the tanks, indicating a major operation executed with military precision.

The hijackers were obviously professionals with a mission, and they had carried it out beautifully. The crew immediately sets to work, carefully disengaging the chains that held the tanks in place and carefully rolling them down the trailer ramp onto the ground. The Jagdpanther once operated by Hans was towed into the warehouse, followed by Otto's Panther.

The gang leader with the deep voice was giving orders, taking charge of his men like any commander would, and once he felt the situation was in hand, he walked into the warehouse and entered a small office, picking up the phone and dialing.

"We have them," he said, and listened for a moment before hanging up.

The man starring at Dr. Hermann Schreck listened to the good news on the phone, "Good work," he said, fidgeting with a Cross of the Teutonic Knights. "The Americans did what we could not, but now we shall finish the job. I'll have operational information shortly," he continued, turning briefly to look at Schreck, whose breathing was labored as he sat, still bound, beneath the lamp on the other side of the room.

"Keep me posted," he ordered and hung up, turning back to Schreck.

"We are almost finished with our business here, Herr Doctor," he said. "Most excellent news for us both, yes?"

Jonathan just stared at the two old men. He looked at Petra, but he could tell from the look on her face that she was just as shocked as he was. She'd probably never heard their crazy story, either. These were two war heroes, well, heroes for their side, and apart from the unbelievable story about tanks with supernatural powers and secret ceremonies, they both seemed pretty lucid for their age.

He looked down at his desk at the picture that had been in the sealed envelope, an old black and white photo of Otto standing beside one of the very tanks that had been pulled out of the lake. It was dated 1945. On the back was written, *The pride of our Panzersoldaten.*

The crew in the warehouse worked feverishly to open the hatches of both tanks, but had no luck. The tracks and other moving parts seemed to be in pristine condition after their steam cleaning, almost as if the tanks could be fired up and driven immediately.

If they could only open any of the hatches.

The gang leader was growing impatient, barking out orders and demanding others try, but it was almost as if the hatches were somehow bolted or sealed from the inside.

"Bolted from the inside?" he exploded. "Preposterous!"

He shoved aside the man who'd shared that ridiculous theory and climbed on top of Otto's tank himself, clambering on the turret and staring at the hatch as if he could open it with the sheer strength of his will.

He even got down on all fours and sniffed around, as if there were clues to be found emanating from the cracks and crevices between the hatch and the surrounding metal.

Suddenly the surface of the turret grew hot, and the man with the deep voice sat back on his haunches. A bright glow emanated out of the tiny space between the hatch door and its frame, casting a ghostly green pallor across his face.

Suddenly the 700 horse Maybach engine began to turnover and the tank roared to life, its powerful engine very nearly throwing him off with the vibration.

The crew on the ground all froze in their tracks, staring at the phantom tank like it was an alien craft. The man with the deep voice instinctively grabbed onto the barrel of the main gun for purchase and it was at that exact moment the tank fired, blowing a hole into the wall of the warehouse and sending him flying across the warehouse floor.

The noise was deafening as the men all dropped to the floor or ran, staring at the massive hole in the wall. Almost together, they looked at the Jagdpanther as if expecting it to start up also, which it did, as if on cue.

Now there was no one on the floor; they were all running for the doors. The Jagdpanther turned its barrel on the opposite wall and fired, blowing a gaping hole into the other side of the warehouse, almost as if it was simply trying out its armament after a long sleep.

Flames and smoke poured from their exhaust ports and as the drive sprocket took up the tension on the track signaled an awakening from a long hibernation as the two tanks began to move towards the double doors through which they'd entered the warehouse, now closed but providing little resistance, the resurrection of the two tanks was complete.

The tanks blew through the doors and part of the exterior wall like a hot knife through butter, running over several crewmembers and the torso of the deep voiced man, which had been separated from his legs with the initial blast.

The Phantom Panthers now unleashed their supernatural birthright. The glacial coaxial machine guns now commenced spewing a blazing hail of red hot lead. Everything in their field of fire was decimated with flaming tracers of death.

The Panther's coaxial machine gun mounted in the mantel of the turret next to the main cannon added to the carnage, the turret now began to rotate, the 75mm cannon blasted holes in the building structure and the machine gun now laid down a field of enfilade fire that swept the interior of the building.

PHANTOM PANTHERS

Anyone not shielded from fire was met with a continuous stream of machine gun bullets. All of the equipment, vehicles and interior offices were torn to shreds.

One of the men was able to get to the small office, and dialed a number on the phone, a number someone in his lowly position was only allowed to call in case of an emergency.

"*Kalugin here, what is it?*" demanded the voice on the other end.

"The tanks!"

Outside, the two tanks stopped at the edge of the clearing.

"*Who is this?*"

"They're gone!"

Outside, the behemoths turned in unison, pointing their barrels directly at the warehouse office and the small communications tower beside it.

"*What do you mean, gone?*"

The lowly crewmember never had a chance to answer.

The Phantom Panthers disappear into the Black Forest of Central Germany.

The line went dead and the tall man in the Wewelsburg Castle's make shift torture chamber hung up the phone, not quite understanding what he had just heard. The guards in the guard post ran for their lives as the two giant machines crashed through their guard post without hesitation and then disappeared into the night in the black forest of central Germany.

Jonathan was about to ask Hans and Otto again why they thought the tanks were dangerous, why they thought they were the only men alive who could stop them and more importantly, why he shouldn't throw the lot of them out of his office, when the phone rang. He picked it up and listened as the voice on the other end made an inquiry, "*Major, this is Blankenship, have the Panthers arrived yet? We've heard no confirmation since their ETA this morning.*"

Jonathon hesitated a moment, realizing that he hadn't heard a word from his personally appointed escort party. "That's a negative, sir. They're not here."

"*Have you had any contact with the escort party since they left the lake yesterday?*"

He searched his head, trying to think of a reason why the tanks might have been delayed, but in the end he had no idea why they were late or where they were now.

Jonathon replied, "No sir, I haven't heard anything."

CHAPTER 14

Jonathan hung up the phone and stared at the two old men, who were looking at him expectantly, as if he should just buy their bullshit story without further question. He was also looking at Petra with new eyes. Or rather, he was looking at *Petra Mader* with new eyes.

"What happened?" Otto asked, oblivious to any semblance of respect for the Major's privacy. Jonathan was just as startled by the old man's perception as he was irritated by his audacity.

Hans had also seen the troubled look on Jonathan's face as he took the phone call and added his own intrusive question to Otto's. "Is it the tanks? Is someone hurt?"

Jonathan quickly regained control of his facial expression, regretting that he hadn't taken the call in the museum's designated Communications Room. *I won't make that mistake again*, he thought.

He wasn't sure which was more disturbing: that 120 tons of heavy armor was mysteriously unaccounted for, or that the tanks' two original drivers were sitting in his office trying to help him find them.

Either way, Jonathan wasn't about to give either man any classified information, regardless of their deductive reasoning skills.

And then there was Petra. Lovely, passionate Petra.

Jonathan looked at her, his mind drifting back to the night before. She smiled at him almost hopefully – a soft, beautiful smile – and he couldn't help but wonder whether or not her charms had all been a ploy. He would never forget the intimacy they shared, but what if it had all been some sort of ruse to help these two old warhorses get whatever it was that they wanted? He didn't like thinking that way, but he was a Major and couldn't afford to be manipulated by personal feelings.

Which led Jonathan to his next thought.

"Help me out here, gentlemen... What exactly do you want with those tanks?" Jonathan asked, trying a cordial approach.

Otto began to interrupt, "That phone call, was it – "

"If you don't mind, I'll be the one asking the questions, Mister Mader," Jonathan cut in, a little more sharply than he meant to. He avoided Petra's look of recrimination; he'd deal with her later.

Otto ignored his tone. "Call me Otto, please," he said.

Jonathan let a smile splay across his lips and nodded at the old man's gesture of goodwill. He had a feeling that Otto had held something back from his already-fantastic story, and he intended to retrieve that information using whatever means necessary. *The best way to catch a fly is with honey*, he thought, *two can play at that game.*

"Of course, Otto," Jonathan said in a gush of amiability. He looked to the other old man. "And may I call you Hans?"

"Mister Krieger will be fine," the old man replied, with more than a hint of gruff.

"Hans, please," Otto interjected. "We want to cooperate any way that we can! Think about what's most important."

Jonathan ignored Hans and spoke to Otto. "And what is it, exactly, that's most important? I've heard your story, but I still don't understand why you're here."

"Are you kidding me?" Petra exclaimed in an angry outburst. "You heard what my father said about those tanks!"

"I wasn't talking to you, Pet – Petra," Jonathan answered, his forced calm not helped by the fact her father clearly noticed the term of endearment.

Petra noticed the nickname too and increased her volume almost as if to erase what had come before. "Those tanks are dangerous," she said forcefully. "You heard what he said!"

"Let me tell you what I heard," Jonathan said, beginning to let his suspicion and anger spill out. "I heard two old men tell a ludicrous story about Nazi blood rituals and weird batons and rings. I heard your father describe supernatural tanks from World War Two capable of melting entire platoons without taking a scratch. Maybe you all have a mind for fantasy, but what I heard sounds more like something from the Twilight Zone than anything based in reality!"

At that, Petra burst out of her chair. Behind his desk, Jonathan did the same. "How could you possibly say something like – " Petra began to retaliate. But she was interrupted before she could finish.

"Children!" Hans said loudly and the force of his command caused both Petra and Jonathan to hold their tongues. In unison, they looked down at him, then at each other, then they sheepishly sat down to the bemusement of the two old men. Everyone in the room could tell the difference between a lover's quarrel and a productive conversation.

"It is obvious," Hans said, more quietly this time, "that the two of you have things to… Discuss."

Petra blushed. Jonathan averted his eyes from Petra, looking down at his desk.

"However, now is not the time or place for such discussions," Hans continued. "We can answer your questions, Major, but only if you give us a chance to answer them. Perhaps you will listen to my old friend here for anther moment or two, and leave more private matters for another time?"

Duvall's office was quiet for a few moments as Hans' curt request hung in the air. Otto couldn't help but smile at his former second-in-command; he was a quiet man, but when he spoke, he always made an impact.

Otto broke the silence. "I was asking about the phone call because I discerned it was troubling to you. That's all, Major. Was I wrong?"

"The phone call did leave some loose ends," Jonathan said tightly. He'd lost all advantage now, he knew that. Otto and Hans clearly weren't about to reveal anything that they didn't want to reveal.

"We have nothing to hide, Major," Otto continued, as if he had read the younger man's mind. Jonathan also noticed that he'd addressed him by his formal military title, which was clearly an invitation to informality. He had to admit, this old man was good.

"Please, call me Jon," he said, going along. *Honey catches the fly*, he reminded himself.

"Jon. Very good," Otto said. "Jon, I would never ask you to provide information you're not allowed to divulge; both Hans and myself are intimately familiar with the nature of classified information. But, what if you just *listened* while I drew my own conclusions — neither confirming nor denying them, of course — on the off chance that I'll be able to provide helpful insights for any problems you might be facing?"

Jon thought for a moment, trying to assess who was in control of this discussion. "I'm listening," he said, deciding that it didn't really matter.

"I gather from your reaction to the phone call and our questions that whatever you know is proprietary, which of course, will be respected."

"Go on."

"But, none of this prevents me from telling you what I know."

Jonathan nodded deliberately.

"So, let's assume for a moment that the phone call had something to do with the tanks you recently discovered, and whose unusual history I have shared with you."

Jonathan said nothing, but he did not stop him, so Otto continued.

"Let us further assume that the objects you were referring to on that phone call – the ones which you said haven't arrived – are Hans and I's former tanks."

Jonathan did his best to keep his face a blank mask, giving away nothing. But, Otto couldn't be dissuaded.

"Major Duvall, if I have guessed correctly, it is absolutely imperative that we find those tanks," Otto said, leaning in, his voice laced with urgency.

Jonathan didn't know what to say. After a few seconds, he decided that he'd had enough of tip-toeing around bureaucratic lines. He just wanted to know more. "Alright Otto, let's say you're right. For the sake of argument, let's say these two tanks *are* missing. Why do they so urgently need to be found? I'm sure they're valuable, but they're 30 years old and their insides are completely water-logged. Even if they could be made operational, aside from you two, nothing on this planet could use them with any kind of fatal efficiency – they're antiques!"

Otto looked at Hans and the two men shared a grim look, as if they knew something that no one else did.

"Major Duvall. Jon. If those tanks are ever made operational, they will never be contained," Otto said, looking directly into his eyes. "We must not allow that to happen. The tanks must be destroyed."

U.S. Army Armored Operations, Grafenwohr Training Base

Colonel Morrison surveyed his tank commanders. Each of the six men headed a platoon of four tanks, and each had been selected for special duty by the base commander in conjunction with his recommendations. There wasn't a man among them with whom he would not have willingly trusted his life. They were the finest tank commanders in the entire 1st Armored Division, as far as he was concerned, and he was about to reward them for the months of testing and training on the brand new M1-Abrams Tank with their very first live fire exercise in the magnificent new machines.

After the hooting and hollering was finished, he called them back to attention and went over the ground rules for the pretend Soviet invasion forces from the forests to the east, mimicking an attack from the Czech border.

As an added bonus, Uncle Sam had even sprung for some T-54 facades, which was the current generation Soviet battle tank. While the men knew they were merely dressed up M-60s, the American tanks the new M1-Abrams would be replacing, they were still pretty excited to finally set their sights on such machines with a full deck.

"Too bad the Germans are on our side now," one of the commanders said to a buddy in the chow line the night before the big day. "I'd love the chance to blow the hell out of one of their Panzers."

Jonathan hung up the phone and began the walk back to his office from Communications. As he bounced down the single flight of stairs that took him to the first floor of the museum, he wondered if there was any good way to break the news that he'd just received. As he strode into his office to find Otto, Hans and Petra awaiting him expectantly, he still didn't have an answer.

"Someone is coming to talk to you."

"About what?" Otto demanded. "I've already told you everything, Jon. Is there something wrong? Time is of the essence!"

"I understand that," Jonathan said. "But you need to tell your story to someone else. I'm not the only one who makes decisions around here."

Otto paused for a moment. "Who?"

"Just wait a few minutes. They're on their way."

"Major Duvall – "

"Jon."

"Jon, these tanks are still out there," Otto insisted. "You don't know what they're capable of."

"But you already told me," Jonathan answered. He felt bad for the old man, but not so much that he'd relinquish control of the situation at hand. "I told you, I'm not equipped to make these decisions."

"What *decisions* need to be made?" Otto exploded. "I'm telling you, these tanks are unstoppable. Do you understand what that means? We used these tanks; they have the power to destroy anything and anyone. And they will! The only *decision* to be made is how deep into hell we should bury them!"

"Otto, if you'll just wait a few minutes – " Jon began.

"Minutes could mean lives!" Otto shouted. "What don't you understand? What can I say to convince you?"

Jon was quickly growing tired of this. "That's what I'm saying, Otto. It doesn't matter if you convince me – and I'm certainly not saying that you have. Stop wasting your breath on me when you really need to worry about my superiors."

That seemed to do the trick. Otto slumped back in his seat while Hans and Petra stared on in silence.

"You think you've lost them," Otto murmured ominously, "but you know nothing. There are others in this world who saw the savage destruction wrought by these tanks and very few of them share our pure intentions. You don't *lose* 90-ton war machines – they're not your keys. They've been stolen, I swear you that. If you didn't suspect the same thing, we wouldn't be talking about this."

Otto stood up and moved to Duvall's desk. More loudly now, he said, "You don't have to reveal your classified intelligence, it's written all over your face. I'm not stupid, and neither are you. Let's at least agree on that."

This was too much. Jon stood up, ready to tell the stubborn old man exactly why he didn't agree with that statement, but Hans beat him to the punch.

"Otto," Hans said quietly, so softly that both men had to strain to hear what he was saying. "They're not coming to *listen*."

Otto stared at Hans for a moment, then looked back to Jon in realization. He slumped back in his seat once more, defeated. Or maybe ashamed; Jon couldn't tell. A moment ago, Otto had been like the lion that he undoubtedly was in his youth. Now, he looked every bit his age.

Out of the corner of his eye, Jonathan could see Petra looking back and forth from her father to him, but neither man had the courage to meet her gaze.

At that moment, two MPs entered the office.

"Mister Mader, Mister Krieger. Come with us, please."

Jonathan watched as Otto and Hans slowly stood up from their chairs to be led out of the room. After the military personnel closed Jon's door behind them, silence consumed the room for too many seconds.

"Weird to think that this time last night, we were eating cheesecake at Marlene's, right?"

Petra only stared at him. He couldn't tell if she was angry, sad or worried, but he knew one thing she wasn't – happy.

At Grafenwohr, Colonel Morrison lifted the field binoculars and surveyed the area where the war games would commence in a matter of minutes. The sky was almost blindingly blue, with crystal clear visibility for miles, not a cloud to be seen.

He nodded to his aide, who barked the order into a radio, and the rumble of 24 fully armed M1 Abrams battle tanks echoed throughout the valley.

Morrison smiled and turned to his second-in-command.

"Beautiful day to blow something up."

Otto sat in a small interrogation room across a table from a stone-faced man in plain clothes, who he presumed was with American G-2, military intelligence. He knew there was no point in speaking to such a man, since clearly his superiors were on their way. Otto had calmed down considerably, not sure why he had lost control like that. He told himself that he would not make the same mistake twice, no matter what happened.

They'll know soon enough, he thought. *You've done everything you can, Mader.*

The first inkling that anything was wrong came from the lead surveillance pilot.

"HQ, HQ, unidentified vehicles detected in northeast quadrant. Section nine-jay-three."

Morrison grabbed the radio from his second and barked into it. "Repeat."

"Unidentified vehicles approaching from the northeast, approximately three clicks out, moving fast."

"How fast?"

"I'd say thirty clicks per hour, sir."

"*What* are they?"

"Not sure, sir. Going back for closer look."

Colonel Morrison clicked off and turned to his aide. "Get on the horn to Roberts and ask him what the hell's going on out there."

He turned to a map along the folding table set up on the hill, which was held in place by four rocks to prevent the wind from taking it. He looked over the northeast quadrant, which was heavily wooded. Only one back road led to the area.

"What the hell?" he muttered just as the lead pilot rechecked. "HQ."

Morrison grabbed the radio. "This is HQ."

"They're armored vehicles, sir. Tanks."

"Tanks?"

"Near as I can tell, sir."

"How near was that?"

"Could a buttered their biscuits before they disappeared under the trees, sir."

Morrison would have laughed if wasn't so shocked at the intrusion. Security was tight all around the installation all the time, but especially during war games.

"I need eyes on the perimeter, son."

"Yes, sir."

Morrison's aide interrupted. "Colonel, there's no answer at entry six."

Entry six was the back entrance along the old logging road. In the northeast quadrant. Morrison clicked back to his lead pilot.

"Entry six, I need a report."

"Yes, sir...sir?"

"What is it?"

"They looked like Panzers."

Morrison shared a look with his aide before quickly going back to the radio. "Come again?"

"The tanks coming your way. I think they were German. World War II."

Morrison nearly dropped the radio.

PHANTOM PANTHERS

~~~~~

This is commander Morrison, my platoon will be point, the remainder will follow my lead on my signal, do you copy? The tank commanders replied over the intercom, we copy sir.

Tabor head out north by northeast towards nine jay three. As the platoon moved into a large clearing the first tank encountered the Phantoms Panthers and there was barely a moment of confusion among the American crew inside the machine before the Jagdpanther fired a shell that pierced its newly forged armor and exploded in the gunner's lap, killing the entire crew instantly.

Commander Morrison barks out commands from his vantage point, "Masters target 1 o'clock, fire at will!" Master Sergeant Burns yells into the radio as he turns from the scope. "Driver stop!"

The driver wrestled the massive machine to a standstill. To their flank was the Panther, which was much closer and made a better target.

"The loader chambers an AP round and yells, loaded and ready!"

The gunner locked on the Panther, which was just turning to face them across the tiny clearing. "Target identified."

Fire at will, the loader screamed.

"Fire!" the commander ordered and practically dove back into the scope, the metal ridge of the sight graticule pressing so deeply into the skin around his eyes that the marks would have been visible for several days had he lived.

The commander couldn't believe what he saw. A direct hit on the Panther and after the smoke cleared, no damage. None at all. He turned his attention to the second tank.

He was still staring into the scope when the Jagdpanther fired, its cannon engulfed in smoke. He watched as the 88mm shell grew larger in the viewer. His first thought, beyond the shock of his own crew's impotent attack, was that the incoming shell looked almost like something out of one of those Roadrunner cartoons his five year-old son loved to watch on Saturday mornings.

He never managed a second thought.

The maneuver field now was ablaze with burning hulks and smoke that inundated the area. The Phantom Panthers settled into a macabre rhythm, the Panther pulling in close to take fire with its larger, more powerful brother, the Jagdpanther, the tank killer, continually did just that. An entire platoon of America's finest laid waste.

Morrison called in air strikes, which were just as ineffectual against the Phantom Panthers as their beautiful new M1 Abrams, which fell one by one.

"What the hell are they?" Colonel Morrison screamed to his second in command just before the Jagdpanther blew apart their position, sending him and his camp into the crystal blue sky he had so admired merely an hour before.

The last living witness to that year's war games was Morrison's aide, who managed to repeat the Colonel's question and describe the carnage just before he bled out on the hill overlooking the terrible, metal-strewn clearing.

The last thing he saw were the two Phantom Panthers, disappearing together into the dull gray smoke, their stacks belching clouds of fire on their way back into the dense forest.

CHAPTER 15

"I want to see my father and Hans."

Jonathan sighed. "They're just answering a few questions. They'll be done soon."

Petra remained stone cold. "I don't understand why it had to be like this."

"Petra, it wasn't my call, I swear."

She slumped back in her chair. The two of them had been alone in his office for over an hour now, Petra not giving him a single icy inch. Neither made any mention of what Jonathan and he hoped, Petra were both thinking: *I thought we had something.*

"Pet, I just – "

"Don't even try that," she said, cutting off the nickname she'd so clearly enjoyed hearing him whisper in bed the night before. *Last night? Seems like a year ago.*

Jonathan was getting angry. "You know what I don't understand? How you had such perfect timing. Pretty convenient that you happened to seduce me the night before your father shows up knowing classified information even before I do."

"Are you kidding me?" she replied. "I didn't even know who you were. And you hit on me first, remember Mister So-You-Like-Em-Big?"

"Please," he said, "As if any man could keep himself from flirting with a beautiful blonde like you."

She stared at him as a slight red flush crept up her neck. He had her. "That's the worst line I've ever heard," she said weakly.

"I said it was convenient, I didn't say I didn't like it," he went on, ignoring her jibe.

"Well, I guess it was convenient in *some* ways," she finished coyly. At that moment Jon knew she was right there with him, thinking about their activities from the night before. A tiny smile crossed her lips before she could stop it; fortunately, Jonathan had the presence of mind to pretend not to notice.

He waited a moment, enjoying his memories, before returning to reality. "I'm really sorry, Petra," Jonathan said sincerely. "It was just bad timing."

He saw the look in her eyes and corrected himself immediately. "For your father. I mean, the timing with the tanks and that picture." Now it was Jonathan's turn to blush. "Not, you know, our timing," he stammered. "That was good. Timing, I mean…and, you know. The other stuff."

She sighed and reached her hand across the table. "It's okay, as long as he's not in trouble," she said. "You're lucky your so cute."

Jon smirked, relieved to have warm, kind Petra in his office instead of the cold one. "No, no, he's not in any kind of trouble, I promise. I can tell you that much. They just want to ask him some questions."

"But you can't discuss those with me."

"Right," he said, nodding sheepishly. He gripped her hand a little more tightly. "But Petra, I really don't want this to get in the way of…"

Just then, Jon's office door opened. The same two stone-faced MPs who had removed Otto and Hans now led them back in, not bothering with a cordial knock. Jonathan and Petra quickly pulled their hands apart, leaning back in their chairs and trying to look professional.

The MPs looked at each other, shook their heads, and left.

Otto was not nearly so circumspect. He turned to Hans, "The young ones these days fall in love so easily."

"Papa!" Petra blurted, her face beet-red.

Hans put his hands on her shoulders and guided her to her feet. "Don't pick on her, Otto." He put his arm around her shoulder. "We'll have plenty of time for picking on love birds later. Right now we have other obligations to attend. Your superiors want to talk to you now."

<hr />

The lead fighter pilot was being debriefed by his incredulous superiors in the office at Grafenwohr that, only hours before, had belonged to Colonel William Henry Morrison, a seventh generation soldier originally from Roanoke, Virginia.

"Do you mind repeating that, Sergeant?"

"I know it sounds crazy, sir, I know it," the pilot said. "But those things were vintage. World War II, I swear. German Panzers."

"And you say you scored a direct hit?"

"Wasn't just me, sir."

"Who else?"

"Me and my wingman."

The two men stared at the pilot, whose baby face and wide eyes made him look almost comically young, as if some high school kid had somehow gone through the rigorous and extensive hours of training everyone in the room knew had been undertaken to get the young man to that point.

None of the observers doubted his story; it was just that it was so incredible they didn't want to believe it. Two World War II era German tanks had apparently wiped out a platoon of America's finest and all the latest technological advancements that went into the development of the Abrams had apparently been powerless to stop it.

And now he was saying that even the fighter-bombers filled with ordnance had also failed.

"All of you?"

"We dropped and fired everything we had on those bastards," he said, his voice cracking. "I made four passes. Bounced off 'em like they were beanbags. Like water off a duck's back."

"How did the tanks fail, son?"

"Tanks hit 'em plenty, sir," the pilot said, his voice strengthening. "At one point they had 'em both backed up against the ridge, lined up like a firing squad." He caught himself. "Sorry, sir."

"That's all right, son. Go on."

"Well, I thought they had 'em for sure. It was some pretty nice maneuvering. Them boys knew how to drive," he said, his voice breaking again.

"Were they friends of yours, Sergeant?"

"Some," he answered, wiping his eyes.

"Do you want some water, Sergeant?"

"No, I'm fine, sir," he said. "They all fired at once, and I figured those Panzers were done for, but when the smoke cleared they were just sitting there, almost like they were laughing."

"Laughing?"

"Then they both let lose all the way down the line and they blew 'em all to hell. Just mowed 'em down." He looked from man to man across the table. "That was just before they hit the observation camp."

At that point, the pilot broke down into tears, and was inconsolable for several minutes before he could continue.

"Colonel Morrison was like a father to me," he said. "To all of us. I damn near kamikazied 'em after that. Would have, too, if I thought it would a stopped 'em."

The man asking the questions stood up, and the pilot did, as well. "Get some rest, son," he said. "We'll have more questions for you later."

"Yes, sir," the pilot said, saluting. His superior returned it, and escorted the pilot to the door.

The younger man turned before leaving and said in a voice practically quivering with the fierce conviction of the converted, "Those tanks are evil, sir," he said. "Pure evil, straight from the halls of hell."

After the pilot left, the men heard slightly different versions of the same story. To a man, the pilots debriefed seemed to believe the German tanks possessed some kind of supernatural power and could not possibly be of this world.

It was 21:30 by the time Jon, Otto, Hans and Petra got to leave the museum. They were all so exhausted that Jon offered to pay for a taxi to get them back to his hotel. They had a quiet dinner in the adjoining restaurant before he checked Otto and Hans into the room which his superiors had arranged for them. Jonathan's conversation with the hotel clerk was the most that anyone spoke throughout the entire evening.

Jon tried hard to hide his disappointment when Petra insisted on paying for her own room, but he noticed Otto looking at him out of the corner of his eye. Ultimately, Jon decided it was probably better for everyone that they spend the night separately.

As Jon went through his usual bedtime rituals, he reflected once more on his time with Petra, just one night before. As he stared in the mirror, brushing his teeth, he resolved not to let that night be the last that they spend together.

Jon awoke to the sound of someone banging on his door. It was still dark. He turned to see that the clock on the bedside table read 12:30. He'd only been sleeping for an hour.

If that old man tries to show me one more tank picture…

When he opened the door, though, it wasn't Otto. But it was a Mader.

"Petra?" He asked.

She didn't reply, she just kissed him, and pushed him back into his room.

<hr />

Jonathan awoke to find the Petra had returned to her room, but that wasn't enough to sour his mood. Not even close.

At breakfast, the group made small talk about the hotel amenities. It wasn't the most thrilling conversation, but it was a lot more enjoyable than argument or silence, so nobody seemed to mind.

Since they were too exhausted to drive back to the hotel, they had to take a taxi again back to the museum. During the drive, Otto tried to ask what they were going to do about their problem, but Jonathan refused to say anything until they were out of range of any unnecessary ears. Plus, he didn't actually have an answer yet.

By the time they all had made it back to the museum and into Jon's office, he still didn't know what to tell Otto and Hans, so he was more than relieved when a note on his desk requested his immediate presence in the communications room.

"This will probably take me about 20 minutes," Jonathan said, making up a number out of thin air, "Feel free to look around the museum while you wait. Or, you can just stand here."

Relieved to have some time to himself, Jonathan tried hard not to think about Petra on his way up to Communications. *You're distracting yourself, Duvall, you've got more important things to worry about.* Even in his head, though, the words seemed hollow, and he thought about her all the same.

After going up one too many floors in his reverie, Jonathan finally made his way into the Communications room.

"Good morning Major. You have an urgent tele-type from HQ Communications," said the assistant communications officer. He was a plain-looking young man who wore the same thing every day – black slacks with a white shirt and black tie. His thick glasses made his eyes look disproportionately large, and even though he was several years Jonathan's junior, the Major still always felt uncomfortable under his magnified gaze.

"Urgent? Is it about the tanks? Have they located them?"

"I wouldn't know, sir. The communique was marked classified, for your eyes only."

"Of course it was," mused Jonathan to no one in particular, "God forbid I be allowed to delegate my responsibilities." He took the manila folder containing the tele-type from the assistant. "Well, no peeking then Mister."

"I wouldn't think of it," replied the communications officer with not a hint of humor.

Jonathan sighed and pulled out the single-sheet communication:

CLASSIFIED – URGENT

To: All US Military Personnel
From: US Military Directorate, Bonn West Germany
Date: August 14th, 1974
Subject: Hostile Incident – Grafenwohr Training Base

Yesterday at 13:00, an unknown force of armored vehicles was detected during a routine training exercise. Full reconnaissance was dispatched to investigate, but results are as yet inconclusive.

No further information is available at this time, updates to follow. All US military personnel put on Stage 4 Alert protocols. Maintaining a state of high preparedness is advised.

-end communication

Jonathan folded the communique in half and stuck it back in its folder. *An unknown force of armored vehicles? Could it really be…?* Duvall didn't allow himself to finish the thought.

He returned to his office on the first floor, manila folder still in hand. Petra, Otto and Hans were right where he left them, talking quietly as he came in. He looked at his watch… It had only been 10 minutes since he made his trip up to Communications.

Jon didn't say a word as he flopped the folder down on his desk and slumped back in his chair, but Otto clearly knew something was wrong.

"What is it, Major? What's in the folder?"

Jon didn't have a reply. Instead, he stood up and walked over to the window behind his desk, staring out into the courtyard adjacent to his office. All the museum offices had been arranged around the courtyard to give everyone an outdoor view, but right now it only made Jonathan feel worse. It was dark grey outside, as if the air could be replaced by a torrent of heavy rain drops at any moment. *How appropriate*, Jonathan thought.

"Papa!" Petra's exclamation cut into his thoughts.

He turned around to see that Otto had the manila folder open in front of him with the communique in hand. Before Jonathan could say anything, he'd placed it back in the folder and returned it to his desk.

Otto didn't say a word. He just looked at Jon, his old eyes as piercing as ever. Hans also seemed to know exactly what his friend had read and sat by stoic as ever, waiting for someone else to say something.

"I'm so sorry Jon," Petra began, "He had it open before I could stop him, we didn't mean to – "

"It's okay Pet," Jonathan interjected, calmly. "It's nothing he didn't already know. In fact, why don't you go ahead and read it for yourself. There's no reason to hide anything at this point."

PHANTOM PANTHERS

Jonathan picked up the manila folder and extended it out to Petra. But Otto interjected before she could take it.

"Wait," said Otto. "If you believe me, then let Petra be innocent of this situation. There's no reason for her continued involvement."

What Otto said made sense... Jon certainly didn't want to endanger Petra in any way. But, before he could concur with the older veteran's opinion, Petra burst from her chair and seized the folder with astonishing speed. Her father and Hans scrambled up to keep her from reading it, but she poured through the contents of the communique in a matter of seconds, too fast for anyone to stop her.

"There, now you can't un-involve me. You men... Thinking you're the only ones who can solve problems. Remember, father, if it weren't for me you would never have gotten this far with the Major." She turned to Jon. "And you... You should know better than to believe I'd just let you try and resolve this situation without my help. I'm a Mader too, you know."

Jonathan thought for a moment. "I suppose you're right. I can't say I'm happy about it, but I'll take all the help we can get. And, if we're the only ones who truly understand what's going on, then all the more reason to work together."

"So, what do we do now?" asked Otto.

"We plan. The communique said the armored vehicles were last seen in Grafenwohr. If these are your tanks, then that seems like a reasonable place to start our –"

There was a knock at the door.

Jonathan paused mid-sentence.

"Come in." A woman wearing a dark grey skirt and jacket opened the door. She had a nametag similar to Jonathan's on her lapel.

"Ah, Hildegard, how can I help you?"

"Sir, there is an outside call on Line 2 for Herr Otto Mader."

"Who is it?"

"He didn't divulge his name, sir."

Otto looked puzzled and asked where he could take the call.

Hilde responded, "You can take it in here."

Jonathan smiled, "Thank you Hildegard; that will be all."

Hilde nodded, blushing slightly. Jonathan eyed Petra and noticed a barely-contained look of disapproval flit across her face as Hilde turned to leave his office.

Jon picked up the receiver and tapped the Line 2 button, extending the phone towards Otto.

"This is Otto Mader. Who am I speaking to?"

"Herr Otto Mader?"

"Yes, that's what I said. Who is this?"

"This is Standartenfuhrer Dietrich von Mueller. I am liaison officer for Obergruppenfuhrer Fritz Von dem Weise of Odessa."

Otto straightened in his chair, looking across the table at the young Major. "How can I be of service, Herr von Mueller?"

Information for you regarding the 'Occult Korps'. I've delivered this message as quickly as circumstances allowed."

Otto was dumbfounded. He'd never expected to hear anyone utter those two words again.

"The individual asked to be known as 'Herr Dr. S'. He requests your immediate presence at Wewelsburg Castle to further discuss this information."

Otto listened intently, mentally repeating the voice's words in his mind.

"It is my duty to arrange a meeting for 20:00 at Wewelsburg; will you able to meet at this time?"

"Ja Wohl, Herr Standartenfuhrer", he answered smartly.

"Excellent. I've been asked to stress that time is of the essence. That's all, Herr Mader."

PHANTOM PANTHERS

The line went dead before Otto could reply.

※

"What was that?" Petra asked. Jon wanted to know the same thing.

"I've just spoken with an Odessa liaison officer that has arranged a meeting at Wewelsburg Castle tonight with a man identified as Herr Doctor S – I can only assume this is Herr Doctor Hermann Schreck." Hans seemed to have drawn the same conclusion, his eyes sunken into a scowl.

"I know we haven't always seen eye to eye, Major, but we must go to Wewelsburg at once. This could be the answer to all problems," Otto pled.

"But what about the tanks? If the armored vehicles in that communique are our lost Panthers," Jon said, motioning to the folder, "We must proceed to Grafenwohr at once."

"But finding the tanks doesn't do us any good if we can't contain them," Otto countered. "You don't understand the power these war machines possess, Major. The only man who stands a chance of helping us is this Schreck. This is the man who helped us harness the tanks' power in the first place; he could very well be the only man on this planet capable of shutting them down."

Jonathan wouldn't be persuaded. "It doesn't matter if your Doctor can contain the tanks if they're not available to be contained. Grafenwohr is a priority. Then we can consider going to Wewelsburg once we have them under our control."

Otto was about to protest again when Petra jumped in.

"Who says we have to pick one or the other?" She asked.

"What are you saying, Pet?" Otto asked warily.

"I'm saying there are four of us and two places we need to be." She turned to Jon, "Wewelsburg is on the way to Grafenwohr, Jon, you should know that. Why don't you and I go pick up this

Schreck and Papa," she now turned towards Otto, "you and Hans can go on to Grafenwohr to see if you can get information about the tanks' whereabouts. We should only be about an hour behind you after we pick up Schreck."

Both Otto and Jonathon looked at her, not saying a word.

"You know it makes sense – Schreck has to come to Grafenwohr anyways if he's going to do anything to the tanks."

Jon didn't like the thought of dragging Petra into any possible danger, but he had to admit, she had a knack for good ideas. And he certainly wouldn't mind some time alone with her.

"Well, I don't like it, but it does solve our problem." Jonathan said, hesitantly.

"Absolutely not," said Otto. The urgency in his voice heightened as he continued, "We have no idea what we're getting ourselves into. All we know is that it's risky. Very risky. Dr. Schreck was innocent enough during the war, but who knows how he's changed since. And I certainly don't want you getting close to either of these tanks," he said, now looking at Petra. "Wewelsburg is an unholy place; I won't have my daughter set foot on its grounds!"

Hans stood up and walked behind Otto. He placed both hands on his shoulders and said in his characteristic calm, "Otto, you forget. This isn't the girl we found alone in Bad Helmstedt all those years ago. She can take care of herself."

Otto looked at Petra and Jon could see the beginning of tears in his eyes.

"Yes, I suppose you're right, my friend. I've forgotten how old I am, haven't I?"

The room was silent for a moment, both older men clearly lost in deep reflection. Then, in an instant, Otto was back to his old grizzled self, as dapper as ever.

"Well? What are we waiting for? Daylight is wasting!"

CHAPTER 16
Wewelsburg Castle, Home of the SS Occult Korps

Jonathon and Petra completed the two-hour drive to Wewelsburg Castle in almost complete silence. The dark gray thunderclouds that he had noticed earlier in the day now unleashed their torrential downpour; the sound of thunder and rainfall seemed to be enough noise for the both of them. Fortunately, the rain had begun to abate by the time they drove up to the Castle's outer gates.

They sat in Jon's car, waiting for something to happen. For a castle, it seemed awfully quiet. Maybe a little too quiet. He wondered how he was supposed to find this mysterious 'Doctor Schreck' in such an enormous fortress.

"Well, I guess we're not getting the red carpet welcome, then," Jon said, in an attempt to lighten the mood.

"No, I guess we're not," Petra agreed.

"Do you think we should just… Go in?" Jonathan asked.

"I don't really see any other option," Petra replied dryly.

Jonathon stared at her for a moment, then got out of the car. He walked up to the Castle's outer gates and couldn't help but notice that they were emblazoned with the twin lightning bolts of the SS. A slight chill ran down his spine, but in his mind he only blamed the cold, wet weather. The gates weren't locked, and though heavy, flung open easily enough.

Jonathan returned to the car.

"Is that an SS signet?" asked Petra.

"Yep Jon replied."

They drove slowly past the gates and down a small road to the Castle's parking lot just outside the eastern wing. From the parking lot, a narrow bridge ran over a moat leading into what Jon presumed was the main castle entrance. However, the bridge was in the first thing Jonathan noticed.

He voiced the thought that they were both thinking. "Where is everybody? Shouldn't there be cars here?"

Petra was clearly just as confused. But then she grabbed his arm and pointed ahead of them to the far corner of the parking lot, right next to a small stairway leading up to the main bridge.

"There!"

It was a single, lonely black sedan. As they drew closer, Jon discerned that it was a late model Mercedes-Benz, his best guess placing it somewhere around the early '50s.

"Nice car," he remarked, absently.

Not wanting to be too obvious, Jonathan parked several spots down and behind the black Mercedes. He chose a spot in a corner of the lot, surrounded on two sides by trees. He slipped the key out of the ignition and looked at Petra.

"Well, this is it. You wanna go in? No turning back now."

Her only answer was to open her door and get out of the car. He smiled and followed suit. Before locking up his car, he popped the trunk and pulled out a small duffle bag.

"What's that?" Petra asked.

"Protection." Jonathan replied, as he pulled a leather side holster from the duffel bag, as well as his trusty Colt 45, Commander's edition. It had a slightly shorter barrel than a normal pistol and a wider grip-stock, and its weight felt right at home when the holster was secured to his left side.

"Do you really think we'll need that?" Petra asked.

"Better to not need it and have it than to need it and not have it," Jon replied matter-of-factly.

"I suppose you're right," she said.

They began walking towards the stairs leading up to the bridge. As they drew closer to the black sedan, Petra sidled up close beside.

"Don't make it look obvious," she hissed, staring straight ahead, "but there's someone sitting in that car. Look."

Jon sidled closer now too. There was only a single light in the parking lot, but it was enough to illuminate the shadow of a figure in the driver seat of the sedan. Whoever it was looked as if they were sleeping, head resting against the steering wheel.

"Shit," Jonathan said, "follow me."

Jonathan drew himself and Petra over to the opposite side of the parking lot as the sedan, seeking shelter in the shadows of the trees. They carefully made their way closer to the entrance-stairs until they were right behind the sedan.

"Wait here," Jonathan said. He drew his Colt, but kept it pointing at the ground. He jogged from the cover of the trees across the parking lot towards the sedan, trying to keep his profile small and in the shadows, so whoever was sitting in the car wouldn't see that he was armed, should they see him coming in their rearview mirror.

But, even when he had come up right next to the sedan, the figure inside remained motionless. He couldn't be sure, but it looked like something had spilled all over the inside of the back windshield. Jon drew closer, walking up along the driver's side of the sedan. He tapped the driver's window with the barrel of his pistol.

No reply. Not even a hint of movement.

Jonathan now leaned down and pressed his face up against the window, shielding his eyes from the glare of the parking lot's solitary light. It wasn't enough, the windows were too tinted.

He called back to Petra. "Pet, bring me a flashlight, will you? I think were safe. This guy's out cold."

"I didn't bring one," she called back.

"Check the glove compartment, there should be one in there."

Jon watched from across the parking lot as she opened the passenger door and leaned into the car, looking for the flashlight. Even in the dark and from a distance, Jonathan couldn't keep himself from admiring the curves of her body as she bent over.

"Found it!" She called, flashing the light on and off a couple times to make sure it worked. She jogged across the parking lot, and he walked out a few paces to meet her. He took the flashlight and turned it on. Leading the way, he returned to the side of the sedan and pressed his face against the driver's side window, this time shining the flashlight alongside him to see into the vehicle.

"Anything?"

"Well, there's definitely someone in there, but they're not moving."

" Did you try opening the door?" She asked, reaching for the handle. Even as she finished her question, she pulled the door handle and it popped right open.

Jonathan was about to say something about maintaining personal privacy, but the figure – and the smell – inside the sedan made the statement catch in his throat. The man was wearing a thick, black wool coat, but he wasn't napping. There was a crater where the right-back side of his skull should be, and what was clearly blood was spattered all over the driver's seat and the rear windshield.

"Oh my god," Petra gasped, shielding her eyes and reflexively turning back into Jonathan's arms. He held her close as he tried to move past his initial shock and objectively examine the inside of the car.

"Go away by the stairs," he said. He had to know whether or not this was the 'Doctor Schreck' he was here to meet. And if it was, he had to try and find out why he was dead.

Holding his firearm in one hand, he reached down with his other to pull the man off the steering wheel. His thick coat was sticky with blood. He didn't bear any name tag or other identification, so Jonathan had to resort to searching his pockets. He pulled out a thin wallet and looked inside.

"This isn't our man," Jonathan said. "But we're close… This is Dietrich von Mueller, the man who contacted your father."

"Let's just go," Petra said from the stairs. "I don't like this place."

"We can't leave until we have answers. Think about it, Pet, if someone killed this man, then your father and Hans may be in danger too. We should at least go inside and look around… It doesn't look like there's anybody else here, but maybe there are clues inside the castle."

Petra clearly didn't like his answer, but she didn't object either. Jonathan closest to the door of the sedan walked over to the stairs.

"Here, you take this," Jonathan said as he handed her the flashlight. "I want to keep my hands free, just in case."

Together, they walked up the stairs leading to the East wing bridge. It was narrow, and as they crossed cautiously, listening all the while, the only sound they could hear was the faint trickling of the moat below. The main castle gates were wide open, but minimally lit, just like the parking lot.

They proceeded through the castle gates and into the courtyard. It was completely deserted, at least as far as Jonathan could tell. The fortress was built like an isosceles triangle, with an enormous tower on the northern point. Inside its walls, the courtyard was also triangular, although it was hard to tell in the dark. Jonathan counted four electric lights in the entire courtyard, which was easily about 75 yards long and 25 yards wide at its widest point.

"We should've at least waited until morning," Petra said rhetorically, clearly knowing that there was no turning back now.

"What's the matter, afraid of the dark?" Jonathan said, giving her a very slight and playful shove. She smiled at him briefly. Then she paused, her face frozen. She was looking behind him now, and up. He turned around to see what she was looking at.

Then he saw it.

On the second floor of the Castle, almost directly above where they stood now, but on the opposite side of the courtyard, a light shone through a window. But it wasn't a pure, unwavering light like that of the electric lanterns around the courtyard. It wavered, dimming and brightening in a strange rhythm, back and forth.

"You think anybody's in there?" Petra whispered.

Jonathan didn't answer. Instead, he grabbed her hand and pulled her across the courtyard to hug the wall directly beneath the lit window. If there was anyone in there, he didn't want to be seen.

"I don't know if anyone is there, but I do know that we have to find a way up," said Jonathan, more to himself than Petra. They hugged the wall, looking for some sort of stairwell.

"There!" Petra pointed down a hallway that led from the courtyard into the castle interior. On the left side of the hall, Jonathan could clearly see an entryway into a narrow-looking stairwell.

It was pitch black in the stairwell, as the light from the courtyard didn't reach very far into the castle walls. The only light they had was the flashlight, but it was good enough to get them to the top of the stairs. From the second floor landing, a hallway went off to each side. Jonathan turned to the left, the side that should lead to the lit room. As soon as he moved into the hallway, he could see the room in question… The light the spilled from underneath the door was hard to miss in an otherwise pitch black corridor.

"Stay close," Jonathan said as he began carefully shuffling down the corridor, Colt in hand, "And turn that thing off. The light from the room should be enough to get us there, and I'd rather the surprise be on our side."

Now in complete darkness except for the room down the hallway, Jonathan led them slowly towards the light. When they reached the door, it was slightly ajar. He motioned Petra to quickly get on the other side of the doorway. He made eye contact with her, then held up three fingers, then two, then one, then he burst into the room, Petra right behind him. The door slammed against the wall on the inside of the room with a loud *thud*..

Jonathan's attention immediately went to the source of the light – it was a single light bulb dangling from the ceiling by a cord in the middle of the room, swinging gently back and forth. Below that sat a scrawny man in a chair, facing away from them towards the courtyard. He was shirtless, his hands bound behind the chair he was sitting in.

Jonathan moved closer, tentatively circling around the man to get a better look at him. Meanwhile, Petra chose to inspect the rest of the room, as if she could somehow ignore the man sitting in its center.

As he had suspected, the man was dead, but his passing had clearly been much more painful than the Standartenfuhrer's. His face was a bruised and mottled pulp. One of his eyes was swollen shut, while the other was sunken in and oozing blood, as if the eyeball were missing beneath the eyelid. The man's torso was covered in burns and cuts, and it looked like his right ribs had been broken. Caked blood ran down his chin, and Jonathan noticed a pink, spongy appendage on the floor next to the man's chair.

Jonathan shuddered. He walked over to Petra, who was standing over a table in a corner of the room next to where they had come in.

"Is he dead?" Petra asked, although she clearly already knew the answer.

Jonathan only nodded. "I'm guessing this was our Doctor."

"I'd say your guess is right," Petra said, handing him a folder from the table filled with official-looking documents. The first page in the folder was a scanned copy of an official German military ID. The name read Hermann Schreck, and even though the man in the chair barely had a face anymore, it was enough to confirm his identity.

Jon assumed that the other items on the table must have belonged to Schreck, then. A shirt and undershirt had been carelessly strewn across one side, along with a pair of military ID tags and what Jon could only assume was an SS death's head ring. Underneath the clothes, Jonathan found another folder. He picked it up and looked inside.

"Oh, shit."

The only thing inside the folder was an old photo of two young men standing in front of two World War II-era German tanks. He'd seen the photo before – it was the same one shown him by Otto and Hans.

"What do you mean we're not permitted to enter?" Otto asked, irritated. He and Hans had been driving for the better part of the day, straight from Munster to Grafenwohr and now they were being told their trip was for nothing.

"I'm sorry sir; I can't provide any further information. Only military personnel are permitted to enter the base at this time."

The guardsman was no doubt some low-ranking private, but that didn't change the fact that he had complete control over Otto's immediate future.

"You don't understand," Otto tried again, "We are supposed to meet a US Army Major here!"

The guard was completely unswayed. "I'm sorry sir, I can't provide any further information. You're not permitted to enter the base at this time." If you care to wait for your party you can park in the motor pool parking, down the street to your left.

"Fine, thank you for your time," Otto said, curtly. "We'll come back another day."

Otto turned back to Hans sitting in the passenger's seat, deciding that it wasn't worth trying to convince the Private of his good intentions. They backed up away from the guard post that was the only entrance past the fenced perimeter surrounding the main HQ building. He then proceeded to parked in the motor pool. It was where the training facility kept all their military vehicles, and it also served as civilian parking.

"What do we do now," he asked his old friend.

"We have to find a way to verify that a tank skirmish really happened," Hans said, "I guess we should just wait for the Major and Petra."

The two men looked at each other, then simultaneously burst into laughter.

"Feels like old times, doesn't it Hans?" Otto asked, looking off somewhere outside the physical world.

"It does," said Hans. "But I don't know whether that's a good thing or bad."

"Me neither."

The two men sat in silence for several moments, each thinking back to the days of their youth. Otto began looking around, trying to think up some plan to gain entry into the base.

"Well, what if..." Hans began, trailing off.

"What?" Otto asked.

"I'm just thinking... Do we really need the military's help to find our Panthers? It's not like they liked your story before, back in Munster. Who's to say these guys up here will be any different? And besides, if we help them find our tanks, do you really think they're going to want to destroy them?"

"What are you trying to suggest," pressed Otto.

"We should find the tanks." Hans said. "As in, on our own."

"But where would we look? We can't even get into the headquarters to find a map, how are we supposed to find two tanks in the middle of nowhere?"

"I know you're not that old, friend. It's only been 35 years… Don't you remember this place?"

Otto paused, considering his surroundings. It did seem familiar…

"Come on, Otto. Panzersoldaten training… I know you haven't forgotten that nightmarish initiation hell-week. This is where we fell in love with tanks of our Blitzkrieg!"

Otto looked around again with new eyes. The strange light of dusk and the generally unkempt condition of the camp had prevented his recognition. "You're right, old friend… This is our Grafenwohr. Ha! How could I forget?"

Hans smiled that gentle, knowing smile of his. Otto clapped him on the shoulder. "But that still doesn't help us, does it? We have no way to get permission to enter the training grounds?"

"Who said we need permission?" Hans suggested, devilishly quiet.

Before Otto could follow up with a question, Hans opened his door and got out of the car. Then, he turned around and opened the door of the jeep military truck they'd parked next to.

"Look, they're just like ours — military issue and never locked," Hans said from the driver's seat of the neighboring vehicle. "Get in!"

Otto didn't have time to object. Under normal circumstances, he wouldn't dream of such a bold breach of conduct. But these weren't normal circumstances; they had to find their Panthers ASAP. He ran around to the passenger side and tried to climb in as quietly as he could.

"We're just borrowing it, though, right?" Otto said as he plopped down next to his friend.

"Of course," Hans said, feeling around until he found the ignition switch. "We'll bring it right back."

"Alright, well, let's see how good this memory of yours is, then. I'll be no help finding the training ground. We can't go back up towards the outpost; they'll see us." Otto thought for a moment. "Although, I think I remember an unpaved access road that takes us around the back side of the HQ. If it's still there, that's probably our best bet."

"One step ahead of you," Hans said as he backed out and drove away from the main entrance. In just a few minutes they'd reached the access road, and sure enough, it was still in reasonable condition.

"I wonder if anyone ever uses this these days," Otto mused. "Not that it makes a difference. If we get caught, we get caught."

Fortunately, they made it around the perimeter of the fenced headquarters without raising any alarms. Soon they were driving over the rolling hills that Otto remembered as the training grounds on which he first learned to command a tank. *How fitting to come back here after all these years, this time to destroy a tank instead of drive one.*

After a few minutes of driving, they reached the edge of the wooded area that defined the perimeter of the training grounds.

"I guess we should just drive along here until we find something," Otto said. The training grounds were about 10 square miles, so in theory they should be able to cover the whole perimeter within an hour, barring any terrain-related difficulties. And it had been raining all day, so those were likely.

But, it seemed luck was on their side.

"I think we already have." Hans said, stopping the jeep as he reached the top of yet another hill. This one formed a sort of enormous half-bowl against the edge of the woods, so that looking up from the bottom with your back to the trees, you'd be completely surrounded by elevated ground on all sides. Even in the dark, Otto could see scorched craters all over the hillside in front of him. At the bottom of the hill, the ground was mottled with what could only be the result of heavy ordnance.

"Something definitely happened here," Otto observed. "Do you think this is the result of the 'reconnaissance' the Directorate mentioned in the Major's communique?"

"I'd say so," said Hans, "And look down there." He was pointing towards the bottom of the hill, at something in the clearing.

Tracks, Otto realized, *two of them.*

Hans didn't wait for Otto to confirm what he'd seen. He sped down the hill towards the clearing. At the bottom of the hill, they both got out of the Jeep for a closer look.

"These are definitely Panther tracks," Otto said, impressed that he still remembered his tanking days in such detail. Hans agreed. "And it looks like they go back into the woods."

"It looks like there's a building in there too," Hans said. "Or at least, what remains of one. Didn't we have an outpost out here?" The question was rhetorical, Otto knew. "Which means the Czech border wouldn't be that far away," Hans said, pointing east into the woods.

Together they got back into the Jeep and began to tentatively drive into the woods. The outpost was about 50 yards past the perimeter of the forest, but the Panther tracks continued beyond that.

As they drove deeper into the forest, Otto began to notice a strange tingling on the back of his neck. "Do you feel that?" he asked.

"They're here," Hans replied.

PHANTOM PANTHERS

Otto couldn't describe how he knew, but something was definitely pulling them deeper into the woods. They drove on past the outpost, both men silent, as if some ominous doom loomed in front of them.

It was tough to guess how far they'd driven; the rough terrain made the going slow, and the damp, darkness of the woods made it easy to lose track of time. Soon enough, the Panther tracks led them to a clearing. They stopped and turned off the vehicle.

"If you were looking for a spot to hide two tanks, this would be a pretty good place to start," Otto said, trying to add a touch of humor to their task.

It didn't work.

He could tell from Hans face that he felt the same thing he did; the pull was stronger now. He felt both alive and afraid at the same time, as if his very soul were humming in tune with some unheard melody. Which is why Otto had to do a double-take when he got out of the personnel truck and actually *heard* a melody, though faint, come from the clearing ahead. It was a tune that was somehow familiar, but altogether unsettling.

Even though both men knew what they'd find in the clearing, it didn't make it any more incredible when they pass through the final line of trees and saw their two tanks, side by side, sitting like kings on their thrones. Somehow, the music seemed to be both quieter and more cohesive. Otto could make out lyrics floating hauntingly through the air…

Wo wir sind da ist immer vorne
Und der Teufel, lacht nur dazu
Ha, ha, ha, ha, ha!
Wir kämpfen für Deutschland
Wir kämpfen für Hitler
Der Gegner kommt nicht mehr zur ruh

He recognized the song now – an old SS marching song, one from the glory days of Hitler's Third Reich. Not too different from the one he'd sung with his tank squad back in the days when he commanded this metal behemoth. Somehow, it permeated the air around the tanks, as if it were coming from within.

Otto wouldn't admit how terrified he was at this very moment, even though he couldn't realistically explain why. After all, they were just tanks. Hell, they were tanks that each man had driven at one point in their lives. But, clearly, someone was inside them… Someone who knew an old SS marching song.

"This is our chance," Hans said. Otto thought he detected a slight quiver in his voice, but didn't bother pointing it out. "These are our tanks, Otto, we can end this right now. We just have to get inside." Hans began to move towards the Panthers, but Otto reached out and caught his friend by the shoulder.

"No, let me go," implored Otto. "I was your commanding officer all those years ago and it was me who agreed to command these unholy tanks in the first place. It's my duty, to my country and my daughter, to end what I began."

Hans didn't try to argue, but stood silently by as Otto moved in front of him and began walking cautiously towards the tanks. The music was growing louder now, as if whoever was inside was acknowledging his approach. Other than the music, though, the tanks were completely silent – the only light of the forest into the clearing.

Otto was within arms' reach of his Panther. He reached out and touched its side, lightly. No sooner had he made contact with the cold metal than the strange melody completely stopped. The forest was silent once again, the only sound in his ears being that of his own breathing.

The silence made Otto bold, and he moved more deliberately now. He brushed his hand along the tank's side, feeling the

PHANTOM PANTHERS

Zimmerit coating beneath his fingertips. Memories of his days commanding the steel giant in front of him flooded back into his mind. He felt powerful.

This is my tank, he thought to himself with pride. *Now it's time to take it back.*

Otto began to climb up on his Panther, intending to enter through the gunner's hatch and take charge of whatever was giving life to these indestructible instruments of war.

But, as he placed his foot on the top of the tank track, his leg buckled beneath him. To Otto, it almost felt as if he were shoved downward; as if gravity had become ten times stronger for a split-second. He lost his footing and tripped on one of the rungs along the top his tank. He barely heard Hans cry out from the edge of the clearing as he fell to the ground.

Suddenly, the tanks were alive.

Their Maybach engines cranked over and a sickly green glow emanated from their interiors and from all the joints and seams in the tanks' armor. The music was back in the air, louder now and somehow more hateful.

The next thing Otto knew, Hans was pulling him off the ground by his collar. He felt like a sack of potatoes in his arms.

Hans slapped him across the face. "We have to move, now!"

His friend sounded quiet. Distant. "What?"

"We have to move! Now!" Hans said again, more urgently. He turned and began running back to the car.

An explosion followed by an enormous crack is what finally rocked Otto from his shocked trance. He saw one of the trees near their jeep begin to fall, an enormous hole missing from its trunk. Another explosion; the tanks were both firing now.

Otto ran. Hans had the vehicle running by the time he reached the passenger side and the two men sped back through the forest. The Panthers pursued recklessly, filling the trees around them with explosions and debris. Otto latched onto his seat with both hands, and saw Hans staring intently in front of him, all his attention devoted to navigating the underbrush.

The outpost was in sight – Otto knew that they'd be able to outrun the tanks on open field. But, even as they passed the outpost, both men realized that the firing had stopped.

Hans screeched the jeep to a halt. The two men looked at each other, then back at the way they had come. There was no sign of either tank.

Otto looked at Hans, and at once he knew that his friend felt the same resolve that he did. "We have to go find them," Otto said.

Wordlessly, Hans wheeled the truck back around and they tracked the Panthers back to the clearing. But, the tanks were nowhere to be found. In the clearing, they dismounted and followed the tracks that had made deep impressions in the soft forest floor.

Nothing, there were only two pairs of tank tracks. An old faded pair – the ones that they'd originally followed to the clearing – and the fresh pair that the tanks had just made in their pursuit. There should've been a third pair somewhere; something to indicate where the tanks went to in their retreat.

But there were no tracks, anywhere.

They followed the outgoing tank tracks once again. It was easy to see where the tracks stopped, but that was it… They just stopped. It was as if they had somehow vanished into thin air, like phantoms in the night.

Both men sat in silence, completely stumped.

Otto looked at his watch and jumped in his seat. "We've been gone long enough! Pet and the Major are probably waiting for us back at the base – they said they'd only be an hour behind us with Schreck."

As Jonathan stared in disbelief at the photo in front of him, something broke his concentration… He heard the faint sound of footsteps tapping in the hallway. And they were getting closer.

"Give me the flashlight, Pet." Jonathan took the flashlight in his left hand and his Colt in his right, using the one to brace the other. "Get underneath the table," he said quietly, trying to listen to the sound of the footsteps and not wanting to give away his position.

When he guessed that the walker was a few feet away from the door, he burst out into the hallway, gun and flashlight leveled together, pointing straight ahead. The man in the hallway froze, but didn't raise his hands. The white light of the flashlight made him look like a giant ghost, but Jonathan didn't believe in ghosts. His hulking silhouette looked to be garbed in some sort of military uniform, but Jonathan couldn't quite place him with a specific nationality.

"Who goes there?" Jonathan asked of the large intruder. But even before he had finished his question, the ghostly figure turned and sprinted back down the hallway behind him.

"Stop!" Jonathan shouted, even though he knew it wouldn't do any good. He dashed back into the lit room and found Petra underneath the table. "Hurry, grab anything that you can carry and follow me." Jonathan didn't wait for an answer, he just tossed the flashlight on the table and sprinted back out into the hallway in pursuit of the unknown man. Petra was only a couple seconds behind him, running out of the room with secret contraband in one hand, and the flashlight in the other.

Jonathan reached the same staircase up which they had originally come, and heard his mysterious opponent at the bottom. He took the stairs two at a time, his eyes now adjusting to the darkness. As he came out of the stairwell, he saw the back of the man's shoe just turning the corner into the courtyard.

"Stop!" He called after him. He turned to make sure he heard Petra behind him, before resuming his pursuit. He chased the man through the courtyard and back out the Eastern gate. However, he didn't see the man on the bridge they'd used to access the castle. He swiveled his head back and forth, looking for any sign he could follow.

After a few seconds, he heard the sound of a car starting in the distance.

"He's going to get away!" Jon called back to Petra, who was just now coming out into the courtyard. "Hurry!"

He turned and ran across the bridge and down the stairs back into the parking lot. The black sedan was still there, which meant his opponent must have another vehicle of his own.

"Dammit." Jon muttered, "Why didn't I park closer?" He sprinted across the lot to his car, and threw himself into the driver's seat. Keys out, ignition on, reverse gear, first gear, and Jon was ready to go. He drove around next to the black sedan to pick up Petra. "Get in, get in, get in!"

Petra had barely closed the door before Jonathan sped off. He knew that they hadn't seen any other cars when they came in from the south end of the lot, which meant his enemy-in-pursuit must be using a different exit. To the North, he saw a small driveway that looked like it might lead to another parking lot. He didn't have time to weigh his options, so he just drove. Luckily, he was right and he saw the red glow of taillights speeding away just as he entered the lot.

"That's him!" Petra shouted.

Jonathan pressed the clutch and shifted up to second gear, flying across the smaller Northern lot, taking each swerve at maximum speed. Sure enough, a smaller secondary gate led out of the castle grounds. "This must be where he left," Jon said.

The gate led them out onto a cramped country road, navigation of which was only made more difficult due to the darkness combined the rain from earlier that day. There were several spots on the road where rain had runoff from the hill on which Wewelsburg was built across the road and into the river next to it, creating huge patches of slippery mud. But, Jonathan was an American, and Americans knew how to drive. He thought back to his misadventure with Colonel MaClosky, and a tiny smile touched his lips. *Let me show you how it's done*, he thought.

It was only a matter of minutes before Jonathan had his enemy in sight. It was too dark to tell the make or model of the car in front of him, but he didn't really care about that. Instead, he turned to Petra.

"Do you know how to shoot a gun?" He asked her.

"My father took me to a range a couple times." She replied. "Why?"

"Here, take this," Jonathan said, pulling his Colt from its holster. "I want you to roll down your window and aim for his tires. Just pretend you're a cowboy.

Petra turned to him, looking at the gun he'd placed in her hands. "Jon, I don't think – "

"Just do it, Pet. Remember, this man might be after your father. We have important questions to ask him."

Petra looked to him once more, and out of the corner of his eye he could see a look of determination set itself in her face.

"All right, fine. Let's show this ass hole why you never mess with a Mader," she said, rolling down her window. Jonathan slowed down slightly; he was keeping pace with his target, but no longer moving closer towards him. Instead, he focused on maintaining and even trajectory so that Petra could accurately aim his Colt.

The barrel of his pistol blazed loud and bright, twice in quick succession. He saw sparks fly up off the road where Petra's two quick shots had missed their mark.

"It's got a kick to it," he advised, "just breathe and aim carefully."

"I said I knew how to shoot," she said.

After a short pause, Petra fired again, just once this time. Jonathan saw were the shot hit the right side of the car's rear bumper.

"Well, he knows we're behind him, that's for sure," Jon said.

Two more shots – that's five that Jonathan had counted now, already preparing his Firearm Discharge report in his mind. This time, one of the shots hit their mark and the car swerved as its right rear tire went flat. But the driver didn't stop, he just kept going, albeit several miles more slowly now. *He must be a gambling man*, Jonathan thought. Or an armed man, Jonathan thought again as he saw the figure reach outside the driver-side window with a weapon markedly larger than Jon's sidearm. Suddenly, the road around them was ablaze as his target loosed a burst of automatic fire on his pursuers.

Petra instinctively recoiled back inside the car. "Why isn't he stopping?" She asked. "You saw me, I scored a direct hit!"

Jonathan didn't have time to answer, as his military tactical driving training kicked into effect. He pushed Petra's head down into her lap, in an effort to prevent her from being hit. Then, he pressed down on the gas and quickly began to gain on his now-hostile target. The man laid down another burst of fire on the road behind him and this time Jonathan heard one chink against his fender.

Completely unfazed, Jonathan pressed his speed advantage, his low-riding Daimler-Benz able to take the one-lane road's tight turns at a greater velocity than his target's classic luxury sedan. He could tell from their driving patterns that his aggressive pursuit was having the desired effect… They were trying to go faster, but a flat tire and an inferior powertrain didn't allow them the acceleration needed to pull ahead. Jonathan could hear the loud buzz of his target's over-taxed engine from inside his own car.

PHANTOM PANTHERS

Suddenly, the car in front of him began to swerve out of control. Jonathan, only a few meters behind his target, soon understood why – it was a nasty patch of mud. He felt his tires begin to hydroplane and lose traction and in an instant he was spinning out. He pumped the brakes as the darkness spun around him, desperately trying to regain control of his vehicle and praying that they'd be able to stay on the tiny road. Petra screamed, now sitting up in her seat and holding onto her seatbelt for dear life.

Finally, his 'Benz came to a stop. He was facing the complete opposite direction he'd been driving. Petra was staring straight ahead, her face ghost-white. Jonathan started laughing.

It took them a few moments to compose themselves, but when they got out of the car, the red glow of their target's taillights was nowhere in sight.

"Did we lose him?" Jonathan asked.

"I don't think so," said Petra, "Look over there."

Jonathan directed his gaze to where Petra was pointing. The flimsy barbwire fence that separated the road from the steep riverbank below was completely destroyed about 30 yards up the road. Leading up to the hole in the fence was a pair of muddy tire tracks.

Jon ran over to investigate, Petra close behind him. They reached the edge of the road, and saw that their target had indeed run off. Jonathan saw that the front half of the sedan was submerged in the river, while the rear wheels spun against air. Even as he watched, the car sunk slowly into the river.

Jon stated the obvious. "He's dead."

Petra nodded in agreement. "There's nothing we can do."

Back in the Benz, Jonathon inquires, "Did you find anything else in those folders?" Jon asked.

"Only this," Petra said, handing him a military document. It was some sort of identification for a *Colonel Vicktor Kalugin*

"Do you think it means anything? If it does, my father would be the man to know," Petra said as he watched him absorb the document in his hands.

Jonathan pondered for a moment. Kalugin was a Russian name, and this was a USSR Military ID – did this mean that the Soviets were vested in his lost tanks?

He had to talk to Otto and Hans. Surely they would be able to fill in the gaps in his knowledge.

"How much further to Grafenwohr?" Jon asked, trusting Petra's native knowledge of the country.

"It's about 4 ½ more hours – we could be there before the sun rises if we leave now."

Jon looked down at himself, no doubt that his superiors would have something to say about his attire. Covered in mud, blood and sweat, he wasn't looking forward to a long drive in a cramped coupe.

"Fine, but we're going to find a hotel with a shower on the way. I don't care if we have to pay for the whole night – I'm not showing up like this."

"I wouldn't mind a rest stop," Petra said. A twinkle in her eye told Jon that she intended to do a bit more than rest, though.

I guess Grafenwohr can wait a little bit, he thought. *It's good to be alive.*

CHAPTER 17

Their stay in the hotel ended up lasting all night. It was early morning by the time Jon and Petra finally made it to the training facility only to find Hans and Otto awaiting their arrival in the civilian lot. It looked like the two older men had spent the night in their car – even from a distance, Jon could see the dark circles beneath their eyes. It was *almost* enough to make him feel bad for getting caught up in the hotel.

Surprisingly, though, Otto and Hans appeared quite chipper when they noticed Jon's 'Benz and popped out of the car to greet them.

"Did you spend the night out here, papa?" Petra asked as she stood up outside the passenger's side door. "Why didn't you two find a hotel?"

"Well, we didn't know we'd need one," he said. "Don't worry about us - this is a luxury suite compared to the inside of a tank. I've spent too many nights stuck inside a boiling hot cupola to be bothered by anything like this. Hell, I haven't slept this well since leaving for Munster!"

Hans chuckled. "It's good to see you again, Petra. And you too, Major."

Otto paused for a moment, looking around as if he expected a third person to appear behind the young duo. "Where's the Doctor? Did you meet with him at Wewelsburg? Could you not get him to come with you? Is that what took you so long?"

Jon paused, looking to Pet as they both remembered their near-fatal adventures from the night before. "I think it's safe to say that we're on our own for this one," Jon said, "the Doctor was... unavailable... when we found him."

"What do you mean?" Otto asked. "He was the one that wanted to meet in the first place! He wouldn't even talk to you?" The stress of the past few days was beginning to show itself as his irritation fumed to the surface. "That old bastard; I knew I should've gone to Wewelsburg. I would've *made* him talk to me!"

"Well, it turns out someone else had that same idea," Jon said. Otto's look of irritation was replaced by one of confusion. "But we shouldn't talk about this here," Jon said. "Let's go find someplace inside."

Jon proceeded to walk up to the guard post outside the main HQ, automatically flashing his identification as he said, "Good morning Private, could you point me towards the operational map room? My friends and I require a quiet place to confer."

"Yes sir, you'll need to head back out the civilian lot and drive about half a mile down the street to your left. You'll see a group of three buildings; you want the one in the middle. If you hit the main highway, you've gone too far."

The Private's directions proved easy enough to follow, and it was a matter of minutes before the group had made their way inside the map room, which is on the ground floor of the base's Information Center.

The room wasn't huge, but it had everything the group needed. Three rows of tables were arranged to face the front of the room, where a large laminated map hung from the wall. The map was extremely detailed, accurately depicting the terrain and topography of a twenty-five mile radius around Grafenwohr, the east side of the map showing the exact line defining the Czech border.

Jon swiveled around two chairs so that he and Petra could sit opposite Otto and Hans at one of the tables on the back row.

"You're sure we're safe in here?" Petra asked.

"We should be," Jonathan confirmed. He quickly scanned the perimeter of the room, double checking that there were no obvious surveillance devices present.

Otto was eager to hear the rest of their story. "So, no Dr. Schreck? What happened?"

The night before seemed more like a dream to Jonathan than anything else, but he quickly recounted what happened at Wewelsburg. As the two older men listened, Otto riffled through the folder that Petra had retrieved from Schreck's torture room. He stopped when Jon mentioned the name *Kalugin*, the name he'd found on the Russian military ID.

"Kalugin?" Otto asked. "As in, Vicktor Kalugin?" He and Hans shared a look that said the name meant something to them. Something bad.

"Yes," Jon confirmed. He went on, "I'm assuming he was the man we chased in the black sedan. That's a Russian name, isn't it?"

Otto nodded.

"What is it, father?" Petra asked. Jon was curious too.

"Vicktor Kalugin was the name of a feared KGB enforcer during the war. He was infamous for cutting the tongues out of his informants after they'd divulged information." Otto said. Jonathan thought back to the pink, squishy appendage next to Schreck's mutilated corpse.

"But he was executed after the war... His trial was in the papers."

Hans nodded in agreement.

"Are you absolutely sure it was *Vicktor Kalugin?*"

Petra grabbed the folder, riffling to the back. She pulled out the ID and slid it across the table to the two older men. "See for yourself," she said. *Vicktor Kalugin's* name and picture were clearly visible.

Across the table, Hans turned to Otto and spoke quietly, although Jon could still make out the words. "Does this mean the Soviets know about the Panthers?"

Otto thought for a moment, his gaze unmoving from the document on the table in front of him. Slowly he said, "They have to, it's the only explanation."

Jon could see the gears turning in the old man's thinly-haired head as he looked up slowly from the table, his eyes grave. "Jon, it's absolutely crucial that we find these tanks as soon as possible. Hans and I can verify that the Russians aren't in control of the tanks now, but I guarantee you they're moving faster than whatever search party your Directorate is putting together up the road."

"Verify?" Jon's curiosity was piqued. "What do you mean 'verify'? How?"

"We saw them last night."

Jonathan realized that in all the fuss with the Colonel, he had completely forgotten to ask the two older men what they'd been doing exploring private military property in a stolen vehicle.

He listened in awe as Otto quickly recounted their experience in the clearing beyond the outpost and how he'd experienced the aura the tanks and the power that they both possessed. Hans nodded quietly beside him, interjecting when he felt Otto had neglected an important detail.

"They chased us to the outpost, but then, for some reason, they just stopped. When we turned around, they were completely gone. We followed their tracks – twice – but it was as if they just stopped existing." Otto went on, "We would've kept looking except we *thought* you two were already back at the base."

Forty eight hours ago, Jonathan would've laughed at such a story. Now, he took in every word, not wanting to miss a single vital detail. He stewed in silence after Otto finished his story, digesting all the information he'd just heard.

Petra was the first to speak.

"Maybe they're still there."

The statement hung in the air, its implication slowly sinking in.

"I mean, they have to be close, right? Two tanks don't just vanish into thin air," she was looking around at the three men now, waiting for someone to agree with her.

"Well, it's a place to start." Jon said, trying to put more confidence into his voice than he actually felt. "I'll go request one of the jeep's and notify the outposts along the way that we're coming. We wouldn't want to get caught without permission by one of the Colonel's patrols." Jon said, Otto and Hans looking like two children as they exchanged a mischievous look.

It was an hour later when they left the barracks and began the trip towards the eastern edge of the training fields. Jonathan had requested a map of the outposts around Grafenwohr, which made it easy to identify possible locations where Otto and Hans encounter the tanks.

There were three total outposts on the eastern edge of the military grounds, each about 2 miles apart. After the storms from the day before, the hilly fields were slippery with grass and mud, which meant the going was slow. Still, having the map made up for it, and it only took about half an hour to find the half-bowl formation that had clearly been the site of some sort of armored conflict. Jon could see lots of wheel and tank tracks along the hillside, but only three extended back into the forest. Jon deduced that those were the two tanks and the jeep that Otto and Hans had absconded with the night before. He drove down, intending to add his own tracks to the three.

Beneath the trees, it felt like twilight. The sunlight formed miniscule flecks through the leaves overhead. Jonathan turned on his headlights.

They passed the ruined outpost, right where the map said it would be. As they continued, Jon noticed a large amount of destroyed underbrush forming a sort of trail back further into the forest.

They continued driving. Soon, Jon saw what looked like a break in the trees of ahead.

"That's it!" Otto said, pointing from the backseat.

Once they passed into the clearing, it was obvious that there had been another sort of conflict there. Jon parked the jeep at the edge of the clearing and got out, looking around. There certainly weren't any tanks to be seen, but there *were* fallen trees all around the edge of the clearing. Some looked as if they'd been struck by lightning, scorch marks lining the tops of their broken trunks.

"This must have been where they chased us," Otto said, pointing at a line of tracks on the ground and motioning in the direction from which they came. "But see for yourself – there are no other tracks leading in or out of the clearing."

Jon did check for himself, driving up and down the trail between the clearing and the outpost twice, but finding nothing. In desperation, they continued on past the clearing until they hit an old, pockmarked road. But still no sign of any tanks – in fact, it looked like this road hadn't been used in years.

Jon looked down at the map one of the Privates in the Transportation Room had given him back at the base. It didn't show much past the perimeter of the training grounds, but Jon noticed a small farm road northeast of the military property, and it continued off the right side of the map. That had to be where they were.

PHANTOM PANTHERS

"We can't be more than 10 miles from Soviet territory," Jonathan observed, trying to decide whether or not it was worth continuing on.

Even from the backseat, Otto felt his hesitancy. "We have to find the Panthers," he said, "As soon as possible, time is of the essence."

"But what good does it do us to find the Panthers if we don't know what to do with them?" Jon asked, mind already made up. "I don't want to risk running into any unfriendly Reds if we don't even have a clear objective. Plus, we're navigating blind at this point. We still haven't found any tracks and we're at the edge of my map."

Otto was probably about to reply, but Jonathan didn't wait for an answer. He was already turning the military vehicle around to head back to the barracks.

"I know where that farm road is; let's go back and find it in the Operations Room. Then, we can formulate an intelligent plan once we know where the tanks might have gone."

<hr />

Back at the map room, it was easy to find the farm road on the exquisitely detailed map, but that's where the easiness ended. As Jon suspected, they'd been less than 10 miles from the Czech border – 7 miles to be exact – which meant that driving down that road would've put them in range of possible reconnaissance. The Germans and Czechs weren't overtly hostile, but you could never be too careful when dealing with possible KGB involvement.

The last thing you *ever* wanted to do was underestimate the KGB.

"We have to tell Colonel Smithson," Jonathan stressed for the third time. "You two already got me dangerously close to shit creek with your antics last night; I could be discharged if it were ever discovered that I knew about the theft of a military vehicle without saying anything. I don't even want to think about what would happen if anyone found out I were hiding mission-critical information."

"I understand that," Otto replied, once again, "but what is your Colonel going to do? I don't doubt that he could find the tanks, but what then?"

Jonathan sighed, but Otto went on anyways.

"He's going to gather his forces and make an all-out attack, that's what. He's going to try and outgun our Panthers, but all he's going to do is throw away the lives of tens, if not hundreds of men. Is that what you want?"

Of course it wasn't. Maybe Otto was right. From the limited experience Jon had with the new Colonel, he didn't exactly judge him as a gifted strategist. He had no doubt that the Colonel would make an aggressive effort to capture the tanks the instant he discovered their location. And if what Otto and Hans said was true – and so far everything had been – then head-to-head battle with the tanks would only result in a swatch of avoidable casualties, and they still might not re-capture them.

But if all that were true, then it meant that there was no right answer for Jon. Either he did what he was supposed to do – tell his superior what he knew – and in doing so kill hundreds of innocent men. Or, he could do the right thing – find an alternative solution on his own – but risk losing his honor and his career.

"Alright, Otto, you got me. What's the plan? If we can't destroy them with weapons, if they're too dangerous to capture, then what are you going to do?"

"Without Schreck, we only have one choice." Otto smiled. "It all starts right here," he said, pointing to a barely-visible bridge on the enormous map. "And it might not even work."

PHANTOM PANTHERS

Am I really doing this? Jonathan asked himself, not for the first time, as he secured the jeep's winch to the munitions bunker's garage door.

Otto's plan was simple, in theory. He had hypothesized that the two ghostly Panthers felt some sort of grotesque recognition of their original commanders. Otto intended to use that connection as the only weapon they had against the rogue war machines.

And all I have to do is lie to my superiors, help steal explosives, and trust a couple old men to successfully outsmart two autonomous tanks without blowing the whole lot of us to kingdom come.

But even as he got back behind the steering wheel of the jeep, winch now secured to the garage door, he knew he didn't have a choice. He pressed the gas pedal, slowly.

The noise the garage door made as its gears screeched against each other sounded like some sort of desperate, dying animal. Jon was grateful that the base was so short-staffed, otherwise they surely would have been noticed. As it was, they chose the furthest and smallest munitions bunker from which to procure their needed explosives. Otto, Hans and Petra were all outside the jeep, and Jon could see them cover their ears against the metallic screech in his rearview mirror.

Once the garage door was high enough, the trio ducked beneath it and disappeared inside the bunker. Jonathan knew nothing about explosives, so he had to trust Otto and Hans to identify what was needed. Petra was with them to serve as a pack mule.

That brought a smile to his lips. Jon had tried tell her that he should be the one to help the older men find what they were looking for while Petra waited in the car. "What, you don't think I'm strong enough?" she had accused, before socking him hard in the arm. *She certainly knows how to throw a right cross*, he mused.

Petra startled him from his reflections. "Hey! We're all good; come help us load this stuff up," she said, motioning to the pile of explosives they'd gathered outside the garage.

Together, they quickly but carefully loaded up the back of the jeep. The explosives felt foreign in Jonathan's hand – he much preferred the sculpted grip of his Colt 45. He felt around inside his coat, making sure that the sidearm was still safely in its holster. He had decided to bring the pistol with him, finding it hard to imagine regretting the extra firepower.

That thought led him quickly to another.

"You guys finished this, I'll be right back," he said, dashing underneath the garage door and into the munitions bunker. The sparse fluorescent lights overhead seemed paltry and Jon was glad that the sun had decided to come out today, even if it was still trying to hide behind some clouds. The extra sunlight coming in beneath the garage door made it easy for Jon to find what he was looking for and he was back outside right as the others finished loading up the Jeep.

"Here, you should each take one," Jon said, distributing the three loaded Colts he'd taken around the group. Otto and Hans smoothly shouldered the holsters, their military experience showing through their familiarity with the weapons. However, he saw a look of hesitation flit across Petra's face. "Remember what I said in Wewelsburg? Better to have it and not need it than to need it and not have it."

Finally, they were armed and ready to go.

Jonathan detached the wire-cable from the garage door and wound it back up on the jeep's industrial winch. He did his best to press down the garage door and make it look natural, but it was obvious that its gears were thoroughly trashed and would eventually need replacing. He didn't want to think about explaining that the Colonel, so he quickly sped off towards the Eastern outpost to put the thought behind him.

"So what all did you grab back there?" Jon asked as he drove.

PHANTOM PANTHERS

"Nothing fancy... 10 bundles of dynamite, 10 blasting caps and 12 detonator cords – always good to have a couple extra of those. That should be enough for what we need." Otto said, rattling off his inventory at rapid fire pace. Jon barely kept up with what he was saying.

"And you're sure you know how to rig the dynamite?" Jon queried. He just wanted someone to tell him their plan would work; some slight reassurance that he wasn't crazy.

Hans answered, and it was clear from his excited tone that this was a topic he felt very comfortable talking about. "Well, the problem won't be with us, Major, it'll be with your dynamite. The only bundles we could find look like they're at least five years old. I guarantee you this stuff wasn't in storage for live combat – the only reason your Colonel probably kept it around for clearing dams and such around the base."

Jon let the words sink in. "So you're telling me that the dynamite might not work?"

"Don't worry! We brought extra, just in case," Otto said, clapping him on the shoulder, an unsettling glint in his eye.

Jon was *not* reassured, but he kept driving anyways.

CHAPTER 18

It hadn't taken them very long to re-find the farm road Northeast of Grafenwohr; the trip across the training grounds and through the woods on the other side was almost beginning to feel familiar. Jon stopped once they reached the road once again, pausing to let himself and the rest of the group gather their thoughts.

According to the map back in the operations room, the farm road in front of them ran straight East and West. To their left, West, the closest noteworthy location was a small town named Falkenberg. One of the Privates had informed them that the place held little more than a grocery store, a gas station and a place to eat; it was more of an outpost for the area's many farms than an actual town.

None the less, Jon knew they would've heard something if the Panthers had been sighted anywhere near Falkenberg. In fact, the Colonel's search parties were primarily looking North and West – towards Munster, on the way to which being where the tanks were lost. Supposedly. But, as Otto had noted when outlining his plan, if the KGB were involved, then the Panthers were almost certainly located to the east... *Towards* Soviet territory.

That meant they had to go right. Jon knew they had about 10 miles until the Czech border. He only hoped that they would find some shred of evidence indicating the tanks' location before they reached that point. Jon looked over at Petra in the seat next to him, then reluctantly turned left, as if he were taking some blind leap of faith.

PHANTOM PANTHERS

The enormous pot holes that dotted the road did nothing to improve Jon's mood, and he would've driven right past the farmer if Petra hadn't grabbed his arm and made him pullover. The man had been driving a tractor when Jon passed him, but he dismounted and began chasing them, arms waving, as soon as he saw the military insignia on the back of their jeep.

"We don't have time for this," Jon muttered as he watched the man walk towards them in his rearview mirror. The man was clearly some sort of laborer. He wore coveralls rolled up to his knees, with a torn shirt beneath. His billed hat was grimy and Jon could see dirt and filth all over his bare forearms.

"What if he knows something about the tanks?" Petra asked, even as she unbuckled her seatbelt.

Jon wasn't so optimistic. He subtly reached into his coat and felt his Colt snug against his torso. He watched the man approach until he was right outside his window.

"Two *Panzerkampfwagons* the man exclaimed", looking at Jon and pointing back towards his tractor. "two giant Panzerkampfwagons have destroyed my farm".

Jon was lost. He spoke very little German and this man spoke a dialect foreign to him… Something much thicker and more guttural than what he was used to deciphering in Munster.

Petra leaned over, listening closely as the man went on frantically, repeatedly motioning back towards his tractor. "He's a farmer," she said quickly to Jon before leaning further across his seat to speak to the man.

She asked him. Jon looked at him, waiting for his answer.

The man, "Ja, two giant machines".

Jon assumed she was trying to understand the man's problem.

The man spread his arms apart, as if he were measuring something in the air. "Big and terrible machines. Machines with lots of gun". Then he pointed at Jon and his frantic fury seemed to reignite once more.

"Back away," Jon said, motioning with his hands for the man to step away from the truck. "Tell him to back away," Jon said, turning to Petra. Instead, she got out and walked in front of the jeep to continue her conversation with the man. Jon watched from behind the windshield, wary.

Finally, the man and Petra appeared to reach some sort of agreement. He motioned back to his tractor for a final time and began walking back towards it. As he passed Jonathan's window, he said, "I will show you, you'll see what the monsters have done to my farm.

Petra got back into the passenger's seat. "What did he say?" Jon asked.

"Well, a lot," she said, "but, basically he said that his farm was attacked by two machines. He was angry because he thinks they were the military's machines; apparently they had German flags emblazoned across the side."

Petra paused for a moment. Jonathan saw that all four of them knew what these 'machines' must be.

"We're going to follow him back to his farm right now so he can show us the damage. I think he thinks that we don't believe him and he wants someone to take responsibility for the damage to his farm. I think he wants the military to pay for it."

"Ha! We'll see about that," Jon said. He would deal with that potential miscommunication later. For now, he had to find anything he could about the Panthers' whereabouts. If that meant following some crazy peasant-farmer on a wild goose chase around his farm, then that's exactly what he would do.

PHANTOM PANTHERS

The man's farm was located about a mile North from the old farm road that they'd been traveling. It wasn't a huge farm – Jon estimated it at around 50 acres, although he'd never been particularly gifted with geography.

From the moment they passed the gates indicating the border of the property, Jon could tell something was wrong. Even from the jeep he could see that something terrible had carved a swath of destruction right through the cluster of barns and stables near the middle of the farmer's property. As they drove closer, their jeep behind the farmer's tractor, Jon noticed a small flock of chickens running around one of the pastures, clearly agitated. He heard the sound of horses galloping and he heard a loud whinny from somewhere outside.

They had to make way for cows that were meandering aimlessly. Hogs were roaming the terrain hysterical and seeking anything that they could eat along the way.

More peculiar than that, though, was the air. It felt charged with energy, as if it still held some residual trace of the powers that had wrought such complete destruction on this poor bystander's farm. In his rearview mirror, he could see Hans and Otto visibly squirming in discomfort. He guessed that they felt the same thing he did.

The tractor in front of them stopped right outside what used to be some sort of barn. It was evident by the tank tracks running right though it that it was one of the Panthers that had clearly disposed of the farmer's barn. Hay from the loft was strewn all over the place as if a tornado had hit the farm. The farmer got off his tractor and began motioning to the barn behind him and Jon didn't need a translator to guess what he was saying.

He turned to Petra. "Tell him that we're going to look around, and that we're going to find these tanks in order to verify his story."

As Petra got out of the jeep, Jon did the same, followed by Otto and Hans. As Petra went to simultaneously console and interrogate the farmer, Jon and the other two men began wandering around to examine the wreckage.

Jon made his way closer to the destroyed barn. Little pieces of wood and debris littered the ground he walked on, and as he drew closer he noticed a clear line of scorched bullet holes along one of the still-standing barn walls.

As he surveyed the area beyond the barn, he saw more of the same. A long bungalow, which Jon assumed served as the farmer's household, was another similar victim of a tornado hit. In the forest just off of the house or what was left of it was the farmer's wife and two children huddling together still shaking from the terror that they had just lived through. Jon felt a mixture of guilt and anger rise in his gut.

He *had* to find these tanks.

He waved to the shell-shocked family, trying to look apologetic, but instead they turned and looked at this group of strangers with desperation. Jon sighed and a rush of fatigue and hopelessness set over him as he began walking back towards the jeep.

This family is lucky to be alive, he thought. *I wonder if we'll be so fortunate.*

Back at the jeep, Petra was still trying to assuage the disgruntled farmer. She didn't appear to be making very much progress. Jon walked up to the duo and asserted himself – they didn't have time to waste on arguing with farmers, even really, really unfortunate farmers.

"Where did they go?" Jon demanded, talking over the farmer.

The man attempted to begin another ramble, but Jon cut him off.

"The tanks," he said deliberately, "Where did they go?"

The farmer looked blankly at Jon, Otto, Hans and then at Petra. She translated, "Did you see where they went"?

PHANTOM PANTHERS

The farmer paused for a moment, seeming to recognize that he wasn't getting anywhere with his current tactic. He mumbled, "Ja," and slowly mounted his tractor once more.

Back in the jeep, Jon followed the farmer as he drove beyond the wreckage and the bungalow towards the opposite edge of his property. He pulled up next to a small creek and Jon did the same. Once parked, Otto and Hans got out and walked over to the farmer.

"They went this way", the man said, pointing.

Jon didn't wait for any translation, instead following the direction of the man's finger and seeing two sets of tracks on the other side of the creek. That must have been where the tanks went after having their fill of destruction on the farm.

Jon turned to address Petra, Otto and Hans and motioned for the farmer to wait next to his tractor while the group conferred. "We can't help this man right now; we have to find the Panthers." He looked in the sky to check the position of the sun. "Those tracks head east. If we're lucky, we'll be able to intercept them before they reach the Czech border." And say I like you and I arrived I want you all is will you will undoubtedly the sunlight and I assume. You just got a car as you progress is like no He turned back and glanced at the farmer, now seeing and old unfortunate soul instead of a crazy, desperate farmer.

Petra collected the twenty or so Marks that they all had in their pockets, and walked over to deliver the gift to the farmer and express her thanks for his help. He still seemed disgruntled, but he accepted the gift graciously enough. By the time they were all re-situated in the jeep, the farmer had already begun driving back to his homestead. The jeep made easy work of the shallow creek and so they continued following the enormous tread tracks on the other side.

It seems that they had no choice but to do exactly what Jonathan had been trying to avoid. They followed the tracks east from the farm until they led them to a trail. Fortunately, there hadn't been any inexplicable breaks in the tracks as they'd experienced in the woods near Grafenwohr; the tracks continued onto the trail, easy to discern in the midday sun.

Keeping sight of the Panther tracks was not the problem – where they led them to was. They had finally reached the Czech border, marked only by a signpost nailed to one of the trees along the trail.

Vorsicht: Sie verlassen den Americanishen Sektor

But Jon knew that while the sign might be small, the implications of crossing it would be huge. But no matter how Jon tried to look at it, they *had* to cross that border.

The group now weighed their options, it wasn't the first time since Otto had explained his radical plan. They could go back to Grafenwohr and attempt to explain why they believed the tanks were beyond the Czech border.

CHAPTER 19

Attempting to convince Jonathon's superiors was a long shot. If they believed – them and that was a big *if* – then they might be able to join an official search party and get permission to go beyond the border. And again, that too was an enormous *if*... The Czechs weren't known for their desire to help Americans. On top of that, Jon would have to explain why he had hidden his intel from his superiors, as well as why he'd helped two German veterans abscond with military-owned explosives.

In the end, Jon knew that he really didn't have a choice. He was in too deep to turn back and even if he wasn't, he didn't honestly believe his superiors would or could do anything to help. It seemed that trespassing into Czechoslovakia was their only course of action; he just hoped that Petra's or Otto's Russian was as good as their German. If they got caught, they didn't fancy trying to explain why they had ten bundles of dynamite in a trespassing US military jeep.

Here goes nothing, he thought as he revved the jeep past the border. The rest of his party fell silent, all knowing that they were in hostile territory now.

His hope was that they'd lessen their chances of getting caught by staying on the small woodland trail. In fact, he was almost grateful now that the Panthers had chosen to detour through the farm. It would've been impossible to pass the border on the road they'd been on before the farmer stopped them; Czechs kept regular patrols, even on the smaller trails.

Jonathon drove a short distance down the road slowing down and then coming to a complete stop, from one of the command cars a Czech or Russian office approached and signaled the alien vehicle to stop.

"Shit." He said, one word summing up his thoughts.

Jonathan's heart was pounding in his chest. He thought quickly, his mind processing their circumstances at rapid fire pace.

As if the hulk-man could read his mind, he whistled, and suddenly the jeep was surrounded. At least 20 men appeared on either side of the trail. Every single one of them was armed with an AK-47 except for the ogre in front of him and Jon didn't imagine that such a man needed a gun to be lethal.

From his seat, Jon could see sweat glistening on Petra's forehead. They all knew the danger they were in, but there was nothing they could do. So, they just waited as the giant overseer and his assistant slowly approached the vehicle.

The pair stopped about 10 feet from the jeep's headlights. The hulk-man approached as his partner waited, AK-47 aimed directly at the windshield. From his position, Jon knew that he could easily kill him, Petra and probably both Otto and Hans before any of them could so much as raise a weapon.

The Russian behemoth walked around their jeep once, inspecting its contents and looking each passenger over in turn. Finally, he came around to the driver's side window and had to lean down to look at Jon.

"Identification papers". After examining the documents, three German citizens and one American.

"Mr. American, you look lost." The man's voice dripped Red, but any English was better than no English at all. Jon prided himself on being a man who could count his blessings.

"Actually, we *are* lost," Jon said, "Could you kindly gentlemen point us towards American territory?"

The man bellowed with laughter. He shouted something Russian to his comrades and they all joined in his laughter.

Damn, Jon thought, *worth a shot.* He could feel his adrenaline racing as his mind worked on overdrive. He had to think of a way out of this, and fast. He could see Otto and Hans fidgeting restlessly in the backseat. Jon guessed that somehow he was the calmest one in the jeep, whatever good that did. He just had to think…

Once the man had stopped laughing, he looked back down again and pointed back to the explosives piled obviously in the rear of the jeep. "Are those lost too," he asked, his thick Russian accent not thick enough to hide his sarcasm.

The big Russian looked at Jon for a moment, and to his surprise, he stepped back away from the door and walked back to his partner holding the AK-47. The tension inside the jeep was palpable.

"What are we going to do?" Otto whispered from the backseat.

"Just stay calm and follow my lead," Jon said. He knew that he didn't actually have any lead for them to follow, but he hoped that a display of confidence would help ease their anxiety. Whatever was about to happen, he was sure that it collected state of mind would help all of them get out alive. "When I act, you act too," Jon said, trying to make it seem like he had a plan.

The Russian looked at him as he took off his gloves and Jon noticed some sort of ring on his right hand. It looked like it had a sword and shield emblem attached to the band. (supposed to indicate KGB affiliation, also indicating these aren't official Czech forces).

"Poplach!" He heard some of the men begin to exclaim. He had no idea what 'poplach' meant, but when he opened his eyes and looked up, he saw that the Russian wasn't looking at him anymore. Instead, he was looking behind him, down the trail.

Jon looked too, and that's when he saw them – two steel behemoths, rolling through the trees. Even as Jon watched, they stopped.

It can't be…

The trail was still for a moment, and then an explosion obliterated the two Russians furthest from the jeep. The hostile party scrambled into action.

This is your chance, Jon thought and before he had time to convince himself otherwise, he reached into his jacket and drew his Colt from its holster. He was on the ground, which meant that he wasn't in position to aim for a lethal shot, but he quickly found a suitable alternative…

With a loud bang, the huge Russian's knee exploded outward behind him.

The higher they climb, the harder they fall, Jon thought as the gargantuan Russian toppled to the ground in a fit of curses, clutching futilely at his blown-out knee.

Another explosion rocked the trail somewhere in front of him.

The men were too confused to react to Jonathan's attack on their leader. Jonathan was up on his feet now, the pain in his face forgotten. He only needed one eye to shoot, so he let hundreds of hours' worth of target practice take over and quickly headshot the two nearest Russians. He pointed his gun at the enormous leader, still writhing on the ground, but decided against ending his life.

Only then did he look around and examine his surroundings. The destruction he beheld was almost hypnotizing.

Hans and Otto now scurrying for cover in the ditch on the road side yell to Jon and Petra that the Panthers are coming out of the forest and are charging down the road heading directly for them.

Cannon fire now permeates the air. High explosive shells burst in the midst of the Czech and Russian troops. The guard shack and other border buildings now become easy prey for the Panthers powerful guns as they burst into small bits of debris.

Bodies of helpless soldiers fly through the air as if floating on air. The Panthers glacial machine guns now spew out rounds like a giant scythe through the surrounding foliage. The personnel vehicles are peppered with a continuous stream of bullets and their frames collapse as bullets fill their tires with countless rounds.

"Jon, Otto, Hans get in the jeep!" The sound of Petra's voice snapped Jon out of his trance. "Hurry!"

Jon and the others turned to run back into the jeep. Then, he was in reverse, backing away from the carnage in front of them.

The tanks were drawing closer now, their Russian targets seemingly forgotten, even though a few men remained and opened fire. Both cannons were now pointed directly at the jeep.

"Hurry, Jon, hurry!" Petra stressed. Jon slammed the trany into first gear and sped off away from the tanks, back down the way they'd come. Shells exploded around them, sending huge hails of debris down around and in front of them, but somehow, the jeep remained untouched. A single shot would have been enough to detonate the dynamite in the back of the truck, but it seemed that luck was on their side – for once.

They had made their getaway and they all knew that they were in Czech territory. It was only then that they realized the trail was silent behind them.

Jon parked the jeep and got out, looking back for any sign of the tanks.

Nothing. The forest was silent, and the trail was empty all around them. No sign of the Russians or the tanks, or so they thought.

Otto now pulling out the map, his finger lands on the point to where they have to go. The bridge in the Naturpark Nördlicher Oberpfälzer Wald

CHAPTER 20

"They have to be nearby," said Otto. "We should keep going." Jon knew that every minute those tanks were left roaming through Russian territory increased the risk of a catastrophic international dispute. They'd already annihilated a Czech border patrol and it could only be a matter of time until more Soviets showed up. Where there was one Red, there were always more.

Jon watched as Otto opened up their map and began examining it.

"We're closer than I thought," Otto mused, as he looked back and forth between the map and their surroundings. "The Naturpark is actually located just off this road, about 7 miles up, bearing northeast then north."

Petra somehow seemed to be the only one unperturbed by their close encounter with the Panthers. Oblivious to their near-death experience, she said, "We should hurry; we don't want to get cut off again by those tanks." Jon knew she was right, and quickly made a U-turn to direct the jeep northwards.

The road was easy to follow, and the map proved accurate. There was a sharp curve in the road past where they'd skirmished with the border patrol and then they were headed north. The sun was beginning its descent through the sky out to their left; its golden rays filtered through the surrounding trees, glaring intermittently into Jon's eyes as he drove. He squinted to see the road in front of him. Under different circumstances, the drive would have almost felt peaceful.

They heard thunder. At first, Jon thought it was another thunderstorm, but the sky overhead was clear. Another loud boom and Jon realized his mistake – it wasn't thunder at all, but the sound of high explosives echoing in the distance.

It seemed Otto had the same realization. "Sounds like our tanks have found another patrol." His voice sounded grim, but remained laced with determination. Then, as soon as they came around another slight bend, "This should be our park." He pointed to a road up ahead on the left side.

As Jon turned onto the road, he read the sign arching over the entryway:

Naturpark Nördlicher Oberpfälzer Wald

If the drive leading up to the park had felt surreal, then the drive through the park itself was taken straight from a dream. The trees grew thicker, and yet it didn't feel darker. If anything, the lush vegetation made the park feel more vibrant and alive. The trees acted as a barrier to the sounds of combat in the distance; the sound of the jeeps engine almost drowned out the explosions entirely.

Jon drove the jeep over a crest of a hill, and that's when he saw what could only be their final destination – a rushing river ran through the valley below, and over it extended a surprisingly well-kept beam bridge. It stretched from one side of the valley to the other over the river. It looked narrow, but sturdy.

"Are you sure we have enough explosive material for our plan to work?" Jon asked.

From their vantage point above the bridge, Jon counted eight separate support pillars, four on each side. It looked like the two pairs closest to each shore were made from some sort of stone, likely concrete, while the middle pairs were made from some sort of reinforced wood.

Otto got out of the jeep and surveyed the bridge below.

"They've made improvements to this bridge since I last saw it 30 years ago," he said, "but we *should* still be able to carry out our plan. We'll just need to make each and every stick of dynamite count."

Jon really didn't like the word 'should' – it implied chance. Unfortunately, there wasn't much to do about it. He could still hear the tanks rumbling in the distance and he knew that they'd would close on them soon enough. There was no way out of the park except the entrance through which they'd come; if they turned back now, they may get cut off and stuck in the park with no hope of escape from the vile war machines.

"Well, I suppose we should get to work," Jon resigned, "No turning back now."

The rest of the group agreed, a sense of purpose simultaneously providing them with both the motivation and courage to continue. They remounted the jeep, and continued down the hill.

As they drove across the bridge to the other side of the river, Jon noticed Otto looking out the window as they drove. He appeared to be making mental calculations

and every now and then he would lean over and whisper something to Hans, who would inevitably nod fervently and whisper something back. Jon was sure he didn't want to know what the two were saying, so he just kept driving.

Despite his wishes for ignorance, however, Hans noticed his glances towards the older duo in the back seat and mistook them for genuine inquiry. "The middle supports are too far apart for optimal structural integrity," Hans explained, "Otto and I were just agreeing that we should only need to detonate the wooden supports in the middle of the bridge for our plan to work."

There's that word again… 'Should'.

As they reached the western side of the bridge, Petra voiced the concern she saw on Jon's face. "Are you sure Papa? We only get one shot at this, right? Wouldn't it be better to spread the explosives out to target each pillar?"

"We don't have enough dynamite to detonate four concrete supports," Otto said, matter-of-factly, "But if we can lure the tanks to the middle of the bridge and successfully destroy all four wooden pillars there, the weight of the machines should take care of the rest. Not very many bridges can support 60 tons of heavy metal without central supports."

Hans elaborated. "With limited explosives, our optimal strategy will be to target the weakest areas of the bridge. Obviously, wood is weaker than concrete, so that's where we'll detonate."

Not for the first time, the older men's words had done nothing to make Jonathan feel better. Nonetheless, he asked, "Okay, so what do we do now?" He motioned to the back of the jeep, "How do we get these things set up?"

"You and I will take the explosives and secure them to the wooden supports," Hans said, pointing to Jon and himself, "While, Petra, you and your father will handle the wiring."

"Yes, it's only right that the *commander* should take on the most important tasks that the grunts can't handle," Otto said, ribbing Hans. Jon was sure that at a different time he could appreciate the older men's jesting, but now it just annoyed him. "Plus I don't want my daughter handling these explosives if we can help it," Otto said, more seriously this time.

At that, Otto and Hans both got out of the car and began unloading the dynamite from the trunk. Jon looked over at Petra in the passenger seat, and as soon as she turned to return his gaze, he leaned over and kissed her. Hard.

"I really want to make it out of this," Jon said. "I feel like we have unfinished business."

Petra smiled, and in that moment it was the most beautiful thing he'd ever seen. It felt like he'd stumbled onto an oasis; he felt rejuvenated, reinvigorated. "We'll always have unfinished business," she said suggestively. "But now's not the time. We'll have plenty of time for that later." She leaned over and pecked him on the lips once more, then pushed him back and jumped out of the jeep.

Jon watched her go, then did the same.

"Careful!" Hans exclaimed.

Jon was carrying a bundle of dynamite in each hand and had almost tripped as he was going to hand one to Hans. They both knew that any misstep from either man would be quite lethal. Jon was reminded why he'd never considered a career in demolitions... He much preferred the more controllable, focused lethality of a firearm.

Unfortunately, firearms couldn't destroy bridges.

They were at the eastern pair of wooden supports, closest to the side where they'd come from. Each support pillar formed a joint with the side of the bridge, and Hans and Jon were placing two bundles of dynamite at each one. Otto and Petra were waiting for them to finish placing the dynamite before weaving the wiring and securing the blasting caps, all of which would eventually lead back to a master detonator they planned to use from the western side of the bridge.

Jon and Hans made short work of their assigned task. All they had to do was place the dynamite adjacent to each pillar, and make sure the blasting caps were positioned for easy wiring. Otto and Petra were taking longer... Not only did they have to wait for Jon and Hans to finish placing the dynamite, but wiring the explosives took significantly longer than their mere placement. So, after Jon and Hans finished, Hans urged Jon back to the jeep while he went to help Otto.

PHANTOM PANTHERS

"Get Petra to come back with me," Jon called after Hans. "She can help me get this detonator thing ready." Hans looked back and nodded, then ran down to the bridge to meet Otto and Petra. When Hans reached the father-daughter duo, Jon watched as Hans motion back to the jeep and he smiled at Petra's obvious protests. Eventually she turned away, defeated, and came walking back to him.

From the west side of the river, they both watched as Otto and Hans went to and fro across the bridge, various wires in hand, as they ensured that all the caps and wires were properly connected. Within a few minutes, Otto came jogging towards them, a bundle of wires in hand.

"Where's that IED?" He called, still some fifty feet away.

Jon fished the detonator out of the back of the jeep and had it ready on the ground by the time Otto reached them.

"Here – these are the wires for the first two pillars," Otto said, handing them to Jon. "See those wing nuts? Just twist these together and wrap 'em around one of them; we'll use the other wing nut for the second pair of charges. Just make sure they have metal-to-metal contact," Otto explained, pointing out the important area of the explosive.

Just as quickly as he'd come, Otto turned and ran back down to get the other pair of wires from Hans on the bridge. It only took a few moments for Jon to get the detonator wires wrapped around the explosive.

"Here, take this and set us up somewhere under cover," Jon said, handing the plunger detonator to Petra. "We don't want to be caught out in the open whenever these machines finally find us." At that thought, Jon quickly did a double take to ensure that the ever-present rumbling remained distant... The last thing they wanted was to be caught unaware by two highly lethal Panthers. However, try as he might, he could discern no audible sign of the Panthers.

"Do you hear that?" He asked Petra.

She listened for a moment. "What?" She asked.

"Exactly."

Jon quickly handed off the detonator, then turned and ran down to meet Otto and Hans on the bridge.

"Our tanks are silent!" He called as he drew close to the two older men, who were talking frantically on the bridge. "There's no more thunder!"

Otto looked up at him from his conversation with Hans, then listened for himself. "We have to hurry," He said, the phrase beginning to sound like a broken record.

"What can I do to help?"

"Actually, I need you to help Hans insert the final blasting caps. He can show you how, but old shaky hands aren't ideal for handling high explosives."

Jon nodded, and took the remaining blasting caps from Hans. There were only two pillars left to wire and Jon quickly discovered just how elementary dynamite is in its construction.

"It's really easy," Hans said, "Just pick up each stick and you see that hole there?" He motioned to the hole at the top of the stick in Jon's hand. "Carefully – and I mean *carefully* – insert that metal blasting cap into the stick. Then, once you've wired each stick in both bundles, just twist them together to form a cord like we did with the other ones.

"Then we can bring those up to Petra and wire up the detonator," Jon finished for him, "I think I can do that."

It couldn't have taken him more than five minutes to cap every stick on the third pillar. He moved efficiently, but deliberately. Years of target practice had taught him the importance of steady hands, and that part, at least, came easily to him.

Just one more pillar to go, and then we can get out of here, Jon thought.

As soon as the thought left his mind, the ominous rumbling returned to the air, louder now.

"They're in the park!" Otto called to Jon, running over to him. "Hurry and wire the final pillar – this won't work without all four!"

Jon moved more quickly now over to the final wooden support. But before he could start rigging the final two bundles of explosives, Hans came over and grabbed the wires from his hand.

"You guys bring the wiring back up to Petra – I can finish down here." Hans called over the sound of the approaching tanks; the rumbling was loud enough to make hearing difficult.

Jon nodded, and began to run back towards Petra. "Come on, Otto, we need you to set off this detonator!" Otto seemed reluctant to leave his old friend on the bridge, but he knew that his expertise would be more beneficial elsewhere.

As soon as they reached the western edge of the bridge, Jon turned back to see two gargantuan machines roll over the hilltop on the eastern side of the river.

It was them – the tanks were here.

The rumbling grew quieter for a few moments as the tanks idled at the top of the hill and then fire erupted simultaneously from both tanks' cannons. Jon barely had time to think before an explosion rocked the hillside about fifty feet in front of him and Otto. Jon saw Petra scramble away from the explosion, seeking cover behind a nearby tree.

Then another explosion hit. Then another.

The tanks were descending towards the bridge now, firing as they went. Their eerily luminescent canon rounds seemed to penetrate the very fabric of reality as each explosive cratered into the hillside. Each tank took turns laying down suppressive fire with their coaxial machine guns, streams of bullets peppering the hillside around them.

Fortunately, the tanks didn't seem to have very good long-range accuracy, at least not while they were in the process of changing elevation. Jon suspected that would change as soon as they reached the level surface of the bridge. But, of course, by then the trap would be set.

Where's Hans? Jon thought, remembering that the second older man wasn't with them.

He and Otto continued running up to meet Petra behind her tree-cover, then turned back to watch as Hans continued his work on the bridge below, seemingly unfazed by the heavy ordnance around him. Even from a distance, Jon could see his brow furrowed together in concentration as he frantically capped the final sticks of dynamite on the remaining support pillar.

"He's going to finish," Otto said, confidently. Then, remembering the second part of his task, he took the wires from Jon and began threading them around the explosives remaining unused wing nut.

The tanks were nearing the eastern edge of the bridge now and their failure to yet hit a target only increased the urgency of their fire, as if they were somehow frustrated. Round after round of lightning-like explosives echoed out of each barrel, streaking through the trees around them and leaving scorched air in their wake. With an enormous explosion, one round finally found a target – Jon watched as the jeep disappeared in a flurry of fire before his eyes. One moment it was there, the next it was gone.

When the tanks reached the eastern edge of the bridge, they stopped firing, as if reconsidering their approach. For a moment Jon thought they might turn back, somehow aware of the trap set before them.

"Hans, run!" Otto shouted down to the bridge. "Now's your chance!" Hans had finished his task and had been hiding behind one of the concrete support pillars close to the western edge of the bridge. Now he looked up at the group, then back at the tanks, then he began a full sprint for their location.

The tanks responded immediately to his movements and began firing just as abruptly as they'd stopped. This time, though, they seemed to have a clear target. Hans' Jagdpanther took the lead as the two tanks crossed the threshold onto the bridge and it began firing explosive rounds directly at Hans, while Otto's Panther continued suppressive fire on the western hillside. Machine gun bursts complemented the explosions like some sort of deranged accompaniment.

Hans somehow managed to dodge the explosive rounds intended for him and made it off the bridge. He was barreling straight towards their location at full speed. The tanks on the bridge behind him had slowed their approach, moving more deliberately now.

Hans was nearing the jeep now – or at least, the scorched chunk of metal that used to be the jeep. Just a hundred feet or so more to go and he'd be safe behind the trees with the rest of the group. Otto was shouting for Hans to run faster, but Jon couldn't make out the words over the sound of the tanks' engines and heavy fire.

Suddenly, a line of red burst from Hans' chest; the Jagdpanther's coaxial machine gun cut through ground, tree and flesh with equal ease. Hans looked down at his chest, then up at Jon, Petra and Otto. He tried to say something, but only blood gurgled out from his mouth. He stumbled a couple more shaky steps, then collapsed on the ground.

CHAPTER 21

"Hans! No!" Otto screamed. He felt his gut clench as he watched his old friend collapse to the ground, mortally wounded. He instinctively tried to run out to grab him, but someone grabbed his jacket and held him back. Explosions continued to craterize the hillside around them, machine gun fire mowing through grass, wood and scorched jeep metal with equal ease.

"It's too late," Jon said from behind him, "He's dead."

Otto had no reply. He and Hans had brushed with death so many times during the war; he never expected to make it out alive, but somehow he did. They both did.

Otto sunk deeper into his reverie as time on the hillside seemed to slow down. The world seemed distant. If he could just concentrate hard enough, maybe he could somehow go back in time and refuse Hitler's cruel invitation into the order of the Teutonic Knights. The mystical power they'd been promised was nothing more than a hollow gift laced with poison. The tanks gave them power alright, but they didn't win the war and now they may end up starting another one.

Another explosion came dangerously close to the small bunch of trees they were using for cover. Otto felt the heat of the explosion rush across his skin, and it shook him from his trance.

These machines must be stopped, Otto thought, *at any cost. They cannot be allowed to take any more innocent lives. Hans, old friend, your death will not be in vain.*

"Otto, we need to detonate! Now!" The urgency was evident in the Major's voice.

Otto snapped around, looking for the explosive he'd helped wire up. "Give me that," he said to Petra, who held the detonator device loosely in her hands.

Otto took the detonator and set it carefully on the ground. He performed one last cursory check of the wires connection to the wing nuts. Everything was in place and properly connected; now they just had to wait for the tanks to reach the right spot.

Otto watched as the tanks slowly crept onto the bridge and began moving towards the center. *Yes, keep coming closer you fiendish bastards. Just a little bit further.*

Finally, both were completely on the bridge. They're belligerent outpour of ordnance stopped, for the moment, as if they knew the group was trapped and unable to escape their wrath. Bursts of machine gun fire scourged the ground around their cover, but never close enough to score another kill. The lack of high explosives at what was now medium- to short-range for the tanks felt like some sort of cruel mockery.

"Papa, what are you waiting for?"

"We're sitting ducks up here, Otto, press the detonator. Please!"

Otto barely murmured a reply, "Almost… They're almost there…" He was too focused on the Panthers' progress across the bridge to manage more than that.

Finally, both his friend's former Jagdpanther and his own Panther passed the eastern pair of concrete supports.

"Now," he said as he twisted the detonator's handle. He heard that wonderful click and whir as the detonator's generator spun to life, sending a surge of power up through each wing nut and out the attached wires to the dynamite below.

Nothing.

The detonation should have been almost instantaneous, the only delay being the generation of the proper amount of power to release into the blasting caps. He should've just seen eight bundles of dynamite simultaneously obliterate four wooden supports; instead, all he saw was the unhampered approach of two hostile war machines.

"What's wrong?" He heard Petra asked from behind him.

An easier question to ask than to answer, he thought.

"Try it again," suggested Jon.

Otto knew that if it didn't work the first time, it wouldn't work the second, but he humored the younger man regardless. He twisted the detonator's lever back up to the start position; it disengaged with no sign of any mechanical malfunction. Then, he pressed the release knob, more deliberately and smoothly this time, just to make sure he hadn't somehow gone too fast the first time.

Still nothing.

The Jagdpanther was past the first wooden support on the bridge now... *We're running out of time.* If either tank crossed the western-most concrete supports, it would be too late for the detonation of the central wooden supports to do anything.

He knew he didn't have much time for problem-solving. He closed his eyes, and quickly envisioned a schematic overview of their demolition plan. *The detonator is brand-new, and any damage to even a single explosive would surely result in detonation. Since we haven't seen any explosions, the problem must be either with the wiring, or the blasting caps. But I trust Hans; it couldn't be the blasting caps.*

He looked up from the detonator and let his eyes follow the wiring through the grass down to the bridge. The wiring was braided together in one thick strand, so it was relatively easy to follow from his elevated vantage point.

"There," he said, pointing at last, "See that?" Jon and Petra moved up next to him, looking over his shoulder and following his finger to a point on the hill just past the western edge of the bridge where the wire went underneath a piece of scorched metal. "There's our problem," he said.

He didn't wait for the younger couple to figure it out for themselves. "The wiring has been destroyed; it looks like debris from the jeep has severed our connection."

Otto thought for a moment. *If it's just the wiring, I should still be able to use the fail-safe...*

"I have to go down and repair the wire!" In reality, Otto knew that no repairs could be made in time for the tanks to still be in position, but he didn't want to tell the young couple his real plan.

"Papa, you can't go down there; it's not safe!"

"I know darling, because this mission has been so safe thus far," he smiled, "Don't worry about me, sweet daughter, I can take care of myself."

"Otto, let me go, I can run faster and you're not in a fit state of mind."

The sight of his friend's death flashed across his eyes once again – it was a vision he knew he'd never forget. But it didn't make him scared, only more determined to ensure the destruction of these vessels of cruelty. He had to admit, though, that the Major was brave.

"I appreciate the offer, Major, but I'll be just fine."

The Jagdpanther was past the first wooden support now, with the Panther not far behind. They rolled onwards, steadily, suppressive fire bursting forth every now and then to keep their prey under cover.

"I love you Petra," Otto said, "but I have to do this. There's no other way." He gave his daughter one last kiss on the forehead, then turned to Jon. "Cover me, Major," he said with a smirk, "Just try and distract 'em."

Without another word, he turned and made a dash to the next nearest patch of trees, slightly down the hill towards the remains of the jeep. He felt the vibrations of machine gun fire pouring into the ground behind his footsteps. Somehow he managed to stay ahead of the lethal weapons, though. From the second patch of trees, it was another quick dash to the scorched remains of the jeep.

The tanks paused now, as if they were watching him, waiting for him to make his next move. He looked back up the hill to where Jonathan and Petra were still hiding behind the thicket of foliage. He made eye contact with Jon, and gave him a clear nod.

The Major reached ducked around the tree cover and fired several shots in the direction of the tanks. Otto knew the attack was futile. Even if the small caliber bullets of a sidearm could somehow penetrate the armor of the supernatural tanks — the same armor that shrugged off high explosives and armor penetrating rounds like a Sunday breeze — there was no way to secure an effective hit from such a distance. None the less, the attack was loud, and just as Otto had hoped, that was enough to get the tanks' attention off his place of cover. They each turned their cannons up the hill at the hiding duo, and that's when Otto made his run for it.

In five long strides, Otto reached the place where he suspected that the sharp metal debris had sunken into the wiring. It was easy to confirm his suspicions — scorched wiring lay strewn to either side of the sharp metal hunk. *Just as I thought; far too much damage to repair.*

As soon as he'd confirmed the uselessness of the primary wire, he made a beeline for the bridge, staying crouched to minimize his profile. But with just a few strides to the edge, a searing pain shot through his left arm. He fell to the ground, clutching at his bicep. Warm liquid oozed between his fingers; when he looked down at his arm, all he saw was shredded flesh and leather where his arm and jacket sleeve used to be.

Machine guns... Could've been worse... His mind was swimming, and he tried desperately to focus on the task in front of him. *Stop the bleeding... Just stop the bleeding... You have to reach the fail-safe.* Otto was tired. He felt old, now. *Don't die yet,* he thought, and before he lost consciousness, he somehow managed to tighten his belt around his bicep.

<hr />

"Papa!" Petra shrieked. "What's he doing?! Why isn't he moving? Why didn't he repair the wire?! Why would he get so close?!"

She was frantic, but Jon had seen it too – Otto had clearly walked right past the source of damage he'd indicated. He hadn't even bent down to try and repair the wire; one quick glance and he was moving directly towards the bridge and the tanks, where he promptly fell to a strafe of automatic fire. Jon saw him miraculously tourniquet his own arm, but if they didn't get down to him immediately, there was still a good chance he'd bleed out.

The Panthers were moving closer now, both of them almost halfway to the second and final pair of wooden supports. Otto had explained that they could not pass the western concrete supports, which meant they only had a few yards left before their mission would be impossible to complete and before their death would be absolutely certain.

As if the tanks could smell the scent of fear, they began moving faster across the bridge. Both tanks completely stopped firing both their cannons and auxiliary weapons; beneath the thrum of their Maybach engines, Jon could've sworn he heard music on the air.

"I don't know," Jon admitted, defeated. "I don't know what he was doing. I don't know what *we* can do. Maybe there's some other way out of the park?" But they both knew the words held false hope – they'd both seen the map, they both knew the only entrance was also the only exit. The rest of the perimeter was fenced.

All he could do was watch and try his best to comfort Petra, and as he did, an inkling of what Otto's plan might be began to slowly cement itself in his mind.

As Otto's mind flowed in and out of lucidity, some sense of familiar purpose cut into his consciousness.

That music... There's that music again...

It was the SS death march; the very same one they'd heard in the clearing outside Grafenwohr. But somehow he remembered it from before that, strange déjà vu gripping his mind. The voices were too familiar; he recognized them from somewhere else.

Then it hit him.

He and Hans had made a parody to the lyrics of an SS marching ballad, alterations which only he and his tank squad knew. And yet, that same parody permeated the air now, even though the only two men alive who'd known them were he and Krieger. *That's our song! Horst Vessel? Could it be?*

In that moment he knew why the tanks had demonstrated such an affinity for the two old veterans, and why the tanks must be kept from reaching any further into Czech territory.

With one good arm, he pushed himself up from the ground and somehow got his feet beneath him. Slowly, he stood up. His left arm hung useless at his side. Otto knew that the tanks could see him, now. But even as they turned their cannons on them, he raised his good arm into the air.

"It's me!" He called as he approached the bridge, "I'm here!" If the tanks had eyes, he knew they'd be watching him know. He reached the edge of the bridge, arm still raised in surrender. The tanks slowed to a crawl as he approached.

"I know who you are," he called out to them, "My name is Herr Oberst Mader; I am your commander, and I command you to halt!"

The tanks stopped. *Perfect,* he thought, *just behind the concrete supports.*

PHANTOM PANTHERS

He limped onto the bridge... Less than 30 feet separated him from the tanks now. "I know you've been waiting for me," he called out to them, "And I'm glad you've come – Heil Hitler!"

The tanks let out a burst of machine gun fire into the air in some sort of deranged salute. He was getting closer, just 20 feet away now. He eyed the fail-safe, the end of the short, thin wire now between his feet.

"Friends," Otto said overdramatically, feeling slightly ridiculous talking so passionately to two machines, "There are two Allied sympathizers up on that hill. With your help, we could end their lives and bring glory to the Reich!"

He smiled.

"Unfortunately, I love them both, and I can't allow you to do anything like that."

With that, Otto quickly reached to the ground and snatched the fail-safe wire. He gave it a quick tug and before another thought could enter his mind, he was thrown into the air by the force of four simultaneous explosions.

"Papa, stop it!" Petra screamed. "No!"

But it was too late. Jon had suspected what Otto might do, but knew it would do no good to object now. Even as Jon watched, Otto pulled something thin off the ground and yanked it backwards.

The explosion was enormous; it was almost like watching a movie. Even from their cover, Jon saw the dark figure of Otto's body fly through the air as wood and concrete alike splintered and cracked, flying outwards into the river below. Enormous chunks of concrete plunged into the water like cannon balls, each one creating a massive circular shockwave. The wooden debris was more delicate, sprinkling down into the water like leaves. Jon saw the remainders of all four wooden supports detached from the bridge and fall slowly into the lake, making enormous waves as they went.

The bridge wobbled and fractured, looking in this moment more like a flimsy rope bridge than one made of concrete and asphalt. The weight of the two gargantuan Panthers was too much for the remaining unsupported architecture; with a deafening crack, the concrete pillars buckled as the bridge literally tore away from the western shore. Like some sort of dying sea monster, tank and bridge alike crashed into the river below.

"It's over," Jon said as he watched the destruction unfold. "He did it; it's over."

Petra didn't seem to care. She was sobbing, her head pressed against the tree in front of her. As she sobbed, she hit the tree repeatedly, saying "Why, why, why" with each strike. Jon saw blood on her knuckles, and pulled her away from the tree and into his arms.

"It's okay," he said, "It's over now. We can go home. He won."

Mysteriously, Otto could somehow see himself from outside his own body as he sank down into the lake. He could see that his eyes were barely open and his wounded arm was leaving a trail of red blood through the water as he sank. As he hovered next to his body, he saw that a piece of concrete and rebar had lodged itself in his leg. One of his feet was mangled too. But, he felt no pain. In fact, he felt nothing at all.

This must be what it's like to drown, he thought, *with any luck I'll bleed out first.*

As he resigned himself to his death, he took in the underwater scene around him. Debris was sinking everywhere; when he looked upwards, he saw two dark shapes above him. They were enormous, but they swayed back and forth like leaves falling from an autumn tree as they sank, tumbling ever so gently. It looked serene. Even as he watched – he couldn't have said whether it took seconds or minutes – the figures grew larger until they were beneath him, sinking all the way to the bottom of the lake. A cloud of sediment went up around them as they hit the lakebed, and he could see the two dark shapes beginning to disappear into the wet sand as it settled.

Otto smiled and saw the last of his oxygen bubble out his lips.

As he watched the two tanks disappear into the bottom of the lake, he found himself reliving one of his first memories with his tank. It wasn't of combat, but of his return home to Helmstedt after receiving his Panther. He thought about how his wife had run out to greet him and how tightly she'd hugged him; he could feel her arms around him now. He thought about his daughter, and how happy she'd been that day. *Her little smile… Always so adorable.* How he wished he could see that smile one more time.

I hope she can be happy now, he thought as the darkness began to thicken his vision, *God, please let her be happy now.*

And that was the last thought of Otto Mader.

Epilogue

"You almost ready, Pet?" Jon called down the hallway into the bathroom where Petra was applying her makeup.

"Just five more minutes!" She called back. "Will you get the boys in the car while I finish up?"

She looked at herself in the mirror. Her adoptive father had always raised her to be a modest girl, which was easy since modesty came naturally to Maders anyways. None the less, she had to admit she looked good.

Although, I guess I'm not a Mader anymore… I wonder if the Duvalls are a modest family. She chuckled at such a silly idea. Jonathan was certainly *not* modest; if anything, his cockiness had rubbed off on her. Her thoughts continued to wander as she finished applying her makeup,

Her hair was shorter now than it had been five years ago, extending barely past her shoulders, but that just meant she tended towards wearing it down instead of in a tight bun. She'd kept her athletic physique just fine, even after two babies.

For a moment she thought about calling Jon back into the bathroom to enjoy her beauty in private, but thought better of it. *Plenty of time for that later,* she thought.

She finished in the bathroom and retrieved her coat from the bedroom before heading out to the car where she found Jon and her two sons.

"Thanks for waiting," she said as she got in.

"I'll always wait for you, my beautiful wife," Jon said, smiling, as he leaned over from the driver's seat and kissed Petra on the lips, so softly like he always did. She instantly regretted not calling him back for some quick mommy-daddy grown-up time before they left.

As Jon pulled out of the driveway, Petra thought back on her life over the past five years. She inevitably did that a lot around this time of year, so close to the date of her father's death. A lot had changed in half a decade… That much was for sure. Thinking about it made Petra both happy and sad at the same time.

As Petra stared out the window at the hypnotic emerald leaves of the trees as they drove; she soon found herself back in Munster after the Naturpark incident.

In the first few weeks after Otto's death, Petra had been completely lost, sunken into depression. She wouldn't see anyone, not even Jon; she just wanted to be alone in her hotel room in Munster, unable to bear returning to her home. In fact, Jon was the last person she wanted to see because he reminded her of what had happened.

Eventually, though, she just wanted someone to *talk* to; someone who understood what she'd gone through, and who knew her father. It was a tall order, considering the circumstances and there was only one man who fit the description. As it happened, he was tall too.

She remembered the night when she finally returned one of Jon's many calls in tears. He'd been so happy to hear from her and she recalled how kind and empathetic he'd been on the phone. He'd insisted on coming to see her at the hotel when he heard her crying, but after his arrival it hadn't taken long for that tender consolation to transform into rugged passion. They'd spent the night together and they'd later learnt that was the night they conceived the twins.

In the morning, they'd gone to Marlene's for breakfast. They'd spent that whole day walking around Munster, talking and enjoying each other's company. From then on, they were inseparable and they quickly tied the knot once Petra had discovered the pregnancy.

These days, they made a trip to Marlene's an anniversary tradition, even though it was an hour's drive from their current home in Dortmund. Fortunately, they passed a convenient stop along the way.

Petra snapped back to reality as they pulled through the cemetery gates. One of the boys shouted something in the backseat. "Settle down boys, we're here," she said.

The cemetery was beautiful and well-kept. It was small, located out in the country north of Dortmund, just like what her father had always asked for. She liked to imagine that he was at peace here; him and Hans both.

Jon parked the car beneath a tree on the side of the circular drive that ran around the cemetery. Petra got out and opened the back door.

"Come on boys. It's time to go see grandpa and uncle!"

Petra knew the twins didn't really understand what they were doing here – At four years old, they were still much too young to comprehend death and loss. But, they seemed to enjoy the trip anyways, and they excitedly clambered out of the car..

From the car, it was just a short walk to her father's grave. Jon held her hand as they made the trek quietly. The only sounds were the giggles of the boys as they ran around releasing the energy they'd been forced to coop up on the car ride over.

Petra wasn't sad; not really. It had taken her a long time to accept the fact that her father had to do what he did to destroy those tanks. She'd replayed that day in her head so many times over the first few months after her father's death, but she never figured out what they could've done differently. In the end, she decided to accept his death for what it was – a sacrifice that enabled her to live. For the second time, he had saved her life; it's just that this time the cost was his own.

Finally, they reached her father's tombstone:
Otto M. Mader
February 17, 1912 – August 19, 1974
A man who gave everything for those he loved
Beloved Father, Veteran and Friend
And next to it:
Hans V. Krieger
December 2, 1914 – August 19, 1974
A more courageous man there never was; he died selflessly
Beloved Uncle, Veteran and Friend

"Come look boys, do you recognize the names?" The twins ran over and stood in front of their parents, looking down at the tombstones in front of them.

"That's my name!" Otto Jr. said, making the connection before his brother.

"That's right," she cooed in affirmation of Otto's realization. "And look, Hans, see that? That's your name too, isn't it?"

Hans Jr. nodded and smiled up at her. He took after his father, and Petra especially noticed the resemblance when he smiled. She was sure Hans would be quite a lady killer someday, just like his father.

The twins weren't identical; Otto had the rounder face and a dirty blonde hair, right on the edge of brunette, while his brother Hans had a pointy chin with bright blonde hair. Otto was technically born first, a fact he never let his brother forget, especially since he tended to have the quicker wit of the two.

"Do you remember who those are?" She asked the boys.

"Yea! That's Grampa Otto…" Otto Jr. started.

"And Uncle Hans!" Hans Jr. finished for him, determined to get a word in.

"That's right, and do you remember why we come see them?"

Jon answered this time, taking her by surprise. "Because he let us have a family." He put an arm around Petra, and she smiled at him. "That's right," she said.

"Come on boys, let's leave your mother alone. She wants to spend some quiet time with Grampa." Jon herded the boys back to the car, leaving Petra alone standing over the two graves. She'd brought two bouquets of flowers, and she placed one on each grave now.

"I miss you so much, Papa." The statement hung in the air for a moment as Petra thought about what to say.

"I just want to say, thank you. You were the best father a daughter could've asked for. What I'd give for you to be here now." A tear rolled down her cheek, but she quickly wiped it away.

"The kids are doing great; I think they're starting to recognize you now. They're getting old enough to understand what this place is… They started Kindergarten just a couple months ago. I miss them during the day, but they're making lots of new friends and they seem to have fun at school. It works out well; Jon and I won't be able to keep up with them much longer!" She smiled at that, as she heard one of the boys laughing loudly back at the car.

"I'm doing good. Jon is such a wonderful husband and an even better father; I'm so lucky to have found him." She smiled, thinking of the first time she met Jon in the museum so long ago. "I suppose I have you to thank for that, too."

She stood in silence for a little while longer, thinking about her father. She could hear the boys getting antsy by the car.

"Anyways, say hello to mom for me," she said, "And Hans, I hope you're doing well too. Enjoy the flowers."

She leaned down to kiss each tombstone, then turned and walked back to the car.

"You ready?" Jon asked her as she climbed in the passenger seat.

"Yea, I think so." She replied. "You kiddos ready?" She called to the boys in the back seat.

"Yea!" They said in unison.

"Do you know where we're going?" She asked them.

"I know – Marlene's!" Otto Jr. exclaimed, not waiting for Hans Jr. to get an answer in.

Petra smiled. "That's right."

She turned to Jon as they pulled out of the cemetery. "Thanks for coming with me today, baby," she said, "I really appreciate it."

"No problem!" Jon said, smiling. "Anything for my beautiful wife."

"Mmmmmm, your sweet," she said, leaning over to give him a smooch as he took them back onto the country road towards Munster. "Happy anniversary, *Major*." He turned to glance at her, and she gave him a sly wink.

"Ohhhh, I know what we're doing later."

"Getting dessert?" Otto Jr. piped up from the back seat.

Jon laughed. "Yes, something like that."

"I want ice cream!" Hans Jr. chimed in.

He smiled one more time at Petra, then looked at the two boys in the rearview mirror. "What kind of ice cream do you want, Hans?"

As the boys began arguing over the best flavor of ice cream, Petra said one last ancestral prayer:

Father, if you're out there, help me to raise my boys to be men like you.

She didn't hear an answer, but in her heart she felt at peace and a smile played across her face. Another tear ran down her cheek.

"What's wrong darling?" Jon asked, ever observant.

"Oh, nothing, I just love you."

After all the pain she'd experienced, after everything that had plagued her family, finally she was truly happy.

A special thanks to

Tom Townsend, Author of the provacative story, "Panzer Spirit" that inspired me to write my story, Phantom Panthers.